*Damn it all!* Gabriel thought.

He closed his eyes and tried to ignore the ache that had settled just behind his heart.

The more time he spent with Annie, the harder it was going to be to leave.

Yet leave he must.

There was nothing in the way of permanence that he could offer a woman like Annie O'Brien. And she was the sort who deserved a forever kind of man, a home and a lapful of babies.

Gabe couldn't give her any of those things.

All he could do was treasure the time they had together.

And try not to hurt her when it was time for him to go.

Dear Reader,

What better way to start off this month—or any month—than with a new book by *New York Times* bestselling author Nora Roberts? And when that book is the latest installment in her popular Night Tales series, the good news gets even better. I think you'll love every word of *Night Smoke* (which is also this month's American Hero title), so all that remains is for you to sit back and enjoy.

With *Left at the Altar,* award-winning author Justine Davis continues our highly popular Romantic Traditions program—and also brings back Sean Holt, a character many of you have suggested should have his own book. *Annie and the Outlaw,* by Sharon Sala, is another special book. This one boasts the Spellbound flash to tell you it's a little bit unusual—and as soon as you meet hero Gabriel Donner and discover his predicament, you'll know exactly what I mean. Our successful Premiere program continues this month, too, introducing one new author in each line. Try Kia Cochrane's *Married by a Thread* for a deeply emotional reading experience. And don't forget Maggie Shayne—back with *Forgotten Vows...?*— and Cathryn Clare, who checks in with *The Angel and the Renegade.* All in all, it's another wonderful month here at Intimate Moments.

I hope you enjoy all our books—this and every month—and that you'll always feel free to write to me with your thoughts.

Enjoy!

Leslie J. Wainger
Senior Editor and Editorial Coordinator

---

Please address questions and book requests to:
Silhouette Reader Service
U.S.: 3010 Walden Ave., P.O. Box 1325, Buffalo, NY 14269
Canadian: P.O. Box 609, Fort Erie, Ont. L2A 5X3

# ANNIE

# AND

# THE

# OUTLAW

## Sharon
## Sala

Published by Silhouette Books
America's Publisher of Contemporary Romance

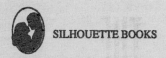 SILHOUETTE BOOKS

ISBN 0-373-07597-9

ANNIE AND THE OUTLAW

This edition published by arrangement with Harlequin Enterprises B. V.

® and TM are trademarks of Harlequin Enterprises B. V., used under
license. Trademarks indicated with ® are registered in the United States
Patent and Trademark Office, the Canadian Trade Marks Office and in
other countries.

Printed in U.S.A.

## SHARON SALA

is a child of the country. As a farmer's daughter, she had a vivid imagination that made solitude a thing to cherish. As a farmer's wife, she learned to take each day as it came without worrying about the next. After she and her husband, Bill, raised two children and too many crops to count, she went from clotheslines to deadlines with a smile on her face. Writing is, for her, nothing more than the fulfillment of a lifelong habit of daydreaming. Giving birth to characters in her mind and then sharing them with those who like to read is the thing she loves best.

During our lifetimes, someone special will cross the paths we are on and forever after change the directions that we take. From that day forward, we will be different. Either in the way we think or the way we live. And from that meeting will spring renewed faith in ourselves and hope for the future.

Without faith—with the absence of hope—we are nothing. We have nothing.

This book is dedicated to those special people who care enough to make the difference.

# *Prologue*

The noonday sun was at its zenith, beaming down with relentless persistence upon the crowd gathered around the hanging tree at the edge of town. A gusty wind did its bit in making what was left of Gabe Donner's last minutes on earth miserable by blowing sand into his eyes and against his cheeks, stinging his already bruised and battered face with a rude reminder that sensations would soon be a thing of the past.

"You cain't just hang him," a woman sobbed, and cradled her belly, swollen to near-bursting with an overdue baby. She threw herself between the angry crowd and the man on the horse who was about to be lynched. "He saved my life. If it had'na been fer him, you people ... you God-fearin', law-abidin' citizens woulda run me down."

"Get back, Milly," a man shouted from the back of the crowd. "He was part of the gang who robbed our bank. Just because he couldn't bring himself to hurt you, don't change the fact that his buddies have done gone and made off with our life savings.''

Gabe cursed and squinted his eyes. It was a hell of a day to die. But he'd been heading toward this for most of his life, and he knew it. Somewhere around the age of twelve he'd taken a step in the wrong direction, and there'd been no one in his life who'd cared to call him back.

The woman called Milly screamed as two men pulled her out of the way. Gabe's gut kicked as the horse beneath him danced sideways from the noise and shouts. The rough fiber of the rope around his neck and hands ate into his skin like a saw-toothed rasp. He winced, aware that losing a little skin was nothing to what was about to transpire.

He stared down at the woman who'd uselessly pleaded his cause and still could not believe he'd done what he had. One minute he'd been riding out of town with the rest of the gang, just ahead of a hail of gunfire, and the next thing he knew, he found himself leaping from the horse and throwing himself onto the ground, using his body as a shield between the pregnant woman and the pounding hooves of the horses ridden by the posse giving chase. He sighed and swallowed another curse. Why the hell couldn't she have been home having that baby?

"Gabe Donner...do you have anything to say for yourself?" a man asked.

He grinned and shrugged as he looked down at the sobbing woman. "Whatever you do, lady...don't name him after me."

In spite of his dusty, blood-stained clothing, a week's worth of whiskers and a badly needed haircut, the smile transformed his face. His handsome features and devastating grin made her sob even harder. It seemed such a tragic waste of manhood.

Wrenching free of the man beside her, she dashed forward. Pressing a shaking hand on Gabe's leg, she felt the jerky tremble of long thigh muscles under stress. "May God have mercy on your soul," she whispered.

And in that moment Gabe felt one small ounce of his guilt lifted and delivered. He winked.

Then, before the stunned assembly, he took away their decision and some of their joy by doing the deed himself. He kicked the horse, sharply jabbing his spurs into the animal's sweaty flanks. The horse neighed wildly, rearing up on hind legs in sudden objection to the pain, and then burst forward, as if coming out of a starting gate.

A couple of curses and then a hush came over the crowd as the man's long, lean body jerked in the dusty wind. One by one they turned and walked away, suddenly shamed by their kangaroo court and the ruthlessness of it all.

The sobbing woman was escorted back to her house, where she fell into bed and promptly gave birth, as suddenly and painfully as Gabe Donner had died.

And then there was nothing but the creak of the rope against the tree limb as the solid weight of his body swung back and forth... back and forth.

A loud roar filled Gabe's ears. Fire swept across his face, and the smell of sulfur scalded the insides of his nostrils and burned his eyelids. Confusion was uppermost within his heat-fogged brain as he tried to decipher the words being screamed at him in a virulent tone.

"You were mine!"

The air around Gabe reverberated from the sound of the voice. He inhaled, then wished that he hadn't, as the sulfuric steam once again scalded his throat and lungs. He stood his ground, unable to move from the spot on which he'd landed.

"Right up until the last moment, your soul was mine! And then what did you do? You ruined it! It might have been excusable if it had only been the woman...but no! You had to go and save a baby! An unborn one, at that! *They* still belong to *Him!*"

The hiss that accompanied the accusations sucked the air from Gabe's body. He began to get the message. The voice screamed and spat, shouting obscenities Gabe had never imagined as he absorbed the implications of his situation.

*I've done it now! I've gone and made the Devil mad! This is too damned scary, even for me. From the way he's spitting and cussing, it seems I don't even belong in Hell.*

The voice seemed to filter through the skin over his bones, insidious by its very nature, imbuing him with a sensation of scorched flesh and degradation. Yet he saw nothing but the constant swirling clouds of fire and steam. If he hadn't been so stunned, he might have laughed. It seemed he was doomed to mess up, even in death.

"Get out! Get out!" the Devil screamed, and Gabe's body quivered from the onslaught of sound. "You don't belong here. There's nothing I hate worse than a sanctimonious sinner!"

And before Gabe could blink, the fire, the smoke, even the voice, had disappeared, and he felt himself being tossed aside as if he were so much garbage. It was as if he were left hanging in a vacuum where no one and nothing existed—except himself.

*God!* he thought, and with the thought came the being.

"Gabriel."

The voice was solace after sin. Grace after a lifetime of gratuitous living, and Gabe shivered.

"I never thought we'd be having this conversation," God said softly.

Gabe shivered. Neither had he.

"You surprised me, my son," God said. "You were one that I thought I'd lost. But right at the last moment, when it actually counted, you did something right."

If an immovable force hadn't been holding him up, Gabe would already have fallen. He'd endured more than a human could bear this day, and yet he was being forced to stand and listen again to his sins and the lack of compassion with which he'd lived his life.

"However, that in itself is not enough for all your transgressions to be forgiven," He continued. "Remember, it wasn't you who begged for mercy on your soul...it was the woman."

Gabe's head dropped, his chin nearly touching his chest. *This is it,* he thought. *I'm about to get the shaft here, too.*

"No, Gabriel. Heaven does not give shafts...only second chances."

Gabe's head jerked up, his nostrils flaring as he inhaled and his mind absorbed the clear, pure sound of God's laughter. He almost smiled. If he'd known God had a sense of humor, he might have tried religion a long time ago.

As badly as Gabe wanted to, he could not speak. All he could do was stand and listen to his fate being handed out.

"This is my command!" God said, his voice deepening with a powerful force as the sentence He had decided to impose was made clear to Gabe. "You will go back. Soul intact, flesh and bones. To the human eye you will seem as all men. But heed me, Gabriel!"

Gabe's body shook, and he blinked rapidly as a blinding light sent him to his knees.

"If you can learn what it truly takes to get to Heaven, then you will be granted entrance and eternal life."

*Dear God...it will take two lifetimes to undo the damage I've done,* Gabe thought.

"So be it!" God commanded. "Then you shall have two lifetimes. One hundred and fifty more years on earth to right your wrongs. But...heed my warning!"

Gabe could not see, only hear and feel, as the air around his body vibrated once again. Yet this time it was as if the motion came from a multitude of wings...as if all the angels in Heaven had suddenly surrounded him and struck him blind as God continued.

"Stray from my path...ignore the way of the righteous...and you will be lost in Limbo, stranded between Heaven and Hell for all eternity with nothing but your conscience for company."

Suddenly all was silent. Gabe tried to stand, and then he felt himself being hurtled backward.

The limb cracked, and Gabe's eyes opened just in time to see the dry, dusty earth of Kansas rushing up to meet his face.

A horse's soft nicker of welcome was his only clue that he hadn't imagined what had just transpired. This was real. Gabe Donnor had come back from the dead.

With an aching groan, he rolled up and over, momentarily surprised that the ropes around his neck and wrists were in the dust at his feet. And then he shuddered, remembering where he'd been, and knew that those ropes were the least of the surprises yet to be had.

He picked up his hat from the ground, dusting the worst of the grime from inside the brim, and called softly to his horse. In minutes there was nothing left to tell of what had transpired that day but a coil of rope lying in the dirt like a snake waiting to strike.

Gabriel Donner was gone.

# Chapter 1

*Oklahoma City, Oklahoma—Present Day*

It was hard to tell where the man began and the machine ended. Black leather and black metal, both well-worn and dusty, covered muscle and motion as the motorcycle and its rider wove their way through the heavy weekend traffic on I-240 on the south side of Oklahoma City.

Just ahead, an eighteen-wheeler swerved to keep from running up the ass-end of a car that was barely doing forty in the fast lane of the freeway. The motorcycle moved smoothly past the near-miss as its rider guided it in and out of the swiftly moving vehicles like a bullet on its way to a target.

The rider in black suddenly shot into the far right-hand lane and geared down to take the next exit, which would lead him toward Dallas, via southbound I-35. The biker leaned into the turn, and as he did, caught his first glimpse of the altercation taking place at the corner quick stop across the street.

His frown was hidden behind the smoke-tinted visor of his helmet. But he didn't like what he was seeing. Without taking his focus from the road before him, he accelerated through a small gap in traffic and shot across all three lanes, coming to a sliding halt a few feet behind the gathering crowd.

The woman's hair was the first thing he noticed. It was a deep, rich brown. And the afternoon sun that shot through it highlighted the chestnut and amber strands until it looked like a coil of coffee-flavored taffy wound around her head.

Because of the business at hand, he manfully ignored the faint but enticing outline of long legs and a slender but shapely body beneath the white, gauzy-looking skirt and blouse she was wearing.

He yanked off his helmet and hung it on the handlebar of his bike as he dismounted. His legs were long and heavily muscled. The lower half of his body was covered in supple black leather, ending with dusty black boots adorned with old-style silver spurs.

He was rock-hard and a deep-to-the-muscle brown from countless years and endless miles on the road. As his fingers threaded through too-long hair, he lightly massaged his scalp along the places where the helmet had ridden, then let the shaggy black length of his hair fall where it would.

Bare to the waist except for a black leather vest laced loosely across his taut belly, he pulled sunglasses from his bike pack and slid them on. It was intentional that their mirrored surface hid much of what he was, while allowing him to see more of what was before him. He'd heard it said that the eyes were the mirror of the soul, and Gabriel Donner was real careful of who he let look inside the man that he'd become.

* * *

Annie O'Brien was nervous. And because of that, she was also mad as hell. She, a grown woman of twenty-nine, had let these sixteen- and seventeen-year-old boys get her goat. Granted, there were more than a few. And also granted, in this day and time, few boys of that age were the innocents that their parents would like to believe. But the gang of boys preventing her from leaving the parking lot was daunting. And as the number in the gang had grown, so had their daring. They were out of control, and she knew it. And because of that, she was afraid.

"Hey, hey, Annie-Annie," the tallest boy chanted. "You know what I'd like to do to you?"

He tossed his head, and as he did, a dirty brown lock of hair fell from behind his ear and caught in one of his earrings. Annie inhaled sharply and tried not to let him know she was afraid. He was a woman's worst nightmare come to life.

Several of the others laughed and hitched at their jeans, swaggering in thought, if not in deed, at the idea of taking this pretty lady down a notch or two, of showing her what real men were all about.

"Just let me pass, Damon," Annie said, trying again, as she had for the past fifteen minutes, to get to her car on the other side of the lot.

"Oh, now... I don't know if I can do that little thing," he said, then smoothed his hand across the fly of his baggy jeans, watching with increasing delight the way her eyes widened and the slight nervous lick she gave her bottom lip. "You're on our turf now, Annie-Annie. Here, you do what we say."

"Like hell," she said softly, and started to push past, aware that she had little time left in which to deal with this situation before it got completely out of hand.

Damon stepped forward; his pale hazel eyes seemed a reflection of his inner self, wild and out of control. And as he moved, the other seven teenage boys moved with him as if they were joined at the hip, their dilated pupils and jerky, foot-shuffling movements a sure bet that they were riding high on more than adrenaline.

Annie's heart pounded, but she ignored her own panic as she tried to push past them. She took a deep breath, certain that she was about to become another crime statistic, then watched in amazement as the boys came to an abrupt halt. All their cocky assurance slipped away as they looked up and over her head.

Someone was behind her!

Terrified that it was simply more of the same, she froze in horror. She saw the man's shadow as it moved across the pavement, covering and then passing her own shadow, to come to a stop somewhere about the middle of Damon Tuttle's knees. It was big and wide, and she had a moment's impression of being swallowed whole. And then he spoke, and she would have sworn that the air vibrated, so close was his mouth to her ear.

"Trouble?" he asked.

His hand rested lightly at the edge of her shoulder. And though the small squeeze he gave her was as much a question as what he had asked, she knew the second he touched her that he was on her side.

In answer to his one-word question, she nodded. She had trouble indeed.

It was instinctive, an urge born of relief, she knew. But she felt a sudden need to turn and bury her face against what she sensed was a big, strong chest and forget everything but the safety she knew she would find there.

Damon Tuttle was one tough dude. All you had to do was ask anybody on the south side of the city. They would tell

you. And if they didn't, Damon would. He had his hand in
a little bit of everything rotten that went on in the area and
still managed to stay one step ahead of the law. It was tes-
timony to his probation officer's persistence that he was
even still in school.

"Okay, boys... back off!" Gabriel said, and even Annie
jumped at the tone of the voice behind her.

He didn't say where, he didn't say when, but the look on
his face made three of the boys at the edge of the gang take
several steps backward in nervous reflex.

"Move, damn it... and I mean now," Gabe said in a
softer, more menacing tone of voice. When they held their
ground, he swiftly put himself between the woman they
called Annie-Annie and the gang.

His fingers curled into fists and his stomach muscles
tightened against the possibility of oncoming blows.

Annie's heart tilted. As he slid past her, she caught a flash
of a wild, handsome face half-hidden behind mirrored
glasses, a dangerous smile, and then all she had left was a
very solid view of his back.

He was tall, so tall. And he was more tan flesh and black
leather than she'd ever seen, even in a gym. She should have
been scared out of her wits, yet she'd never felt so protected
in her entire life.

Damon's skin crawled as he looked into the big man's
face. His thoughts went into free-fall, as if he'd just walked
into a whirlwind and been caught up in the dead-calm of the
eye, waiting for the rest of the storm force to catch up and
eat him alive. Yet he felt honor-bound to hold his ground.
He couldn't lose face in front of his boys, not for just one
man.

"Who do you think you are, man?" one of them sneered,
secure from his vantage point in the middle of the gang.

Damon shivered as the big man's focus shifted, turning that hidden gaze from himself to the boy who'd spoken. And when a slow smile slid across the biker's face, Damon's belly rolled.

"I *know* who I am, boy. I'm someone you don't want to make mad." He took several steps forward and was suddenly nose-to-nose with Damon Tuttle.

"I'm no boy," Damon muttered, trying to maintain eye contact with the man, when he felt an urgent need to cut and run instead. Damon was the type of tough who was at his best with a backup of muscle, and he had a sudden instinctive flash that his buddies were about to bolt.

"Oh, but you're wrong," Gabe said softly.

The biker's motion was so swift, that Damon never saw it coming. He shuddered as hands locked around his arms, the grip iron-hard and unyielding. Looking up and suddenly seeing the terror on his own acne-scarred face mocking him from the mirrored reflection of the biker's glasses was a humbling experience. Damon Tuttle did not like to be humbled. Yet there was no other way to describe the fact that his feet were now dangling inches off the pavement while the biker held him suspended as if he were a child.

"That's exactly what you are...a boy," Gabe said. "And not a very good one, at that." He shook Damon roughly to make his point, ignoring the fact that the other gang members were digging in their pockets for weapons. "Boys do stupid things. Threatening a woman like this is stupid...real stupid, *boy!*"

He emphasized the taunt by glaring over Damon's shoulder at the others, who quickly slid their weapons back out of sight.

"You've gained nothing by frightening her." He dropped Damon as suddenly as he'd picked him up. "And there's something else you should remember." His last statement encompassed the entire gang as he took off his sunglasses and stared them full in the face, no longer hiding behind the mirrored lenses for effect. "Men don't run in packs... but dogs do."

The big man's quiet sneer as he slid his sunglasses back on made all eight boys turn red in anger and embarrassment as they remembered the fear on Annie's face. It suddenly didn't seem as cool as it had minutes earlier.

"Oh, hell, let's go, Damon," another boy said nervously. "No big deal, right, bro?"

"Is it going to be a big deal, Damon? It *can* be one if you need it to be," Gabe said softly.

Damon got the message. This biker could take them apart and reassemble them in new order, and they all knew it. He shook his head and dropped his gaze. He couldn't describe the relief he felt when he saw the biker relax and take a step back.

Damon Tuttle was the first to move as, one by one, the teenagers shuffled away, tossing half-hearted threats and rude innuendos over their shoulders, unwilling to completely acknowledge the fact that they'd let themselves be bested by one man who hadn't even thrown a punch.

And then Gabriel remembered the woman and turned.

"Are you all right?" he asked gently.

Annie nodded, then fainted in his arms.

He sat in the shade of the building, using his bike for a chair as he cradled the woman called Annie who was lying loose and limp across his lap. Her head was lolling against his bare biceps, and he marveled at how thick and soft her hair felt against his skin. He couldn't remember the last time he'd held a woman so intimately or been able to look his fill.

Her nose was small and straight and perfectly fit her heart-shaped face. Her cheeks looked soft, and as he held

her, he absently traced the ball of his thumb across them to
test out his theory. He'd been right; they were as tender and
soft as a baby's lips.

He sighed and inhaled slowly, wishing away the thou-
sand thoughts that instantly intruded, as well as the accompanying ache in his loins. After what she'd been through,
what he was thinking had no place in her life, and because
of who he was, neither did he.

Her mouth was wide, her lips full. They were the kind that
drove a man wild and begged to be kissed without saying a
word. Gabriel Donner had come too far and lived too long
to turn down the unoffered invitation.

Ignoring the busy traffic on the street just beyond the
parking lot, as well as the ebb and flow of customers coming and going in the store behind him, he bent down, opened
his mouth just enough to encompass hers, and then groaned
when she sighed and unconsciously responded.

She tasted of heat and cinnamon, and as his mouth tightened across her lips, he dug his hands into the coil of her
hair, unwittingly sending the pins that had held it in place
flying.

She moaned, and he lifted his head and frowned, instantly aware that he'd trespassed. It was a silent acknowl-
edgment that the good he'd done by helping her had been
wiped out in a heartbeat by the marauding manner in which
he'd taken her favors without permission.

Her eyes were green. That much he remembered from
before she passed out. He looked down at his fingers, buried deep in her thick, luxuriant fountain of hair, and tried
not to think of where else on Annie he would like to put his
hands.

Her hair fell free as he withdrew his fingers and began
trying to smooth the mess that he'd made of it. Guilt at his

transgression made him feel too much like the toughs he'd just run off.

She came to with a start.

"Oh, Lord," she muttered, as she realized where she was and began trying to unwind herself from the man and his bike.

But the action, as well as her panic, was wasted when he calmly stood and then set her back on her feet without a word.

"You fainted," he said.

Annie's hands shot to her head. She felt the long, thick weight of her hair falling through her fingers. Doubtfully, she looked back up at him.

"And the pins came out of your hair," he added.

She frowned. She already knew that. It was the how of the incident that was worrying her.

"I can't see your face," she said, unaware of the nervous tremor in her voice.

His movements were as slow as honey on a cold winter morning. Annie held her breath as he leaned forward until their faces were only inches apart, then slid his glasses down the bridge of his nose and let them drop into his hand.

Oh... I had a feeling this would only get better—and worse, Annie thought.

To go with the starkly handsome features she'd seen only in profile, she now had a pair of eyes so blue that she caught her breath at the color's purity.

"That better, Annie?"

She took a step backward, then swayed. His hand shot out so quickly that she didn't even see it coming. She felt only the firm yet gentle grip as he steadied her on her feet.

"How do you know my name?" she asked.

"Damon the Terrible called you by it several times. I assumed he knew you. Was I right?"

She sighed and buried her face in her hands. Gabe frowned. There was obviously more to this incident than casual harassment.

"Well, Annie-Annie, was I right?"

"Don't call me that," she said sharply, shuddering at the fear that came back with the rude twinning of her name.

"Then what *do* I call you?"

Annie stared at him. There was no reason on earth why she should be telling this bike-riding, leather-clad knight on shining metal a darned thing about her personal life. In fact, everything she'd been told and taught over the past twenty-nine years reinforced that fact.

"My name is Annie Laurie O'Brien."

He held out his hand, then waited to see how much woman she turned out to be. By all rights she should be scared out of her wits by his appearance.

Annie looked down at the long, strong fingers, the wide, callused palm and the tracing of scars across the backs of his knuckles. Surprising herself, as well as him, she reached out and took what he offered.

Gabriel was shocked. His eyes narrowed, and his mouth firmed. He looked down at the way her fingers had curled around his and then back up into her face. He swallowed hard. Oh damn! Not trust!

She was more woman than he'd even imagined. The thought made him angry. Not now! he thought. Don't you do this to me! Not when you know my time is nearly up. He glared up into the sky.

*Gabriel, Gabriel. When will you learn? Everything that happens, you bring upon yourself,* said His voice.

The quiet answer slid through his mind, and with it came the truth slapping him full in the face. He dropped her hand and sighed wearily. How many years had he been on earth, riding the roads and highways, trying to get it right?

"And your name is . . . ?" Annie asked.

At the same time that she was waiting for him to answer, she was thinking that if he'd been accompanied by three other "horsemen" on similar metal, she would have guessed by their motorized mounts that they were the Four Horsemen of the Apocalypse. She squinted her eyes, fancying that he was about to answer by saying "Death," when his deep voice rumbled past her ear.

"My name is Gabriel . . . Gabriel Donner."

Her eyes widened, and her lips curved into a smile. In spite of the fact that she knew laughing in someone's face was extremely rude, it happened anyway, loud and clear.

Gabe knew there must be a joke somewhere. He waited for her to explain.

"I'm sorry," Annie said, squinting and trying desperately to wipe the accompanying smile off her face. "That was rude of me." She shrugged, still grinning. "I have this vivid imagination." She waved her hand up and down his frame as lights danced in her eyes. "An angel in devil's clothing . . . that's what you are. My avenging angel."

His heart skipped a beat. Angel? She thinks I'm an angel? This time it was Gabriel who grinned. Oh lady, if you only knew.

Annie thought back to the past half hour and knew that her troubles were only momentarily solved. When tomorrow came, it would be more of the same from Damon and his gang. And then she had a sudden and shocking thought. She focused on his heart-stopping smile and ignored the warning her brain was sending.

Pooh! she told herself, as she realized that what she was thinking could get her killed. So what! Everyone had to die sometime.

"So, Gabriel, where were you going when you so kindly came to my rescue?"

He shrugged. "Nowhere . . . anywhere."

Her pulse accelerated. Everything kept falling into place. It had to be a sign.

"How would you like a job?" she asked.

Her question caught him off guard.

"Doing what?" he asked, eyeing her carefully, suddenly realizing that he might have rescued a kook. It wouldn't have been the first time, although, to be honest, this time it would be a major disappointment.

"I've ignored the signs for weeks, but after today . . . I think I need a bodyguard." She ignored the shock on his face and continued before she lost both her breath and her nerve. "I'm a teacher. And the gang you rescued me from happens to be part of my homeroom class. I'll be damned if I'll let them beat me. I will not be frightened into quitting at this late date."

Gabe was speechless.

"It would only be for a few weeks," Annie said quickly. "Then school is out for the summer. After that, you could be on your way to nowhere . . . or even anywhere."

The nervous look she gave him sent his heart right to his feet. He couldn't have told her no if his life depended on it.

"Let me get this straight," he said. "You want to hire me to accompany you to school and sit in on all your classes until summer vacation begins?"

She nodded. "Why are you so shocked? Surely it won't be all that bad. Just look at it as a refresher course in basic high school."

"That's just it," Gabe muttered to himself. "I never went to school."

It was hard to say who was the more shocked. Annie for what she'd heard, or Gabe for admitting it.

"You can't read?" Annie asked, trying hard not to sound as shocked as she felt.

"I can read fine," Gabriel said shortly, pushing his sunglasses back on for protection. "I've had a long, long time to read just about any and everything ever written. And believe me, I mean everything."

"Then you're self-educated," she said, somehow greatly relieved that her angel's wings had not been clipped.

"I'm self-everything," he said in disgust.

"Why am I not surprised?" Annie muttered under her breath, then glanced up. "So... is it a deal? Will you be my guardian angel for the next few weeks?" A shadow crossed her face as she lifted her chin, trying desperately not to plead. "When I start something, I like to finish it."

Her voice softened, and Gabriel would have sworn he saw her chin tremble.

"It's real important to me that I finish this school year," she added.

"I'll need a place to sleep," he warned.

The light came back on in her clear green eyes. In for a penny, in for a pound, she thought. Besides, I've never taken a single risk in my entire life. I think it's about time I started...before it's too late. Her hesitation was only slight.

"Follow me," she said as she headed for her car, her slender body swaying gently beneath the loose, gauzy-white skirt and blouse she was wearing.

At that moment he would have followed her to the ends of the earth.

# Chapter 2

Her apartment was everything he'd expected it to be. Ultrafeminine. It was a tasteful display of floral upholstery, small figurines placed in random fashion around the rooms and plants everywhere. There were flowering things, leafy things, spiky stems and flowing vines. He had an urge to duck as he walked through the door, half expecting something to come flying past from her semitropical jungle.

"Make yourself at home," Annie said, and tossed her purse on top of the kitchen table.

All the way home she'd debated with herself about the utter stupidity and careless abandon with which she'd hired him. Off and on, as traffic permitted, she'd caught glimpses of him riding at a safe distance behind her on that devil-black machine, dressed in biker leather, having traded his mirrored sunglasses for a black helmet with a smoke-tinted visor. One seemed no different than the other. She sensed he was using both to hide behind.

But what Annie O'Brien had endured over the past few months had taken some of the caution out of her life. She would finish this school year and her teaching contract, no matter what.

The front door slammed behind him as he shut and locked it. Annie turned at the sound and couldn't hide a shudder. He looked so out of place. A nervous thought occurred to her as she watched him fold his arms across his chest and stare thoughtfully around the room. Had she let the Devil into her Garden of Eden? She bit her lower lip and turned away, hurrying into the kitchen and opening the refrigerator door, then bending down to peer inside.

Gabe heard the tremor in her voice as she invited him in. A wry grimace crossed his face as he dropped his duffel bag beside the couch, then stretched. But he was unaware of her observation and wouldn't have cared if he *had* known. He was used to his appearance making people nervous.

Annie turned, a package of hamburger meat in one hand and a bowl of shredded lettuce in the other. She watched him close his eyes and reach first one arm and then the other toward the ceiling in a halfhearted attempt to work out what she suspected were muscle kinks from long hours on his bike.

"Are you hungry?"

Her question took him by surprise. His eyes opened, and he stared intently at the blank, almost innocent expression on her face. *Yes... but not for food... for you.*

The thought made him angry both with himself and at the situation. He didn't have time for entanglements, especially those of the personal kind.

"Why the hell aren't you afraid of me?" he asked quietly.

"I suppose, if I'm honest, I can't say I'm not." She hastened to add, before he got angry and left, "But let's face it.

The worst you could do to me is rob me, or rape me. Or...maybe torture or kill me."

"Good Lord," Gabe whispered, uncertain how to take her blithe assessment of his presence in her life.

"Those are givens," Annie continued. "And after what I've been through the past few months, I'm not much afraid of givens anymore. Besides..." She shrugged. "Everyone has to die...sometime."

A bitter smile twisted Gabe's face. "You'd think so, wouldn't you?" He'd watched more than one generation disappear from this earth, and he was still here to tell the tale.

She looked up, startled by his strange answer, and then shrugged off the curiosity that might have let her pursue his comment.

"I need you, Gabriel Donner. I need you to get me through the next few weeks of school. After what I've endured at the hands of those boys, I will not let them think intimidation wins wars. And believe me...this is war!"

He grinned slightly at the ferocity in her voice.

"Just stay until my job is over, and then you'll be free to go your own way," she added.

He nodded. Of course he would stay. But she didn't understand why. She couldn't. Leaving someone in trouble wasn't part of the deal he'd made with God. He was honor bound to help her whether she liked it or not.

"Where do I sleep?" he asked.

A faint flush painted her cheeks a rosy hue as she led the way down the small hall.

"This is my spare room." She opened the door and stepped aside as he moved through the doorway. Annie watched as he dropped his duffel bag by the bed and silently assessed the pink comforter draped across it.

"Sorry about all the stuffed animals. I've had them for years. Just toss them on the floor, out of your way. The room isn't much, but it has a separate bath. There are clean sheets on the bed, and—"

"It's fine," he said.

She nodded. "If you want to clean up or... or rest before you eat, feel free. I don't stand on ceremony."

"It's a good thing," Gabe said. "I don't care much for ceremonies." Frowning, he rubbed a thoughtful hand across his throat, feeling the slight pucker of his scar, a memento of a rope that had done what it could to end his life. "The last one I was at didn't serve food."

Her eyes narrowed as, for the first time, she noticed the thin ring of slightly discolored skin circling his neck. Just what and who had she invited into her home? Visions of ax murderers and serial killers sifted through her mind, but she discarded them. Her decision was made, and Annie O'Brien didn't go back on her word. She spun away and headed back toward the kitchen.

"We're having meat loaf," she called over her shoulder.

Gabe shut the door, then leaned against it, a thoughtful expression on his face. Meat loaf!

*Two hours ago I was on my way to Texas, minding my own business, and now I'm in a pink bedroom full of stuffed teddy bears and about to be served meat loaf!*

He began stripping off his clothes as he headed for the shower.

The evening meal had come and gone with surprising ease. Annie's matter-of-fact attitude helped. Also, Gabe had a suspicion that this was just another heaven-sent test. During the past century, he'd endured quite a few. Thrusting a teacher into his face was obviously a none-too-subtle way of telling him that he had more to learn.

He got up from the table and began gathering their dirty dishes. Unintentionally, he and Annie reached for the same bowl at the same time. His fingers slid over the back of her hand, and for a second he felt the panic pulsing through her system. But as quickly as it had come, it passed, leaving him with nothing more than the beginnings of a sleepless night. His body hardened at the thought of spending that night with her, but sanity reminded him that that was out of the question. Getting involved in any way was out of the question.

"Sorry," he said, and calmly reached for another bowl instead.

Annie shivered. His touch had done something to her nervous system that she hadn't expected. For one heart-stopping moment she thought she remembered that same hand cupping her face as soft breath feathered across her cheeks. She inhaled and closed her eyes. Certain she had to be mistaken, she exhaled and opened them, calmly meeting his cool blue gaze.

"Did you get enough to eat?" she asked, ignoring the sexual tension she felt building between them. But the moment she'd said it, she realized she'd only added fuel to the fire.

He smiled. The ache in his body increased.

Oh, damn, I shouldn't be thinking this, Gabriel thought.

Annie forgot what she'd been about to say as she stared at that smile.

His mouth, the one that had been twisted in a wry, almost cruel smirk ever since they'd met, had turned into a thing of beauty. Gabe Donner's smile had turned his mouth into the most beautiful set of lips she'd ever seen.

"What a waste," she muttered under her breath.

"Not for long," he whispered, and moved—too quickly for her to react.

Gabriel captured her between the sink and his body, then leaned down and pressed his lips against the shock of protest he saw coming.

He'd only meant to tease, but the intensity of their joining left him breathless. She tasted of the strawberries they'd had for dessert, and of passion too long denied.

He pulled back and stared long and hard into her face, missing nothing of the fact that her eyes had slipped shut and she was no longer pulling away from him. In fact, at that moment, if she hadn't opened her eyes and realized what had just happened, he knew damn well that she'd meant to slide her arms around his waist.

"Why did you do that?" she asked, trying to work up the good sense to tell herself that she'd asked for it by inviting a total stranger into her home.

"You said you wanted a taste," Gabe said, drawing a finger along the curve of her cheek. "I was just obliging."

"I did not!" she gasped. "I said—" she looked back at his mouth, remembering that only moments earlier it had been pressed against her own " —'what a waste.'"

"Oh," he said, and masked a grin. "My mistake."

"Good Lord," Annie muttered, thinking to herself how close it had come to being a mistake for both of them.

She turned away from the table with a handful of dishes and headed for the sink.

"Forget it," she said, giving him a warning look he couldn't miss.

Not on your life, Annie Laurie, he thought. But he shrugged and continued to clear the table.

"Why do those boys have it in for you?" Gabe asked as he carried the last of the bowls from the table to the sink.

Annie rinsed and loaded the dishwasher with absent skill as she thought about his question. Finally she could only shake her head.

"Honestly...I have no idea. It's been rough all year, but the last two months have been hell. Pure hell! I've been cornered in the halls, in the classroom, even in the parking lot at school. But today was the first time it happened off campus."

Gabe watched her lips tighten as a muscle jerked at her temple.

"Have you reported this to your...uh...whatever?"

"The administrator at my school? Yes."

"And...?"

She looked away. "He told me security would look into it...and to put up my hair and wear more sedate clothing in the classroom."

Gabe frowned. He might have been born in another time, but he was well aware of the implications of what she'd just said. His hand slid across her shoulder, then gently turned her face up to his.

"Are you telling me he was saying that you asked for what was happening? That it was your fault?"

"Not in so many words," she said. And then she turned in sudden anger and thumped her finger sharply against his chest. "But that's what he meant, damn it! Why do men do that?" she yelled. "What is it about the male sex that makes them blame a woman for everything they can't fix?"

Gabe caught her finger on the third jab. "Have a heart, Annie. It wasn't me." He grinned and gingerly rubbed the spot on his chest that she'd been attacking.

"Sorry," she said, and yanked her hand away, trying to forget the way his fingers had heated her skin as they'd curled around her hand.

"Why don't you go watch television or something?" she said, pointing toward the living room. "There's bound to be some sort of ball game on. All men like ball games. You're a man. Go watch one."

Oh, yes, Annie, I am a man. And, thanks to you, a very uncomfortable one.

She shrugged and turned away, mentally excusing herself for being rude. As far as she was concerned, after that kiss he'd stolen, manners were a thing of the past. And she needed him out of her space.

When her back was turned, Gabe leaned forward just enough to inhale a faint whiff of her perfume and considered the thought that he would rather watch her. But after the kiss he'd taken without asking, he didn't think she would appreciate knowing that. When she wasn't looking, he grinned and ambled out of the small kitchen.

Annie breathed a quick sigh of relief. He was so darned big that he swamped everything he came in contact with, including her. She'd never had claustrophobia in her life until he'd started helping her with the dishes. And after he'd kissed her and then turned away as if it was no big deal, it had been all she could do not to burst into tears.

And the strangest thing was, she didn't know why. Although she probably should, she didn't feel threatened by him. And if he did as he'd promised, he was going to make life a whole lot easier for her. She had absolutely nothing to cry about.

She grimaced and tossed the hand towel on the counter. If she looked at it another way, she had absolutely *everything* to cry about. She stomped into the living room, her posture ramrod-stiff and her expression furious.

"I'm going to bed," she said sharply. "Is there anything you need first?"

He stared long and hard at the anger on her face, wondering where the wall had come from that was suddenly standing between them.

"Go to sleep, Annie Laurie," he said quietly. "I'm a big boy. I can take care of myself."

As if I hadn't noticed, she thought as she walked down the hallway toward her bedroom. She couldn't forget the way that wall of man and muscle had pinned her against her own kitchen sink with so little effort.

Therein lay part of her problem. Annie O'Brien had done two stupid things today. She'd hired a total stranger to be her bodyguard. And it wasn't enough that she didn't know him. He had to be a biker...riding the biggest, blackest Harley she'd ever seen. To top that off, she'd taken him home with her like some stray animal and let him kiss her.

And therein lay the root of Annie's problem. She was way too interested for her own good in the male animal she'd brought home. The last thought she had before she finally drifted off to sleep was that he didn't look the least bit domesticated. In fact, if she wasn't careful, he might turn into some wild thing and eat her alive.

"Oh no!"

Annie's quiet dismay as she walked out of the apartment ahead of him sent Gabe bolting out the front door, expecting to have to rescue her again. Unfortunately for Annie, they'd already come and gone.

Her nearly new red Caprice had been vandalized to the point of being totaled. Three separate colors of paint had been sprayed in graffiti-like fashion all over it. All the windows were shattered, the hubcaps were missing, and the tires looked as if someone had taken a chain saw to them. The seat covers had been slashed, and a offensive odor emanated from inside the vehicle.

Gabe stared. The anger that surged through him made him shake. How had this world gotten so rotten? He had a sudden notion that he would have no regrets when it finally came time for him to leave it.

"Call the police," Gabe told her. When he saw indecision sweeping across her face, his voice grew harsh. "Do it, Annie! *Now!*"

She swung around and headed back to her apartment, her posture a vivid statement of her anger at the vandalism, as well as his bossy demand.

After a second brief phone call, this one to the school to let them know she would be delayed, they waited. Several minutes later, a squad car pulled up. The officer's gaze went from the biker who was leaning against the vandalized car to the big black Harley parked beside it.

Gabe had traded his leather pants for jeans, and, in honor of the presence of a lady, he had put on a long-sleeved shirt beneath his leather vest, but it didn't help disguise his go-to-hell attitude, the mirrored sunglasses or the old silver spurs on his well-worn boots. The officer came out of the car with his hand on his gun.

Gabe sighed. One of these days he was going to have to make a change in his appearance, if only to alleviate some of this crap.

"Put your hands in the air," the officer shouted as he slid into a half crouch behind the open door of his car, aiming his revolver at Gabe.

Annie had had enough. "It wasn't him, for God's sake!" she shouted, slamming her briefcase down on the sidewalk as she swept over to the two men. "If it was, do you think he'd be standing there waiting to be arrested? He's with me," she said, and then buried her face in her hands.

Gabe's fingers slid up the back of her neck in a gentle, reassuring squeeze.

"It's okay, Annie," he said quietly. "It's happened before."

The officer made no apology for his misunderstanding as he holstered his gun.

Less than thirty minutes later the report had been made. They watched as the officer drove away with their meager information in his possession. What they had was a vandalized car and a lot of suspicions. But as he'd told them, in his business, you couldn't take suspicion to court.

"I'll have to call a cab," she said, eyeing the ruined car and then her watch.

Gabe shook his head and pointed at her skirt. "Not if you're willing to change your clothes." Her eyebrows arched as his suggestion sank in. "Put on some pants, Annie O'Brien, and I'll get you to work on time."

Just thinking about what her superintendent would say when she arrived at work on the back of a Harley made her nervous, and then a determined glint came in her eyes, changing them to a darker shade of jade.

"Why not?" she muttered, and ran to change.

Gabe smiled. He was beginning to like Annie O'Brien more and more. She was his kind of woman. And then the smile slid off his face. He didn't have women...of any kind. It didn't pay to care when you knew you couldn't stay.

"Wow! Would you look at that?" one of the students shouted, pointing toward the motorcycle and its riders as they turned into the staff parking lot.

Allen Baker, the administrator in charge of the high school, frowned. "They can't park there," he muttered, and stomped toward the bike.

The first bell was ringing as Annie swung her leg over and dismounted. She could hear the bell's shrill peal through the helmet Gabe had made her wear.

I can just imagine what my hair's going to look like, she thought, then looked up in time to see her boss heading toward her. She grimaced. Perfect timing!

She ran her hands through her hair and sighed. It was hopeless. Settling for a redo of her outfit, she began to tuck the tail of her blue silk blouse back into the waistband of her navy linen slacks.

Late-arriving students were making a mad dash across the parking lot. Teachers were strolling through the doors on their way to their classrooms. But Gabe Donner's instincts homed in on the tall, overweight man in a plaid sports coat and navy slacks who was lumbering across the pavement toward them.

"A friend of yours?" Gabe asked, readjusting his sunglasses, then nonchalantly using his fingers for a comb as he thrust them through his wind-blown hair with casual abandon.

"My boss," Annie said, and sighed as she handed him his helmet.

"I say," Allen Baker began. "You can't park here. This is reserved for—" A stunned expression crossed his face as he recognized the face that had emerged from under the shiny black helmet. "Miss O'Brien! What on earth do you mean by arriving in such a . . . ?"

"Mr. Baker. I'd like you to meet Gabriel Donner. He'll be accompanying me to class for the remainder of the school year. Now, if you'll excuse me, I need to hurry or I'll be late."

Allen Baker turned pasty white. He wanted to argue. But nothing more than a gasp slid past his lips as he grabbed her arm, stopping her progress, then stared fearfully at the tall, ominous-looking man who stepped between them.

"What do you mean, he'll be accompanying you to class? We don't allow people to monitor classes without special permission from—"

"I'm not monitoring anything but Annie's welfare," Gabe said quietly, gently removing Allen Baker's hand from her arm.

Baker shuddered as the big man's gaze warned him to look but not touch. As much as he would have liked to, he didn't have the guts to refuse someone who looked as if he'd climbed up from Hell to spend the day on earth.

"I don't understand," Baker said.

"I hired him," Annie said.

"Hired him for what?" Baker asked, wondering what on earth this biker could possibly do that was worthy of a paycheck.

"Bodyguard," Gabe said, daring the man to argue.

Allen Baker had a mental flash of an earlier meeting with Annie O'Brien. He remembered her complaints about student harassment and vaguely remembered telling her to change her style of dress. He looked from her to the bike and back again in panic. This wasn't what he'd had in mind.

"You can't have a personal bodyguard," Allen Baker argued. "Whatever protection a teacher needs is furnished by the district."

"Then why didn't she get it?" Gabe asked. "Why was this woman left to deal with her problem on her own?"

Gabe didn't get an answer to his question, nor had he expected one. They left Allen Baker standing in the breezeway with his mouth agape as Annie hurried away with Gabriel Donner only a half step behind.

"The superintendent's not going to like this," Baker said, as he finally came to his senses and headed for his office. "He's not going to like this at all." And then he frowned and shuddered. "And God help us if the media gets wind of the fact that a teacher in this system felt compelled to actually hire her own security."

He began to run.

The closer Gabe and Annie got to her classroom, the louder the noise level became. Annie gave him a nervous glance over her shoulder as she started inside.

"I'm right behind you," Gabe said quietly.

The deep, level tone of his voice, as well as the reassuring touch of his hand on her shoulder, did what he'd intended. Her stomach settled, her heart rate decreased, and a calm expression spread across her face. She opened the door and walked into the room.

Damon Tuttle's hand slid up her arm, and in spite of the fact that she'd been braced to fight, she found herself being thrust against the blackboard behind her. His pale face, rank odor, red-rimmed eyes and cold stare told her more than she wanted to know. Even if he wasn't high now, he'd obviously spent most of the night that way.

"Take your seat, Damon," Annie said firmly, pushing him away from her.

He grinned and let his gaze rake her body from head to toe in a rude, sexual manner.

"I'm a little surprised to see you, Annie-Annie. Thought you might chicken . . ."

The sneer slid off of Damon Tuttle's face as his gaze went from Annie's nervous expression to the man who'd walked up behind her.

"Now, why would you think something like that?" Annie asked. "I haven't missed a day of school this year."

Damon flushed and looked nervously away as the big biker from yesterday pulled off his sunglasses and started toward him. In spite of his determination to remain belligerent, he felt himself backing away.

"Hey, *boy,*" Gabe said softly, for Damon's ears alone. "I thought we settled all of this yesterday."

Damon tried to bluster his way out of the fact that, step-by-step, the biker was backing him all the way down the aisle to his seat, but it was no use. The obvious fact was that he was scared out of his mind.

"What's he doing here?" Damon asked loudly, and pointed toward Gabe, who refused to budge from his personal space.

"Who? Oh! You must mean Mr. Donner," Annie said in an offhand manner. "Just pretend he's not here," she said, quickly taking charge of her class. "Students, please take your seats."

Gabe grinned at Damon, and the boy shuddered at the feral gleam in the big man's eyes.

"She's right," Gabe said, sweeping his hand out to encompass the class of gaping students who'd suddenly realized he was there to stay. "You won't even know I'm around."

And then he stunned the entire class as his whispered warning swept across the room. "But so help me, if one of you has one cross word to say to her...or looks at Miss O'Brien with anything other than a question about school on your mind, I'll take care of you myself." There was a long pause before he finished. "Have I made myself clear?"

They nodded as one, while silently absorbing the fact that their teacher had obviously hired herself a big gun. And then a tall, skinny youth at the back of the room stood up, making a subtle but daring move as he shoved his hands in his pockets while waiting for permission to speak.

Gabe's gaze swept over the young black man, and then he nodded. "You have something you need to say to me?" he asked softly.

"All I'm saying is...Miss O'Brien is one fine lookin' lady...if you know what I mean. So if you see me lookin' at her and you don't like the way I'm doin' it...then you just better bust my chops now, man, cause I can't help admiring the obvious."

Gabe chuckled, ignoring the flush that swept up Annie's face. "Yeah, man. I know what you mean, she is pretty. But the deal is to respect her, not take her apart . . . if *you* know what *I* mean."

The young man nodded and shrugged, then grinned and sat back down. A sprinkling of soft laughter flowed from one end of the room to the other, setting the mood for the rest of the class.

Finally the bell rang for classes to change and the students left. It was obvious from the quick, sideways glances Gabe got, and the near-silent manner in which the newcomers took their seats, that word had spread swiftly in the halls of the high school.

And when noontime came and the teachers drifted through the halls on their way to lunch, Annie O'Brien returned the favor by staring down any whispered comments about Gabe's presence and quietly introducing him to what he assumed were some of her friends and co-workers.

If it hadn't been so pathetic he would have laughed. Here he was, for the first time in his life able to experience what ordinary life was all about, and it was too late. For Gabe, it would always be too late.

The day was nearly over. Gabe sat at the back of the class, silent as a monolith, barely moving, never speaking, yet the entire day, his eyes had rarely drifted from Annie O'Brien.

He knew to the inch exactly how far up the blackboard her arm had to stretch before the fabric of her blouse cupped her breast and faintly outlined the nipple behind the cloth. He also knew that if she was facing the class when she smiled, the slight dimple at the left corner of her mouth wasn't evident. However, if her head was turned just so . . . and if she was really lost in what she was saying . . . it darted in and out like a pixie playing hide-and-seek.

He'd watched the sunlight play havoc with the hidden textures and colors of her hair until he'd had to mentally restrain himself from ignoring the fact that there was a classroom full of students watching every move he made. He'd never wanted anything in his life as much as he wanted to bury his face in her hair. To inhale the scent of her, to feel her heat and taste the texture of her skin.

He shuddered at the thought and shifted uncomfortably in his seat, stretching his long, jeans-clad legs out in front of him to ease the pressure behind his zipper.

What he'd expected to be unmitigated boredom had turned out to be a treat. He'd read history. Hell, he'd even lived part of what she'd taught earlier in the day. But he'd never expected to fall under the spell of being taught that there was more to it than dates and events. Too much of his life had been wasted just trying to survive, and when that had failed, the rest of it had been—and was *being*—spent on doing what he'd been sent back to do.

Ancient history seemed to be her favorite class. Sixth period and the Trojan War brought her to life. He, along with the students, began to visualize the great wooden horse slowly being rolled to the gates of Troy.

He smiled along with them as Annie related how the Greeks remaining outside must have waited impatiently for the soldiers encased within the bowels of the gift horse to climb out, drawing a picture with her words of how they'd emerged during the black of night and opened the great gate so that the Greek soldiers could come inside and conquer.

The great devastation of the siege that followed was presented as if she'd actually been there. Gabe wasn't the only one to be jerked rudely back to the present when the bell rang for classes to change.

"So the next time someone tells you, 'Don't look a gift horse in the mouth,' you'll know exactly what they mean."

And then she added, "Don't forget that you have to finish reading *The Iliad* by Friday. It will be part of your final exam."

She laughed at their dismayed objections and took their good-natured grumbling as it was meant. One of the girls even paused on her way out the door to whisper something to Annie, and then ducked her head when Annie impulsively laughed and hugged her before shooing her out.

But Gabe was oblivious to the students' groans on the subject of finals. He was too busy trying to get past the realization of his own devastation as he watched Annie hug the teenage girl.

He was jealous. He wanted her to smile at *him* and share whispered nothings in *his* ear. And as he looked past the thought to the emotion behind it, he decided that he'd finally lost his mind.

He'd heard of the phenomenon, but mistakenly imagined that it only befell *little* boys. But Gabriel Donner had been mistaken. Regardless of his age and the reason for his presence, he'd only spent one day in a classroom and already he'd fallen for the teacher.

In sudden panic, he grabbed his sunglasses from his pocket, slid them quickly onto his nose and glared through their darkened lenses, daring anyone to see through the mirrored reflection to the truth behind.

He couldn't be in love. For Gabriel Donner there was no future in loving. His future had ended the day the rope tightened around his neck. And regardless of the fact that he'd been returned intact to the earth on which he'd been born, for him, a future no longer existed. Only time . . . a waiting period that was soon coming to an end.

Annie gathered up the papers from her desk, sighing as she lifted the stack that would have to be graded tonight.

"Let me," Gabe said, and took them from her arms before she could object. "You did all the work today," he said by way of explanation, and stood aside for her to precede him from the room.

"Another day, another dollar," Annie said, and gave him a weary smile that made him stumble in his tracks.

Luckily for him she didn't notice him falter. She was too busy focusing on the two men standing at the end of the hallway.

"Oh, great," she muttered.

Gabe looked up, expecting to see Damon Tuttle and some of his friends. Instead, he recognized Allen Baker, the school administrator, but he didn't know the other man.

"Annie?"

The question in his voice stopped her progress, and she turned to face him. If he hadn't known Annie's fighting nature, he might have imagined he saw tears in her eyes. But that couldn't be. After facing down a gang of toughs and calmly dealing with the fact that her car had been demolished, surely two well-dressed men wouldn't be what it took to bring her down.

"It's the school superintendent," she said. "He's everyone's boss."

"Not mine," Gabe said quietly, and offered his elbow as they started down the hall.

Annie took a deep breath. It was odd what strength she'd gained from Gabe's two small words.

"Miss O'Brien." Censure was thick in Millard Penny's voice.

"Mr. Penny."

Annie stood steadfast, unwilling to give an inch. And with Gabe by her side, it was incredibly simple, after all.

"I don't like what I've been hearing," Millard Penny said, glaring at Gabe.

"I can imagine," Gabe answered, surprising everyone, including Annie, with his interruption. "What startled you most?" he asked. "The fact that one of your teachers was being assaulted and sexually harassed on a day-to-day basis . . . or the fact that Baker here chose to ignore it?"

Allen Baker stiffened, as if someone had just shoved a hot poker up his rear. Annie stifled a grin and slid one step closer to Gabriel as he continued.

"As I'm sure you've already realized, or you wouldn't be here, the media would have a field day with that information, wouldn't they?" Gabe asked.

He paused while Millard Penny digested his announcement, then grinned engagingly, tossing the problem right back in the superintendent's lap with his next remark. "What exactly did you have in mind? I can assure you, as Miss O'Brien's bodyguard, I'm willing to work in conjunction with any other security you authorize."

Penny was speechless.

And then Gabe's smile disappeared, and his eyes grew stormy. "However, you *do* realize that I am not budging from her side until she, and she alone, decides to dismiss me. I take my work seriously . . . very seriously."

Millard Penny stared. First at Annie, then at Allen Baker, then back at Gabriel. He wiped his hand across his face, dislodging the jowls hanging over his too-tight collar far enough that his chin quivered as he answered.

"I can see that this incident is going to take further study." He glared at Baker as if suddenly willing to lay the blame for the entire mess at his feet. "And as far as my teachers' security goes, you can rest assured that that is always uppermost in my mind."

"Thank you, Mr. Penny," Annie said. "I'm glad you've recognized my side of the problem." She stared pointedly at Allen Baker, then looked up at Gabriel.

He saw her determination being replaced with exhaustion. It was that moment when he knew that as long as Annie O'Brien had a fight that needed to be fought, he was her man. Like it or not, love be damned, she needed him. And it felt good ... real good.

Gabe handed her his helmet. "Put this on, Annie. We're going home."

They left the two men arguing in the hall.

# Chapter 3

After the hectic day and the constant state of defense in which they'd spent it, the apartment was a welcome haven. Gabe was beginning to understand Annie's love of plants. They were something alive with which she could share her space, and they didn't talk back.

Annie's face was pale, the tension lines around her mouth deep and drawn.

"You look beat. Why don't you take a nap?" Gabe suggested as he set the papers to be graded down on the kitchen table.

She gestured toward the stack and tried to smile, but a muscle jerked at the back of her neck, reminding her that the headache she'd been trying to ignore all day was about to take over.

"Maybe I will lie down for a minute," she said. "But I don't have time to sleep." Her lip trembled, and she looked everywhere but at Gabe. "Not yet. Not this soon."

He looked down at his watch. "At least rest until I get back. I've got an errand to run."

She shrugged and handed him her keys. "You'll need to get back in," she said, stumbling toward her bedroom as the pain at the back of her neck overwhelmed her.

Gabe looked at the keys and frowned. He couldn't understand her apparent lack of concern regarding his presence. She treated him as if she'd known him all her life. It just didn't make sense.

And as for her headache, he'd seen others like it before. He stuffed her keys in his pocket and followed her, afraid she was going to need help getting where she was going. He was right. He caught her as she staggered.

"Annie, are you all right?"

Uncertainty filled him as her head lolled against his shoulder. Only hours earlier she'd been ready to fight tigers...and Damon Tuttle. Now she couldn't even get herself to bed.

"I stubbed my toe," she mumbled, unwilling to admit how weak she felt, and covered her ears with her hands, dreading the sound of her own voice. "My head hurts."

"I know, Annie," he said softly. "I know."

Without a word, Gabe lifted her into his arms and carried her to her bed. Her face was a contorted mixture of misery and embarrassment as she struggled to help herself.

"Let me," Gabe said, and pulled off her shoes. "Got anything for the pain?" he asked, as he entered her bathroom and began shuffling through the shelves of her medicine cabinet.

"Brown bottle...bottom shelf," she mumbled, then groaned as the words vibrated against her eardrums.

Gabe picked up the bottle and frowned. Prescription medicine. No over-the-counter stuff for Annie. He read the label and frowned again. *Strong* prescription medicine. He hoped she wasn't hooked on the stuff. She wouldn't have been the first to get unintentionally addicted.

He filled a glass with water, then carried it and the bottle back to Annie's bed. The mattress gave beneath his weight, rolling her gently against his thigh as he scooted close beside her.

"Open," he ordered, and slipped the prescribed dosage between her lips. By that time her teeth were chattering from the tension, and a few drops of water slid out the corner of her mouth as he tilted the glass.

She swallowed, then dropped back onto the pillow with a groan, unaware of Gabe's fingers gently blotting the trickle of water before it stained her blue silk shirt.

He swallowed harshly as his hand touched her skin. Just as before, her body was satin to his touch. As her eyelids fluttered between the daylight and dusk hovering at the back of her mind, he cradled the side of her cheek, absently testing the pulse at the base of her neck. It was racing.

Gabe leaned back, smoothing her tousled hair away from her forehead, and felt tiny beads of sweat across her brow. Something was wrong. He hoped to God she wasn't getting sick. He knew even less about healing than he did about school, but today it seemed as if he was about to get a dose of both.

She sighed as blessed sleep claimed her, missing the tender touch of his hand and the fire that kindled in his eyes as he leaned down and kissed the curve of her cheek.

"Just rest, Annie. Rest," he whispered. "I'll be back."

Annie opened her eyes. The glow from the streetlights coming through the slats in her blinds told her that it was dark. Where had the evening gone? Then she remembered the headache and vague impressions of being put to bed like a child. She bolted up as if she'd been shot and raced out of her room and across the hall, half expecting to see that a big man and his duffel bag had gone missing. She was right.

"Oh, no," she groaned, and ran toward the living room, afraid of what she would find next. What she didn't expect was to hear the hum of her washer and dryer in the alcove off the kitchen, or the smell of warm pizza drifting in the air.

"I saved you some pizza," Gabe muttered, pointing toward a half-open cardboard box. "It's a good thing you woke up. I've graded as far as I can go. I was never much good at stuff like this, but I can at least follow your key." He waved her answer sheet in the air, then leaned back and grinned.

Annie stared. This was the last thing she'd expected to see. He was grading her papers...and he wasn't wearing enough clothes for her peace of mind. And then she remembered the pizza.

"You bought food?"

He nodded.

"I'm sorry," she muttered, running a shaky hand through her tousled hair. "You're spending your money on me, and we haven't even discussed salary."

Gabe noticed the nervous way she kept glancing at him, then remembered his disheveled state and grinned.

"Sorry about my, uh . . ." He waved toward his near-bare body and shrugged, as if to say he had no choice. "I'm doing laundry."

His grin told her that he was obviously lying. He wasn't sorry about a thing, and Annie knew it.

"What exactly is that you're wearing?" she asked, trying not to stare at all that expanse of tanned body and hard muscle.

"Your tablecloth. It was the only thing big enough to wrap around me. I don't think flowers do much for my manliness, but..." He shrugged and waved toward his makeshift sarong to make his point.

He could have saved himself the trouble. It was impossible to ignore his manliness... any of it. Annie tried not to stare in the direction the sweet-pea-and-ivy print was climbing, but she couldn't help noticing that it had climbed right up his leg and wrapped itself around his...

"Supreme," he said.

You certainly are, Annie thought, and then jumped as her own thoughts reminded her that she was losing control. "What?"

"The pizza," he said, pointing toward the box again. "I got supreme. And you'll have to grade this stack," he said, as he shoved the papers toward her.

"I can't believe you did that, but thanks," she said, pointing toward the papers, and then took a bite of pizza. She muttered a near-silent curse as a string of cheese fell onto the edge of her collar.

Gabe stood up. And as he came toward her, bells and buzzers began to sound. Annie's eyes widened. So much man in so little fabric.

Fear interceded as she watched him coming closer and closer. She began backing up, until the kitchen wall halted her flight and left her helpless and pinned, the slice of pizza clutched tightly in her hand.

Without saying a word, Gabe reached out, lifted the string of cheese from her collar and dangled it in front of her lips. Stunned by the unexpected action, Annie opened her mouth like a baby bird as Gabe dropped the cheese inside.

Her heartbeat rode her racing pulse like a winded jockey as she watched him, certain that he was about to eat her...or her pizza, whichever came first. He did neither.

Instead, he gently moved her aside and opened the door behind her. It was then that she realized why she'd been hearing bells and buzzers. The washer and dryer had finished their cycles simultaneously. He was merely getting his clean clothes out of the laundry.

"Why don't you sit down to eat, Annie?" he asked. "You need all the rest you can get. I never realized that teaching could be such a headache."

He grinned at his own wit as he disappeared down the hall in a swath of sweet peas and ivy. He returned a moment later, dragging long-legged blue jeans along the carpet, with a handful of white cotton briefs clutched against his chest.

"I *am* going to sit down to eat," Annie said unnecessarily, and plopped down in the chair he'd just vacated.

The chair was still warm from his body, and the suggestion it sent drifting into her mind had her out of it in seconds and into the one on the opposite side. She'd had all the excitement she could take for one day. Thinking about big bikers and their warm behinds did nothing for her peace of mind.

The evening passed without further upheaval, as did the next few days. One week turned into two, and then, before she knew it, they'd actually developed a routine of living together that was almost comfortable.

It was his proper, almost blasé attitude and her own casual acceptance of his presence in her life that—most of the time—made her forget how truly male he was. But she was reminded all too vividly one weekend when she looked up from the chair in which she was sitting to see him burst through the door, half naked and mad as hell.

"Where is your shirt?" It was the first thing that came to mind, but Annie knew the moment she'd asked that it was the worst question she could have asked.

Gabe grinned, but not with humor. He stalked past her and continued down the hallway toward his room without answering.

Annie got up from her chair, pulling absently at her white T-shirt and shorts to straighten them as she followed. It was then that she saw the small path of blood splattered on the floor in his wake and felt a moment of panic as she realized that it had to be Gabe who was bleeding.

Ignoring propriety, she burst into his room without knocking and caught him leaning over the sink in his bathroom, trying to wash a long, angry slash on the back of his arm.

"You're bleeding!"

He turned. His eyes pierced her, blue shards of icy fury pinning her in place.

"Not as much as I was before," he drawled, remembering the puddle of blood he'd left beside his bike, along with what was left of his shirt in the garbage can outside. He winced when the cold washcloth slid along the tear in his flesh.

"Oh, my God," Annie said, and moved. Before she could think, she'd taken the cloth from his hand and pushed him backward onto the commode. "Sit down," she said, and leaned forward, peering over his shoulder to see if there was further damage to his back that she hadn't noticed.

Gabe hit the seat with a sigh, wearily giving in to the exhaustion and pain he was experiencing, and wondered how much longer his body could endure what he put it through. In the same thought, he realized the silent question was moot. If his calculations were correct, his time on earth was nearly up. It was that thought, and the knowledge that he couldn't have the forever that he wanted with this woman beside him, that made him react as he did when Annie cupped his chin with her fingers and started to wipe the cool, damp cloth across his face as she would a child's.

He took the cloth from her hands and flung it into the bathtub, and before she knew what was happening, she was in his lap, and his hands were on her face. She had one moment of fear, and then it swiftly disappeared as he groaned, leaned forward and covered her lips with his own.

Annie shuddered. It was like feeling steel melt against her lips. At first his lips were hard and hot, and then they shifted, softening, testing the corners of her mouth, her chin, even the hollow at her neck.

"Gabriel," she whispered, and then, when she could breathe again, she realized that he'd only begun. His body trembled beneath her fingers, and as her hand slid down the front of his chest, his heartbeat thundered beneath the skin, rumbling like the Harley's engine on a wild ride to heaven . . . or hell.

He scooped her into his arms and stood. Without words, he carried her into his room and then stopped by the side of his bed. His gaze went from her face to his bed, then back again. In spite of the question in his eyes, Annie could not speak. It was all the answer he needed.

The bedspread was cool and slick against the bare skin on the backs of her legs as Gabe deposited her with little aplomb. Annie shuddered and moaned as his hands swept down the front of her breasts, molding the thin fabric of her T-shirt to her generous curves. He straddled her body, positioning himself so that her womanhood was in perfect juxtaposition to his own aching need, and then leaned forward and pressed his mouth across the protesting bud he'd made of her nipple, which protruded upward beneath the cloth.

With mouth and hands, he moved across her body like a marauding outlaw, and just when Annie thought he would take without asking, he stopped, buried his face against her belly and started to shake.

"Gabriel?"

She traced her fingers across the taut, corded muscles of his neck and shoulders, feeling the tension and the emotion he was trying to control.

"I want you, Annie." His voice was low and guttural, muffled against her belly as he struggled with the red-hot need to rip the clothes from her body and bury himself deep inside her heat. "But it isn't fair to you. You deserve promises I can't make. A love I can't give. You don't deserve this . . . to be taken in want and need. And right now—" a shudder ripped through him as his fingers tightened in the flesh at her waist "—all I'm feeling is need."

It killed him to admit the truth of his feelings, but it would have been the end of him later if he'd taken her in a lie.

Tears squeezed from the corners of Annie's eyes as her hands gently stroked his shoulders and down his back until she actually felt the anger dissipating beneath her touch.

"It's all right, Gabriel," she whispered. "It's all right." *I would have been willing to settle for need,* she told herself as she watched him roll off her body and walk back into the bathroom. *There's no time in my life for promises, either. Not anymore.*

She got off the bed and walked out of the room.

It was only days later, standing in line at a local supermarket, that she learned what had happened to him. That he'd walked into a robbery at a gas station not three blocks from her home and wound up in a fight that might have cost him his life.

When she heard the story, Annie stared at the box of cornflakes in her hand and then down at her basket and tried to remember what she'd been about to do. But she couldn't. All she could hear was the woman praising an unknown biker for saving her husband's life, and all she could see were the events that had ensued.

It was then that Annie thought she understood where Gabriel's intense need to have sex had come from. It must be a natural emotion to want to feel alive, when only a short time earlier you had come so close to being dead.

The cornflakes fell from her limp fingers onto a loaf of bread as Annie closed her eyes and swallowed past a lump in her throat. She could think of no better way to feel alive than to experience the blessed rush that came from the joining of two bodies with one purpose...making love.

Time continued to pass with little mention ever made of the near miss they'd had and the wanting that hung between them. Gabe's presence in Annie's world had become so solid that she could not imagine life without him. Yet always, at that thought, came an overwhelming sadness, because for Annie, there would be no future with Gabe. When school was over, he would leave her. She had to face that fact. It was the only way she could get through the days they had left.

Sirens screamed, matching a woman's terrified shriek. Annie sat straight up in bed, heart pounding, eyes heavy with sleep as she tried to imagine why she was still hearing a nightmare when she was wide awake.

A door banged across the hall, and Annie realized that she wasn't having the dream alone. Gabriel's footsteps moved quickly toward the living room. It was only when she heard the front door open and then slam shut behind him that she knew she was truly awake. She bolted out of bed and ran to the window.

Her first thought was that she was hearing police sirens. But when she parted the curtains and looked outside, her heart sank. Fire trucks were everywhere.

"Oh, God! The complex must be on fire," she moaned, and ran to the closet. If she was going to lose everything she owned within the next few minutes, she didn't want to be nearly naked when it happened.

In less than a minute she had on jeans and a sweatshirt. With socks and shoes in hand and shaking from the rush of fear and adrenaline, she stuffed her personal identification in the hip pocket of her jeans and ran for the door.

In the back of her mind, she was both surprised and disappointed that Gabriel had left the apartment without even warning her of the danger. But then, as she raced toward the parking lot where the other residents were gathering, she realized that she'd misjudged him completely. The danger was not to her own building, but to the one two buildings over and closest to the street.

Using the bumper of the nearest car for a makeshift seat, she quickly put on her socks and shoes, shivering nervously as she struggled to tie the strings without making knots, still wondering where Gabriel was and why he'd disappeared so fast.

Firemen were wielding their hoses and making way for the paramedic unit that had just arrived. The paramedics rushed out of the ambulance and, with skill born of long years of practice, quickly cleared a space in the crowd as they began setting up a first-aid station. Another ambulance arrived, available, if needed, to transport the injured. And then a woman's horrified shriek silenced the crowd's rumble of dismay.

"There's a child in that apartment!"

All eyes turned toward the third-story apartment facing the parking lot. A small girl, probably no more than nine or ten, was outlined by the flashing lights from below as she stood at the window, pounding on the glass with both hands. It was like watching terror in pantomime as she struggled helplessly against the glass barrier, unable to lift the window.

The onlookers, Annie included, felt sickened and helpless as they watched the child through the glass. Gabriel's whereabouts was momentarily forgotten in her shock, until she saw a tall, dark man slip through the crowd, run past the fire fighters and into the smoke-filled doorway.

"Gabriel!" Annie screamed, but her shout was lost in the noise around her.

Few people even acknowledged her cry as they stared transfixed toward the child, who was now moving helplessly from window to window in the room.

A handful of firemen held a net directly below her, but she was still unable to break the window. The people could only watch and hope that the man would be able to rescue her in time. Annie increased her own silent but terrified pleas for help as they waited and prayed.

"Oh, my God," Annie whispered, pressing shaking fingers against her lips, unable...unwilling...to believe that she'd really seen Gabe run into the building.

Frantically, she began moving through the crowd in the parking lot, certain that any minute Gabe would grab her arm and spin her around with that heart-stopping smile on his face, chiding her for her fears. But it didn't happen, and she had to face the fact that it *was* him that she'd seen.

A local news crew, which had materialized out of nowhere, had also seen the man, and cameras were instantly trained on the last place he had been seen, as well as the girl in the window.

Fear such as Annie had never known enveloped her. This was worse than anything she'd ever experienced. Fear for herself she could cope with. But this fear for another human being, one who'd come to mean more to her than he should, nearly overwhelmed her.

Ignoring the intermittent tails of smoke that blew toward the crowd in which she was standing, Annie stared at the child in the window and prayed as she'd never prayed before.

Long moments that seemed like hours passed, and then suddenly another gasp went up through the crowd. Flames could now be seen behind the child, and they all knew it was only a matter of moments before it would be too late.

"There's someone in there!" a man shouted and raised his arm, pointing toward the child as a second figure appeared at the window.

Moments later glass shattered onto the firemen below. But they stood their ground and waited, bracing themselves and holding on even tighter to the net. Seconds later, two figures stood in the opening. A man leaned out, holding the limp body of the child. Just as the camera crew focused, he let go of the child, and she fell through the air, as silent as her earlier plea for help had been.

With hardly a thud, the firemen deftly made the catch and then transferred her semiconscious body to the arms of a paramedic, who turned and made a dash toward the waiting ambulance. The man came next. With the flames licking at his feet and no time to maneuver, he leapt headfirst out the window.

Gabe landed on his back, unable to believe that he was still in one piece as he stared up at the smoke-filled night sky.

"You crazy son of a bitch," one of the firemen said, as they rolled him out of the net and slapped him roughly on the back. "You could have been killed."

Gabe staggered to his feet as he gratefully drew long draughts of clean air into his lungs. A man in uniform began heading toward him. Unwilling to explain himself, Gabe turned and quickly lost himself in the gathering crowd.

Annie had watched until she saw him stand up. Then she buried her face in her hands and fell to her knees, unable to move for the relief that coursed through her body. Hands appeared from the crowd around her, quickly pulling her to her feet, then moving her to the edge of the pack.

"Are you all right, miss?" a voice asked.

Annie looked up into the face of a man she recognized as living in her own building. She nodded.

"You sure?" he continued. "It looks as if they've got it under control. I'd be glad to walk you back to your place."

"No, no, I'm fine," Annie muttered, and began looking for Gabe. He was nowhere to be seen.

She pulled away from her neighbor's grasp and started running. Something told her that Gabe wouldn't stick around for an interview. She headed for her apartment.

Her legs were shaking along with her hands as she struggled with the doorknob, trying to make it turn. And then finally it gave and she burst into the living room, only to hear the sound of water running in the shower down the hall. Without sparing a thought for what she was about to do, she slammed the door behind her and began to run. Seconds later she was in his bedroom.

A heavy mist floated out of the shower stall. A pile of smoke-tainted clothing lay in the doorway. The faint but unmistakable outline of a tall, male figure behind the frosted Plexiglas door was all the impetus she needed.

Gabe was leaning with arms outstretched against the wall, bracing himself beneath the flow of water, letting it wash away the acrid stench of smoke and fire. He leaned forward, closed his eyes and sighed as the steady stream rushed over his head and down the back of his neck, easing the muscles he'd strained only moments before and soothing the tiny scorched places on his skin. And then the door flew open and he moved away from the water's force, staring in shock at the look on Annie's face.

"You could have been killed," she said in a broken whisper.

Ignoring the fact that she was fully dressed and he was not, she stepped into the shower and into his arms.

"Annie! My God!" Gabe groaned, as his body betrayed him.

Water pelted down on top of them. Several seconds passed as Gabe stood in shock before he thought to reach over her shoulder and close the door to keep the floor from being flooded.

"Back off, Annie!" His voice thickened as her hands moved up and down his back in a desperate, searching motion, as if she couldn't believe he was actually there and in her arms.

But his warning was useless. She was as glued to him as her clothing was to her own body. With a muttered oath, he reached over her once again, this time to turn off the shower.

Suddenly there was only the sound of Gabriel's harshly indrawn breath as she stepped back and looked at him. Everywhere. Once again his body betrayed him, and this time there was no way he could hide what her nearness had done.

Annie closed her eyes and let the sensations of what she'd seen fill her. And when she opened them again, it was to feel him pulling her wet sweatshirt over her head.

"You have about thirty seconds to get the hell out of here," Gabe said. "Or it'll be too late . . . for both of us."

She shook her head and slid the palms of her hands up his chest as the sweatshirt fell to the floor of the shower with a soggy plop. Her bare breasts tingled as a draft of air moved

across them, tightening the nubs in their centers to a jutting
pout.

Gabriel groaned and bent forward, testing them with the
end of his tongue. She sighed as his lips moved over her and
leaned against his body when her knees went weak, bracing
her hands on his chest, where his heart pounded wildly beneath the skin.

"It's already too late, Gabriel. It has been since the day
we met."

He wasn't certain it was tears that he saw on her face. It
could have been the lingering remnants of their shower. But
the trembling of her lower lip told him all he needed to
know.

"Annie...I can't promise you anything," he said harshly,
still unable to make the last and final move toward the inevitable.

"I don't need promises, Gabriel. Promises mean a future. You and I don't have that. All we have is now...and
it's all I need."

The shower door flew back, slamming with a sharp thud
against the wall as Gabriel picked her up and carried her to
his bed. There, in a tangle of teddy bears and bed sheets, he
stripped her of the rest of her clothing and covered her body
with the fierce determination of a warrior claiming his prize.

He was everything she'd imagined and more than she
could have dreamed. His hands moved with gentle finesse
across her body, lighting fires in places that had never been
ignited before. Every curve of her skin became a flash point
of nerves. She struggled beneath him, trying to return the
favors of his loving, and then found herself unable to do
anything but simply hang on to his shoulders as he took
them both to a place where time ceased and sensation was
the beginning and end of everything.

"Annie, Annie, Annie."

Her name was a chant on his lips as his hands slid between her legs. And then a roar began in her ears that blocked out everything but the feelings building beneath her skin. Fire bursts came in sudden, intense jolts, starting from the center of her being and emanating outward, melting her bones and her senses until she could no longer move or think. All there was in her world was Gabriel's hands, his lips, and the feel of his body moving up and then over... down and inside.

Gabriel slid between her legs, shuddering with every breath as his mind raced his body for control. But Annie's own loss of control was unbelievable, unexpected, and too much to resist.

Her hands said what her lips could not as she grasped his shoulders and urged him on. And when her hips lifted from the bed and begged him to come closer, he did. By then he was too far in and too far gone to remember to prolong anything but the need to breathe.

Annie's heart raced, her body burned, and Gabriel kept touching matches to the fire with intensifying thrusts.

When the first tremors began inside her, moving along his manhood in tiny, convulsive jerks, Gabriel groaned from the pleasure. Through a sensual fog, he watched as Annie closed her eyes, bit her lower lip and arched upward, trying to engulf him. And then everything exploded around them as the world tilted on its axis, and Gabriel held on to the woman beneath him to keep from flying away.

The last thing Annie remembered before falling asleep was Gabe's arms enfolding her and his faint whisper drifting across her ears.

"This wasn't supposed to happen, Annie Laurie," he kept saying. "This wasn't supposed to happen."

Hours later Annie felt herself being taken from the warm bed and carried across the hall. A sharp, unwelcome pain surfaced behind her eyelids when she realized that Gabe had put her back in her own bed. She all but held her breath, unwilling for him to know that she was awake. The hurt was too fresh and too swift as she realized that he hadn't even been willing to awaken with her in his arms.

Finally she heard his footsteps receding, and then the door to her room closed. It was then that the tears came, and with them, the knowledge that she had no reason to cry. He'd warned her that he had no room for promises in his life. And yet Annie knew that she wasn't actually crying because he couldn't promise her anything. She was crying because it wouldn't have mattered if he had.

The next morning the newspapers and television stations were full of the phantom hero who'd dared the fires of hell and saved a child from the burning building. The grainy footage of the rescue was played and replayed the entire day, but luckily for Gabriel, the thick, billowing smoke had hidden his face.

Annie didn't understand his reticence and wondered again if she was harboring a man who was on the run from something . . . or someone. She didn't want to think that Gabriel had a lurid past. But all she had to do was catch him unaware and look, really look, at the hard expression he wore when he thought no one was watching, and her fears came back twofold.

The intercom buzzed, an indication that an announcement from the principal's office would be forthcoming. Annie paused in the middle of her lecture and waited without looking at the back of the room, where she knew Gabriel was watching her every move. Since the night they'd made love, little more than quiet politeness had passed between them. Each evening, immediately after they got home, Gabriel would disappear into his room and come out only to eat or run the occasional errand for her. Yet his looks had gentled, and she would have sworn she saw constant regret coloring the expression on his face.

Twice she'd tried to pay him for his duties as a bodyguard, and each time she'd yanked the check back, his anger so fierce that she'd half expected to see that he'd lopped her hand off at the wrist.

While part of her understood that something had changed between them, the other part of her needed to fulfill her own promise and alleviate the guilt she felt over what had happened the night of the fire. She'd all but begged him for intimacy, and after he'd warned her there was no future in it for either of them.

She fumbled with the papers on her desk as she waited for Allen Baker to make his announcement, desperately trying to ignore the feelings that had returned with her thoughts of making love with Gabe.

Gabriel's eyes narrowed as he watched her look at everyone and everything but him. In a way he understood her need to maintain the distance between them, and in another way he resented the hell out of the fact that she'd been able to do it. Since the moment she'd opened the shower and walked into his arms, she'd been more deeply imbedded in his senses than the heat and smoke from that fire.

"This concerns all graduating seniors," Allen Baker said, his voice slightly distorted from the microphone. "Please remember that graduation practice will be right after school today. Try to attend. It will help the actual ceremony go much more smoothly this weekend."

He signed off with a short witticism that no one laughed at, leaving the class oddly silent.

Damon Tuttle fidgeted in his seat and stared at Annie with his old hatred as she turned her back to the class and began writing an assignment on the blackboard.

Gabriel sensed an imminent eruption, and still he was surprised by the anger with which it came.

"You bitch!" Damon Tuttle shouted as he stood up from his desk and threw his book toward Annie.

Gabriel bolted for the front of the room, but not in time to stop the book. He winced, then breathed a quick sigh of relief as he saw Annie duck. Two students near the door jumped up and ran into the hall.

Gabriel heard their footsteps echoing toward what he hoped was the principal's office. He had no time to be dealing with anything except the fact that Damon Tuttle had just pulled a knife and jumped over two desks in an effort to get to Annie.

"Annie, run!" Gabriel shouted, then said a prayer as he made a flying leap, catching Damon at the back of the legs and sending them both falling across desks and then rolling onto the floor.

The piny scent of cleaning solvent came up and hit Gabriel in the face as he and Damon rolled over and over on the floor, fighting desperately with each other for control of the knife.

Damon Tuttle's pupils were dilated, his nostrils flared, as venomous curses poured from his mouth.

A security guard burst into the room, with Allen Baker right behind him. Among the three of them, they managed to subdue Damon Tuttle without anyone being injured.

And when the knife in Damon's hand fell to the floor at Allen Baker's feet, he could only stare in stunned disbelief.

The security guard slapped handcuffs on Damon as sirens were heard in the distance.

"I'll get you, you bitch," Damon kept shouting. "You won't get away with this. You'll be sorry you gave me grief!"

Gabriel shook as he grabbed the youth's arm and yanked him around to face him.

"She didn't give you anything but a chance at a better life," Gabe said.

Damon spat on Gabriel's boots, then looked up with hate-filled eyes. "She didn't give me nothin'. Anything I have...I gave myself," he yelled back, screaming and kicking out at the guard and the principal alike.

"Take him out of here," Allen Baker ordered, and then he stepped aside in undisguised fear as Damon's glare of hatred was turned on him.

Damon was still screaming and cursing when they dragged him out the door and into a patrol car.

"Is anyone hurt?" Annie asked quickly, searching the room as students began rearranging their belongings and moving desks back into place. The tremor in her voice was evident, but no fear showed in her movements. As usual, in her classroom, Annie was in total control.

"No, ma'am," several students echoed.

"Then please take your seats. Turn to the last chapter of the book and begin reviewing the quiz. Test tomorrow."

With that she walked out of the room and into the hall. It was there that Gabriel caught her.

His arm was on her wrist as she spun around. The look in his eyes was wild. A thin trickle of blood ran from the corner of his lip. Annie dug in her pocket for a tissue. She had started to blot the blood with shaking hands when Gabriel stopped her.

"Why the hell didn't you run?" Gabriel asked, his voice rough with dying panic.

"Because it was my classroom. Those are my students. If I'd run, one of *them* might have suffered, instead."

"Oh, God, Annie," Gabriel said, and pulled her into his arms. For the first time since they'd made love he was holding her, and he knew then that it wouldn't be the last.

"He hurt you," she said, and buried her face against his chest.

"He didn't hurt me, Annie. I hurt myself."

She looked up. His blue eyes were blazing with a fire she could not miss. At that moment she knew that what he'd just said had nothing to do with Damon and everything to do with them.

She sighed and then let him pull her back into his arms. For whatever time they had left, she would not deny him, or herself, anything.

## Chapter 4

Their feelings were out in the open. The knowing and the wanting no longer had to be hidden. But it didn't make that first step toward each other any easier.

Glances were swift, smiles easier, but still uncomfortable, and the air between them was thick with unspoken emotions as they drove home from school.

Annie went straight to her room to change, while Gabe lingered in the front of the apartment, prowling from kitchen to living room and back again, uncertain which way to go with the shift in their relationship.

He'd promised her nothing, and she'd accepted that...and whatever else he was willing to give. But the professional Annie O'Brien was at odds with the one he saw at home. The one at school let no one intrude on her territory. She was proud and protective of all her students. Except for Damon Tuttle, she even made excuses for the troublemakers.

But that Annie didn't fit with the Annie who'd taken a total stranger into her home, offered him a bed, and then slept only feet away with nothing more than a few yards of carpeting and a couple of doors between them. Why had she taken such chances with her own safety? He could have been far more of a danger than three Damon Tuttles.

Gabe stalked to the window and stared out into the street, fingering his lip, which had been cut during the fight, and remembering the night of the fire and the abandon with which Annie had come to him. His gut kicked as his body reacted to the memory of them together in the shower, wet and naked, and the way she'd calmly accepted his warning of "no promises."

He frowned. Either she was lying to herself or to him about her feelings, because in all his long years, he'd never known another woman who would accept his making love without also making promises. And knowing he couldn't make them made him sick. Never before, in the millions of miles that he'd traveled, had he ever regretted the fact that he couldn't say what he was sure Annie needed to hear.

He leaned his forehead against the windowpane, letting the lingering warmth from the heat of the day soothe the ache between his eyes as he wished that his life had been different. And then, at that notion, he laughed aloud.

*Hell! If it had been different, I would have been dust long ago and never have known my Annie.*

At the same moment that he realized he'd thought of her as his, she walked up behind him. It was the shock of that realization and the feel of her hands on his back that made him react as he did.

"Are you all right?" Annie asked, remembering the viciousness with which Damon had fought and the strength that Gabe had used to subdue him.

"No," Gabe growled, and pulled her off her feet and into his arms.

Her own reaction was instinctive. Annie held on. She had no other choice as he carried her down the hall toward his room.

"You shouldn't be carrying me," Annie said. "You may be hurt."

"I *am* hurting," he said, as he reached the side of the bed. He turned her in his arms and slid her body slowly down against his own as he set her back on her feet.

"I hurt here," he said, emotion thick in his voice, as he took her hand and splayed it across his chest, watching with intensity as her fingers traced the feel of his heartbeat. "And I hurt here," he continued, and took her hand, moving it from his chest to the growing ache between his legs.

Annie gasped at the seductive familiarity and then found herself cupping him instead of withdrawing, instantly drawn into the promise of passion hovering behind a curtain of blue jeans.

At her touch, Gabe lost control. If only she'd pulled back or made a sound of complaint, given any indication that he'd overstepped a boundary, he might have stopped. But she hadn't moved except to trace the power of his need and caress it even more as it pushed against her hand.

"Annie!"

Her name echoed loudly in the silence, and then she began to shake as his hands tore at her clothing, yanking at buttons, struggling with zippers, furious with whatever stood between him and the need she'd created.

With every garment he pulled off, her own passion grew. By the time she was naked, her hands were trembling. She unzipped his jeans and felt him, shivering from the onslaught of feelings that swept through her. She felt omnipotent, as if she were holding on to lightning, just waiting for the thunderbolt that would take her to heaven. Her legs went weak as she tried to pull the shirt from his back, suddenly anxious for the feelings that she knew he was capable of creating within her.

"No," he groaned, as red pinpoints of light began to appear before his eyes. He was too far gone to take the time to undress. "No time," he said, and braced his legs as he lifted her up and then impaled her on his engorged manhood.

Annie's gasp slid across his senses as she braced herself against his chest.

She felt his mouth at her temple and sighed with anxious expectation for what was coming. Just as the room began to spin, she inadvertently looked down and saw how their bodies were melding. The image was staggering, and her head snapped back in an instant need to see his face, to know if what he was experiencing was as powerful and out of control as she imagined. She wasn't prepared for his desperation.

His eyes were burning, blue fire in a face gone taut with passion. His nostrils flared, and the perfect cut of his lips had thinned as his need for this woman sent him out of control.

"Don't move," Gabriel said harshly. Blood pounded against his eardrums, rocketing through his body in a wild, near-vicious flow as he struggled with his own lust in a need to give her pleasure.

But Annie didn't—or couldn't—heed the warning. Her legs wrapped around his waist, and as they did, she drew him even farther into her heat.

Honey flowed around him, moving him too far inside to pull back. With a groan, they fell onto the bed in a tumble of arms and legs, and without missing a beat, Gabriel began to thrust.

Unable to prolong the passion, unwilling to wait for the thunderous climax he knew was coming, he closed his eyes, wrapped his arms around Annie and let the storm overtake them.

The suddenness with which it struck left her breathless, with tears washing her cheeks in wild abandon. Her neck arched, her hands clung, as Gabriel rode her toward madness.

The end came without warning. No buildup of sensations, no increasing fire. Just a blinding flash of heat that seared their bodies, then seeped through their systems, leaving them weak and shaken.

Gabriel felt her tears on his face and knew a moment of terror. Had he hurt her? How could he have used her so viciously without a thought for her own needs? With a groan, he lifted himself from her body and stared down into her face and the wild tangle he'd made of her hair.

"Annie, Annie...sweet Lord, but I'm sorry. Don't cry. Please don't cry."

She shuddered and pulled him back into her arms.

"How can I not?" she asked, as emotion shook her voice. "Beauty always makes me cry."

Her words stunned him. Shamed by the giving nature of the woman beneath him, he covered her face with gentle kisses of thanksgiving and knew a terrible moment of regret that they would never have a lifetime together.

Moments later he rid himself of the rest of his clothing and then fell back into bed, wrapping her tight within his embrace as he pulled her head beneath his chin. Slowly her body relaxed against him, and he knew almost to the moment when she fell asleep. It was only then that he could speak, and when he did, he kept repeating the same words softly...over and over.

"Annie...my Annie."

*   *   *

Saturday came and went with little notice. It was the next morning before Gabriel realized what Annie was doing. She'd retreated from his bed to her own room shortly upon waking. Now his brow furrowed thoughtfully as he listened to the water running in her shower.

*Just what does she have to do this morning that's important enough to take her out of my arms?*

Gabe rolled out of bed and headed for his own shower. If she was going somewhere, she would still need him at her side. Although Damon Tuttle had been booked and jailed, the judicial system was notorious for releasing the wrong people at the wrong time.

Minutes later Gabe headed for the kitchen, wearing nothing but a pair of Levi's and a frown. He poured a cup of coffee and then turned with it halfway to his lips as he watched Annie come up the hallway and into the kitchen. She looked different. Suspicion continued to grow.

"You put up your hair," he said.

It was more accusation than observation. Gabe took a slow sip of coffee while trying to decipher her nervousness.

"Is there any more coffee?" Annie asked, knowing full well that the pot had just been made.

Gabe rolled his eyes and handed her his cup. "Take mine," he said. "You look like you need it worse than I do."

Her features froze. The moment he said it, he saw her pain. At that instant Gabe wished himself into the next century.

Annie set the cup down and turned away. Her dress billowed out around her legs as she walked toward the window. Gabe stared at the slender, seductive outline of her body beneath the fragile yellow fabric and wished he knew what he'd said that was so bad. He'd already learned that when Annie hurt, so did he. That he'd caused it made the pain nearly unbearable.

"What? What on earth did I say?" he asked as he followed her to the window, cupping her shoulders with his hands and pulling her toward him until her back rested against his chest. He felt her momentary slump, and then all the muscles in her body tensed as she answered him.

"Wrong? Nothing's wrong," she mumbled. "It's Sunday. I'm just going to church . . . that's all."

He grew still. *Church! Oh damn.*

Even now, churches still made him nervous. All he had to do was walk into one, and every feeling he'd suffered from the time he'd been hanged, until he came to facedown in the Kansas dirt, returned in full. Everything he'd seen and heard ricocheted inside his head like a nightmare until he could exit the building.

He had a feeling that it was God's way of reminding him why he'd been given a second chance. What he was having trouble reconciling was the fact that for the first time in nearly a hundred and fifty years, Annie had given him a reason for living, and it was too late to care.

"Great . . . church," he muttered, unaware that she heard him.

"I don't remember asking you to go," Annie said shortly.

Gabe stared. Something was terribly wrong. If he hadn't known better, he would have sworn that she didn't want him along.

"You can't ride on the back of my bike in that dress," he said, choosing to ignore her rudeness.

"I called a cab," she said, and shrugged out of his grasp.

"I don't have anything to wear," he said.

Annie smiled in spite of herself. "That's supposed to be my line," she said, and turned.

Gabe stared down into green eyes welling with tears. Whatever was going on, he had no intention of missing it. He took her chin between his thumb and forefinger and tilted her face so that she couldn't miss what he was about to say.

"You do not go without me," he ordered, and disappeared.

Annie sighed. She should have known he would be like this. She kicked her toe furiously into the plush gray carpet and then winced when a small pain shot up her leg. How could she have known that hiring a solitary man like Gabriel Donner would become so complicated? Why did he have to come into her life when it was too late to matter?

A yellow cab pulled up into the parking lot of the apartment and honked. Annie looked out the window and then went to get her purse. She would only warn him once. If he missed the ride, it wouldn't be her fault.

"Cab's here," she said, barely loud enough for him to hear, and started out the door with her purse strap slung over her shoulder.

"Got your keys?" Gabe asked as he grasped the door at a point just above her head.

She swiveled around and glared, and then dug into her purse to check. She pulled them out and slapped them into his outstretched hand, then walked away, leaving him to shut and lock the door.

She was already in the cab when Gabe came sauntering down the walkway as if he had all the time in the world. For a big man, he moved with unusual grace. Annie tried not to stare, but it was impossible. She knew only too well how much man there was inside that denim. And in honor of the day, he'd somehow unearthed a near-white shirt and a soft brown leather bomber jacket she'd never seen him wear.

She knew his entrance was going to make a quiet commotion in church, but there was absolutely nothing she could do about it. And then later, after they'd arrived and Gabe slid into the seat beside her and quietly clasped her hand, she knew that she wouldn't have changed a thing about him if she could.

Night slid across the horizon with little fuss. A car horn sounded from the parking lot as an impatient driver tried to hurry a dawdling friend. Gabriel set the last clean glass in the cabinet and then turned. The kitchen was clean. The leftovers had been covered and stored. The evening meal had come and gone with little more than polite conversation.

He sighed and slapped the dish towel down on the counter and went in search of Annie. She'd left nearly half an hour earlier to take a phone call, and she'd never come back.

The door to her room was slightly ajar. He pushed it aside and then stood in the doorway, frowning at the small lump she'd made of herself in the middle of her bed.

Curled knees to chin, her arms hugging herself to keep from coming undone, Annie lay wide-eyed and quiet, staring without blinking at the opposite wall.

Gabe inhaled sharply. A sick feeling came and went in the middle of his stomach, although there was no obvious reason for his uneasiness. A person had a right to quiet times. He could accept that. But the memory of her fixed attention during the church service that morning, and the near-panic he'd seen more than once in her eyes as she'd listened intently to the sermon, made him wonder. He was certainly no expert on religion. But the last time he'd checked, people weren't supposed to be afraid of it.

"Annie, are you all right?"

She jerked as if she'd been shot, unwound herself and sprang from the bed.

"I'm fine," she said, and turned away to smooth the wrinkles she'd made in the spread.

"Who was on the phone?" he asked, determined to get to the bottom of her withdrawal.

She shrugged. "A policeman. He called to tell me that Damon Tuttle made bail."

A rich chorus of unusually descriptive curses fell from Gabriel's lips. Annie turned and smiled at him in spite of herself.

"It's no big deal," she said. "Besides...I don't think it's humanly possible to do what you just suggested."

Gabriel glared. "If that punk comes anywhere near you again, I'll show you—and him—what a little imagination can accomplish."

"It doesn't matter," Annie said. "In two days school will be over. After that, it's immaterial what happens."

Gabriel covered the distance between them in two strides and took her by the shoulders.

"I don't get it," he growled. "Why the apathy, Annie? For weeks you've acted like all that matters is finishing the damned school year, and now you don't care about anything...not even saving your own hide."

She yanked herself out of his grasp and turned away, unwilling to look at him when she answered.

"School matters...at least to me. Besides," she said, and bit her lower lip to keep from crying, "this time next week you'll be long gone and I'll be forgotten. Right?"

Tears blurred her vision as she pulled aside the curtain in her bedroom and looked out into the street. Cars sailed by on a river of asphalt, honking horns in warning, like buoys bobbing in a sea of darkness, to let other drivers know they were passing.

Gabe slid his arms around her and pulled her hard against him until her shoulder blades dug into his chest in mute objection. He rested his chin at the crown of her head and closed his eyes against the pain.

Now it comes, he thought. Here's where she begins to blame me for making love to her without promises.

"Is that what's wrong, Annie? Are you mad at me because I didn't say I...because I can't promise that we'll..."

She laughed and spun in his arms. He saw the sheen of tears in her eyes and felt like a heel.

"Lord, no!" she said, and threw her arms around his neck. "You are what you are, Gabriel Donner. I wouldn't want to change you...even if I could."

He let himself absorb the feel of her body against him, tried to ignore the dampness on her cheeks as she lifted her face for his kiss, and knew that she was lying. And as he took advantage of what she offered, he hated himself for not being able to call her hand.

The bell rang. At that same instant, the entire classroom full of students erupted into a shout of gladness. School was out!

Gabe stood at the back of the room and grinned, watching as the bulk of the class headed for the door in a single motion. They were a mass of humanity on the move. The noise level was just below painful as desks scooted and students shouted playfully back and forth to one another while continuing toward the exit.

Annie fielded comments and accepted the customary token gifts from several students, while waving goodbye to others.

Gabe moved toward her with a single intent. The worry lines around her mouth had deepened during the past two days, and try as he might to assure her that Damon Tuttle would threaten her no more, he felt he'd been unsuccessful. Surely, now that the students were gone and her responsibilities would soon end, she could relax.

Although her students had become accustomed to his presence, a few that had lingered behind slipped aside as he moved down the aisle, giving him the wide berth that his icy demeanor demanded.

Gabe sauntered past her desk on his way to the window, gazing absently toward the parking lot and wondering where he went from here. Leaving seemed inevitable... and impossible.

Bits and pieces of Annie's conversations with her students floated through the air above the noise, and then suddenly he homed in on a conversation that sent him spinning toward her in shock.

"Oh, Miss O'Brien, my little sister is so excited," one of the students was saying. "She's going to be in your class next year. I told her you were the best. She can hardly wait."

Annie's expression froze. The smile on her face never wavered. But the light in her eyes went out as certainly as if someone had taken a gun and blasted it away.

"That's quite a compliment," Annie said. "But I'm afraid your sister will have to take history from someone else. I won't be here next year."

"But why? You can't leave! It just won't be the same without you," the student cried.

Annie's chin quivered. It was all Gabe needed to see.

"What's left to do here?" he asked, his deep voice breaking into the round of complaints.

Annie shook her head without answering and started needlessly sorting papers on her desk as the last of the students drifted away, murmuring to themselves about the loss of a favorite teacher. And then they were alone.

"You didn't tell me you were going to quit."

The accusation hung in the air between them. Annie looked up, her face full of anger, her words sharp, cutting the distance between them in short, staccato bursts.

"My contract was with the school district, not you. I didn't have to tell you anything. You're leaving... remember?"

Gabe slapped the desk with the flat of his hand, and Annie had to force herself not to jump backward in response to the fury in his voice.

"Why, Miss O'Brien! Is that you I hear sounding so bitter...and resentful...and just possibly mad as hell? I guess you needed promises, after all." Gabe's words stung as his drawl ate into her conscience. "Why am I not surprised?"

Annie couldn't look him in the face. After all he'd done for her, she'd been reduced to lying to keep from begging him to stay. The echo of his harsh laughter was all he left behind as he walked out of the room, slamming the door after him.

She sank into her chair, crossed her arms on the desk and buried her face in them, unable to deal with what she had done. But it was her only option. She'd already faced that and the other facts bearing down on her with ominous persistence.

A dry sob burned her throat, but she refused to let it out. An old rhyme from her childhood floated to the surface of her memory, and she found herself muttering, "If wishes were horses then beggars would ride."

But no one was there to question the insanity of the comment or wonder why Miss O'Brien, who taught history on the south side of Oklahoma City, was taking out the contents of her desk drawers and methodically throwing them into the trash.

Nearly an hour later Annie left her classroom, refusing to admit that it was for the last time, and walked into the hallway, expecting to make the long walk to the front door alone.

Her heart skipped a beat as Gabe shoved himself away from the edge of a locker and fell into step beside her without speaking. A small catch in her breathing was all the notice she gave as he reached out and took her by the hand.

"Come on, Annie Laurie. Do what you have to do and then brace yourself. Tonight I'm taking you out."

She couldn't have been more shocked if he'd told her that he was getting a haircut and buying a three-piece suit.

"But..."

He frowned and pointed toward the principal's office, where a gaggle of teachers was gathering.

"Go on...do your thing, teacher. When you're through, I'll be waiting."

Annie couldn't watch him leave. She was too focused on not crying in front of the others as the words "I'll be waiting" echoed inside her head and then settled into a hard lump in the center of her heart.

*Oh dear God,* Annie thought. *Why now? Why did you do this to me now, when you know how futile it is?*

But there was no answer, and, for Annie, no hope. She moved into line, smiling and nodding, thankful that most of the other teachers were unaware of her decision not to return. It saved her the anguish of making excuses she didn't have.

With dinner on the horizon and a rumbling in her stomach that reminded her about the lunch she'd skipped in order to check in textbooks, Annie fought with Gabe for a fair share of the full-length mirror in her apartment.

It was then, between his chin and the bottom of the mirror, that she looked up.

"Where are you taking me?" she asked.

"Are you through with your two-thirds of the mirror?" he asked, smiling a little to himself as he noticed that his snide remark got her goat.

"Be my guest," she said.

"I already am," Gabe said, and winked.

Annie stepped aside, then bowed dramatically. She would bite her tongue before she let him get the best of her.

She buckled the belt on her blue jeans and then ran a fingertip down the front of her plaid shirt, checking to see if she'd gotten all the buttons when she realized that he hadn't answered her.

"So... where are you taking me?" she asked again.

Gabe stood behind her, peering over her shoulder and combing his thick, dark hair. He stopped and looked, staring intently into the mirror until she was forced to meet the reflection of his gaze.

Her eyes widened, turning them an even deeper shade of jade.

"Well?" Annie wouldn't give an inch.

His gaze slid across her face, as if imprinting it forever into his memory. The heat from his gaze made her shiver.

"With me," he said.

For Annie, it was answer enough.

Minutes later she followed him outside to his bike, and then put on the helmet he handed her without comment, wondering as she did why she'd bothered to fix her hair.

He squatted down beside the monstrous metallic ride to check it, unaware that Annie was taking in every aspect of his body and clothing.

Heavily muscled haunches stretched the denim tight across his legs as he stood and leaned across the seat to tighten a strap. Annie was thankful for the helmet's tinted visor, aware that she could look her fill without detection.

It was then that she began to realize how much Gabriel could see without being seen when he wore it himself. She shuddered. He saw entirely too much for her peace of mind as it was.

The long sleeves of his blue-and-white striped shirt were unbuttoned and rolled halfway up his forearms. He wore the same black boots he'd had when she met him, only now they bore a month-old shine. They were sporting the same single-roweled spurs.

The black leather vest he wore over the shirt was open and loose across his chest. In essence, he was still the same menacing man she'd first met in the parking lot of the quick stop. And yet, in Annie's eyes, he would be forever changed. She now saw beyond the obvious. Beyond the outer layers of his disguise to the man beneath. He had the appearance of a devil but the heart of a lion. Strong and faithful and constant.

Annie caught her breath as he moved toward her. The setting sun caught on the crown of his head and turned it to a halo of glittering jet. He winked and smiled at her, as if he could see beyond that smoky Plexiglas to the woman beneath. She shivered at his depth of perception.

The smile was almost the same one he'd given her the day they'd met. But not quite. While the change in their relationship had added to its texture, the last two days had given it a certain caution, as if he wasn't quite sure whether to share it with her or not.

"Are you ready?" he asked, and slung his leg over the seat, straddling the bike in an unconsciously enticing movement that reminded Annie of the way he covered her in bed.

Annie nodded. There were no words to say what she was feeling inside. She simply slid on behind him, wrapped her arms around his waist and waited.

Moments later the engine roared to life beneath them, and Annie inhaled, reveling in the joy of the moment, in just being alive. As the bike threaded into the traffic, Gabe's body moved beneath her hands, a powerful ripple of man and muscle.

She swallowed, closed her eyes and let herself pretend she was in control. It was as close as she'd come to lying to herself in months, and she knew it. Gabriel Donner wasn't a man to be controlled...or loved. He wouldn't stand for the former and couldn't return the latter. Either way, Annie was on a one-way ride, with defeat as her destination.

*What else is new?*

A wry grin tilted the corner of her mouth, but it was lost behind the helmet.

# Chapter 5

"**I** should be the one paying the check. You've yet to accept a dollar from me, and it's just not right, Gabriel. After all, I *did* hire you to do a job."

Annie's words held a hiss of resentment and a lot of guilt as they stood beside the desk, waiting while the cashier totaled their bill.

Gabriel didn't even bother glaring as he paid for their meal. In his mind, they'd gone way past an employer-employee relationship, and there was no going back. Besides, to him, money was nothing more than a necessary evil. He took jobs when he needed them, and when he had enough money to last him awhile, he simply crawled on his Harley and never looked back. Accumulating worldly goods had no place in his life, although Annie would have been shocked at how much he'd managed to save over the years.

He took the change the cashier handed him, stuffed it into his pocket and cocked an eyebrow at Annie, grinning when she pursed her lips and gave him what he privately thought of as her "schoolteacher look."

"It's not going to work, Annie. I'm not behind on my schoolwork, so you can't suspend me. And I'm pretty sure you're not going to fail me. After all—" his drawl held her attention long after it should have, and made her miss the look in his eyes as he continued "—some of my abilities are beyond reproach, aren't they, sugar?"

He leaned forward and, in front of everyone standing at the door waiting to be seated, pressed a firm, sweet kiss directly on her pouted lips.

"Gabriel!"

Annie blushed two shades of red and glanced nervously around, checking to see who was watching. She should have saved herself the embarrassment by not looking, because everyone else *was*. Several giggles and a chuckle or two mingled in her mind with the fact that he'd just referred to their lovemaking and they both knew it.

She stared at a spot somewhere over his shoulder, then down at the floor, and finally breathed a sigh of relief when he took her by the hand and led her out the door of the steak house.

"You are impossible," Annie said, relishing the cool night air on her heated face.

Gabe grinned. "Nothing's impossible, Annie. I thought we'd already covered that subject—in bed."

She grinned in spite of her embarrassment and made a face.

He smiled and cupped her cheek with his hand. "It's good to see you smiling, Annie. I've missed it . . . and you."

Breath caught in the back of her throat. This man had a way of cutting past all the excess, polite conversation. He went for the jugular every time.

"I've just had a lot on my mind," she said. "I'm sorry."

Gabe nodded and then leaned forward and whispered against her lips just before he kissed her, "Enough said. Climb on, woman. The night's not over yet. I know where there's a soft bed, empty and waiting to be used."

Annie's heart thumped once in anticipation and then settled back into its regular rhythm. She put the helmet on, slipped on behind him and wrapped her arms around his waist in anticipation of the ride and what awaited her at home.

Gabe closed his eyes and tried to ignore the ache that had settled just behind his heart. The more time he spent with her, the harder it was going to be to leave. Yet leave he must. There was nothing in the way of permanence that he could offer a woman like Annie O'Brien. And she was the sort who deserved a forever kind of man, a home and a lapful of babies.

Damn it all, anyway, he thought. He couldn't give her any of those things. All he could do was treasure the time they had and try not to hurt her when it was time for him to go.

Gabe was the first to see the lights. The parking lot of Annie's complex was full of police cars and emergency vehicles. For a moment it was like the night of the fire all over again.

"Oh, no," Annie gasped as she jumped from the bike and yanked the helmet from her head. "Something terrible has happened! Gabe...what do you suppose...?" And then she gasped and dropped the helmet into Gabe's hands. "Those officers...they're coming out of my apartment."

Gabe followed the direction of her gaze and knew that the burning sensation in the pit of his stomach was a warning sign that their night wasn't going exactly as he'd planned.

He took her hand and moved toward her apartment, ignoring the roped-off area, as well as an officer's warning shout.

"Hey, mister! You can't go in there."

"My name is Annie O'Brien. I live here," Annie said, pointing toward the partially opened doorway.

"Hey, Harvey!" the officer shouted. "Get a detective out here. The property owner just showed up."

As the officer spoke, Gabe's sharp gaze quickly caught sight of a body on the ground just beyond the bumper of a parked car. A sheet of yellow plastic had been pulled over it, but the outline of a pair of tennis shoes was unmistakable.

Gabe frowned and slowly changed position so that he was shielding Annie from the sight. That was the last thing she needed to see.

"Miss O'Brien?"

Annie nodded, her eyes huge, her chin trembling as she let the detective lead her toward the breezeway sheltering the door to her home. Gabe followed.

"What happened?" Annie asked, and then swallowed a scream as she took an instinctive step back when she looked through the door.

Gabe caught her retreat and steadied her, his hands firm and reassuring on her shoulders as the detective began to talk.

"Officers responded to a break-in when your security system went off," the detective said. "They were too late to prevent what happened, but they got the perpetrator. Damnedest thing, too. When they searched the body, they didn't find anything of value on him. All he did was mess up the place and then run when he heard sirens."

"Body?" Annie began to shake. The events of the last few weeks were about to send her sanity caving in.

The detective nodded. "Some teenager. He started shooting at the squad car the minute it turned into the parking lot. Didn't even give the officers a chance to make an arrest. They didn't have a choice. No matter what their age, the perps are better armed than we are every time."

"Oh, Gabriel," Annie whispered, and stepped inside her apartment. "Who? And in heaven's name, why?"

Gabe held her firmly, afraid that she was going to come apart in his arms. Her beloved plants were lying everywhere, uprooted and broken, the dirt from their containers strewn about the carpet. Huge slashes had been made in all her furniture, and the stuffing had been pulled out through the ripped fabric until it was hanging like topping melting on a cake. Broken crockery and an open refrigerator door told him that the man had left nothing untouched. Items of her clothing were visible from where they stood, and Gabe knew that their bedrooms were probably a mirror image of this destruction.

"Miss O'Brien..." The detective pulled out a notepad and pen. "I know you're upset. And rightly so," he added. "But I need to ask you some questions. We found some jewelry on the bed in one room, and some money in another. The perp obviously saw it, but he didn't take it. From my point of view, this looks like a gigantic case of revenge."

Gabe's pulse skidded to a halt as his heart skipped a beat. Revenge! A horrible thought occurred to him as the detective continued.

"So, Miss O'Brien, I have to ask. Do you know anyone who would want to...?"

"Detective...I want to see the body," Gabe said coldly.

The interruption was unexpected. The detective glared at the big man.

"Now, see here," he began, and then he realized he didn't know the big man's name. "I don't believe I got your name, mister." His pen was poised above the pad, awaiting Gabe's answer. It didn't come.

Gabe stared down into Annie's face and watched as the same thought suddenly occurred to her. Tears welled, and she began to shake harder.

"No," she groaned. "He wouldn't. He couldn't."

"Honey, he tried to cut you apart in your own classroom, in front of a room full of witnesses," Gabe reminded her.

"Who tried to cut who?" the policeman growled.

"She'll tell you," Gabe said as he moved away, and when Annie started after him, he turned and pointed his finger at her. "You wait! I'll be right back."

The look on his face made her sick. She'd never seen so much suppressed fury in her life. Moaning softly to herself at the unbelievable string of disasters that had been dumped on her life, she staggered backward until the wall behind her stopped her progress. Only then did she allow herself to give way as she slid to the floor and buried her face against her knees, unable to face any more horror.

Gabe walked outside toward the body. His hand shook in anger as he bent over and lifted the plastic. The pale eyes staring sightlessly upward were familiar, as was the face and everything that went with it. He dropped the sheet and turned to find that the detective had followed him.

"Damon Tuttle." Gabe's voice was rough, his breathing shallow. He had an insane urge to hit something...or someone.

The detective's eyebrows rocketed to his hairline. He obviously hadn't really expected Gabriel to come through with anything useful.

"How do you know him?" he asked Gabe.

"A few weeks ago Miss O'Brien hired me as a body-guard because several of her students had been harassing her to the point that she'd become afraid."

"She's a teacher?"

Gabe nodded. "And that—" he pointed to the body on the ground "—was one of her students. He was arrested after he pulled a knife on her in the classroom."

"Damn." The detective scratched his head, then looked back at Gabe with new respect. "I take it you were what stopped him?"

"He made bail. The system just let him walk," Gabe accused, ignoring the detective's question.

"I guess it's a good thing she had an alarm, otherwise he might have sat inside and waited for you to come back so he could finish the job," the detective said.

"I'm taking her to a motel for the night. I've got to get her away from this," Gabe said, and headed back to the apartment, unaware and uncaring whether the officer had other ideas.

"Annie!"

His shout shook her. She looked up and saw him coming toward her. She didn't have to ask if they'd been right.

"Oh, my God," she moaned, and started to cry.

"Stop it," Gabe growled, and pulled her from the floor and into his arms. "The son of a bitch wasn't worth it."

Annie saw the room starting to spin. In reflex, her hands reached out for balance. But it was no use. For the second time in their short acquaintance, she was going to faint at his feet. The last thing she felt was his arms beneath her body and his breath upon her face.

It was the steady, rhythmic vibration of a heartbeat beneath her ear that woke her. For a moment she lay quietly, absorbing the gentleness of the man in whose arms she lay.

His hands moved across her like a shadow stealing across the floor, gently smoothing a stray hair away from her face, carefully straightening her clothing, quietly readjusting the hold he had on her to assure himself that it was secure.

But it was the gentle whispers she heard coming from his lips that made a fresh set of tears come into her eyes. He was making promises she knew he couldn't keep. And when she looked around the strange, sterile room and then up at Gabe and caught him looking back, she remembered.

"It wasn't just a bad dream, was it, Gabriel?"

"No, it wasn't a dream. But it's finally over. There's nothing and no one left to fear."

Annie tried to smile and then caught back a sob. *Oh Gabriel...if only that were true. You don't know the half of my hell.*

"Don't cry, Annie." His voice was harsh as he wrapped his fingers in the hair cascading down her back and pulled her closer against him. "It makes me crazy. I'll do anything to put a smile back on your face."

Annie looked around at the room, felt the bed beneath their bodies, and wondered where they were and how they'd gotten there. The ride she'd taken in a squad car to the nearby motel had come and gone without her notice, while she'd been blessedly out for the count. A terrible sense of doom overwhelmed her. Another tear tracked toward her chin. She was incapable of a smile.

Gabe groaned. "Baby...please...just tell me. What can I do to make this better?"

Annie felt the palms of his hands swiping across her cheeks as he tried unsuccessfully to remove the traces of her misery from his sight. And then something he'd said triggered a notion she hadn't considered. She took a deep breath, and before she knew it, heard herself telling him, "I want to go home."

Gabe sighed and nodded as he pressed a helpless kiss at the corner of her lips.

"Tomorrow...when it's light. I swear we'll go back and clean everything up. Before you know it, it'll be good as new. You can buy new plants...and you said you had insurance. We'll shop for new furniture, and..."

"No!"

Her abrupt refusal left him speechless. She'd just asked to go home and in the next breath refused. What was going on?

The headboard of the motel bed dug into the small of his back, and he cursed softly as he tried to find a comfortable position in which to sit.

At the same moment Annie pulled away and rolled off the bed. Seconds later he caught her in his arms as she paused at the curtained window of the motel room.

"What is it, Annie? I thought you said you—"

"I want to go home...to where I was born."

Gabe was dumbfounded. "You don't have any family there. I remember you telling me once that your parents were dead."

Annie winced at the word and pulled the curtain aside, staring blindly out into the night.

"They are. But the house is still there...and it's mine...waiting beneath that stand of trees Daddy refused to cut down." She shuddered and closed her eyes, picturing the last time she'd seen her childhood home. "I miss the trees. There are lots of trees in the Missouri hills."

The curtain fell from her fingers, once again shutting the night out and them in as she gave Gabe a last ultimatum. "If you still want to help, then take me home.... Take me to Missouri."

"I don't get it, Annie. It isn't like you to run away."

Annie's short bark of laughter was anything but funny. "That's a hoot," she said derisively. "I couldn't run far enough and fast enough to escape my fate. Besides—" she wrapped her arms around herself and stared down at the shadows on the floor, made by the faint light coming through the curtains behind her "—I'm not running away. I just want to go home."

Gabriel sensed that there was more to her request than what she'd admitted, but it was beyond him to press her for answers. Not tonight.

"Then you will," he said, and unwound her arms from around her waist and rewrapped them around his. "But tonight…just let me hold you. You may not need it, but I sure as hell do."

Annie's legs went weak. She would always need this man. For as long as she lived, she knew she would never get over that need. She buried her face against his chest and nodded her acceptance of his plea. *For as long as I live,* she reminded herself.

It took ten hours on the back of Gabe's bike. Hard, hot, grueling hours with few stops. Stops in which she crawled off the back of that bike certain she would never be able to walk again, and then, when it came time to move on, equally certain that resuming her seat behind Gabe would be impossible.

But she'd done it. And as they turned off the two-lane highway onto a narrow dirt road, Annie's stamina was disappearing as fast as the sun setting behind them.

"Is this it?" Gabe asked as the bike rolled to a stop. He stood upright, with the bike balanced but still grumbling quietly between his legs, and stared at the small frame house nestled in the midst of a thick grove of oak and pine.

"Yes."

One word. A single statement that to Gabe's ears sounded awfully flat, considering the fact that she'd been so hell-bent on coming.

He sighed, killed the engine and moved the kickstand in place with the toe of his boot. Annie got off first and handed him her helmet as she began brushing dust from the legs of her jeans and the sleeves of her denim shirt.

Gabe slid his sunglasses up, letting them rest on the top of his head as he watched her start up the walk alone. Something about the way she moved told him that she would not welcome company. Not now.

He swung his leg over the bike, untied their duffel bags and slid the straps over his shoulder. They'd traveled light, taking only what would fit on the bike. Everything that Damon Tuttle had not destroyed was being shipped. Annie had left with assurances from her insurance company that a check for her vandalized car as well as the damaged personal property would be forthcoming.

He remembered thinking it was strange that she hadn't seemed to care. In his experience, and God knew he had plenty of it, women took great stock in "things." But Annie O'Brien had simply walked away from all her belongings and ridden off on the back of a Harley with a man she hardly knew.

He cursed softly beneath his breath and followed her up the walk. Maybe here she would find peace; then he could leave knowing she was safe and well.

It was the thought of leaving that made him move angrily past her and up onto the porch, leaving the sound of his footsteps to echo loudly into the odd silence of the woods.

"I don't suppose you have a key," he growled, as he twisted uselessly at a doorknob that wouldn't give.

Wordlessly Annie moved him aside, then stood on tiptoe and reached above the door frame, running her finger lightly across it. Moments later she stepped back, a dusty key in hand. She thrust it into the lock.

"Don't ever put that damned thing back up there," Gabe said harshly, imagining an intruder hiding inside at some future date, awaiting Annie's entrance. "It isn't safe."

"No place is safe. Safety is merely a state of mind." Annie walked inside.

Dust motes highlighted by the fading light coming through the curtained window shifted as a draft of fresh air moved through the house. Everything inside was covered in draped white cloths, lying unused and lifeless, waiting, like Annie, to be needed again.

Annie hit a light switch beside the door, and, surprisingly, a dull, dusty glow illuminated the dingy room. Although the utility bills came regularly and she paid them faithfully, she still hadn't expected anything to work. She looked up and saw that only a single bulb remained in what had once been her mother's pride and joy. A small, four-section *faux* crystal chandelier hung from the ceiling, emitting all the light it could from its forty-watt source.

Gabe grunted, surprised by the fact that the power was on, and dropped their bags beside the door. Without asking permission, he went from room to room, pulling back curtains and opening stubborn windows. Soon a cool draft of air was slowly circulating through the small frame house.

Ignoring him, Annie walked with single-minded intent down the narrow hallway to the room at the end of the hall. Her hand shook as it touched the door. She took a deep breath, letting her fingers slide down the surface as they tested the texture, until they came to the knob. She gripped it and turned.

The last ten years disappeared in a heartbeat as she walked over the threshold. Were it not for the drop cloths over all the furniture, she could have imagined that it was only this morning when she'd left for school. She walked to the bed and pulled back the cloth. The faded pink coverlet was still in place, while a single old teddy bear—her first—reclined against the headboard, one ear missing, along with most of its stuffing. She tried to smile, but she hurt too much inside for the feeling to come.

She walked to the corner opposite the bed and pulled another drop cloth away. It fell to the floor in a cloud of dust, revealing antique maple and a row of snapshots lining the dusty mirror of her dresser.

She inhaled, blinking back tears as she traced the curling edges of the old photos. Her parents smiled back at her. Instinctively she returned their smiles and then realized they couldn't see. They'd been dead for years.

She bit her lower lip and moved on to the next picture, whispering her best friend's name to herself as she remembered well the day it had been taken. Molly on graduation day! There was a picture of Rufus, her daddy's hunting dog, and one of her mother out back working in the garden. Everything seemed so ordinary... and so long ago.

"Annie...I'm going to backtrack to that little store a few miles back and get some food."

She spun around. He was silhouetted in the doorway. A dark, menacing figure of a man with a beautiful smile and a gentle voice. To Annie he represented stability and safety in a world in which she was fast losing ground. She flew into his arms before she thought.

Gabe held her. He didn't understand her fear, but he recognized it just the same. For a long moment neither spoke, and then he felt her withdraw as suddenly as she'd come.

"Are you all right?" he asked softly, willing himself not to react to her fears.

"Are you coming back?"

He drew a slow, deep breath, letting the shock and anger he felt at her question slide back to a safer place inside him.

"I'll pretend you didn't ask that," he said shortly. "And I'll be right back."

She listened to the door slam and then the sound of the bike as its motor was revved more strongly than necessary before he slipped it into gear.

"Oh, my God," Annie whispered, and turned back toward the mirror. The teenager who had been there moments ago was gone, along with the memories. There was nothing left but a woman wearing guilt on her face.

"How could you have done that?" she muttered, as she leaned forward to stare accusingly at her own reflection. "After all he's done...you still doubt him?" A bitter smile twisted her mouth. "You don't doubt *him,* you fool. It's yourself you doubt."

With that she pushed herself away from the dresser and walked out of the room without looking back.

By the time Gabe returned, Annie had cleaned the refrigerator and wiped off the stove. It was time to put the past behind her. She had no more choices to make.

After all these years, the night sounds in the hills were strange to Annie and made it impossible for her to sleep. She tossed restlessly on her bed, grimacing when the old springs squeaked protestingly under her weight.

Gabe shifted beside her in his sleep, and then unconsciously reached out, trying to settle her back safely against him. But Annie resisted the comfort of his touch, as well as the safety of his strength. He'd done what she asked and brought her home to Missouri. And although this was only their first night here, there was no way of telling how much longer he would stay.

Annie knew that she was going to have to find a way to exist without him, and there was no time like the present. The sooner she got used to being alone...and lonely...the better off she would be. With that bitter thought in mind, she rolled out from under Gabe's arm and left the bed.

The old wood floorboards creaked beneath her feet. Thorough cleaning would come in the days ahead, but the sweeping they'd gotten earlier had served its purpose. The floor was smooth and cool to the touch and, to Annie, vaguely familiar. Without thinking, she stepped over the board just left of center in the doorway, knowing that it would protest loudly under her weight.

A heavy, throbbing pressure was building at the back of her neck as she walked through the house toward the front door, a warning she'd come to recognize and hate.

Anxious for the welcome coolness waiting just outside on the porch steps, she rolled her head, rubbing her neck as she did and wincing as her muscles protested the action.

*If I only had access to a hot tub,* she thought. This misery had to be caused by exertion and exhaustion. All she needed was a good night's sleep and it would be better. Surely it wasn't a portent of things to come. Not yet. She wasn't ready.

Her fingers curled around the doorknob at the same instant that the first wave of pain struck. The moan that slid from her lips was soft and frightened, but it was enough to awaken Gabe, who sat up in startled silence, wondering how long he'd been alone in her bed...and why.

Wearing nothing but a pair of white cotton briefs, he bolted through the house without trying to mask the noise he made.

"Annie! Where are you?" he shouted, and then wondered why he felt such panic when they'd left the person who'd threatened her far behind and six feet under.

The pain was so sudden...and so intense. If she could have caught her breath, she would have screamed. As it was, she leaned against the door and braced her legs to keep from falling. At that moment, standing was all she was capable of doing.

"Oh, God," Gabe breathed as he saw her in the shadows, unable to walk, swaying by the door like a broken butterfly trying to fly.

And then he saw her clutch her head and tilt forward. He caught her just before she crashed to the floor.

"My head...my head," Annie groaned, and dug her fingers into her scalp. All she wanted was to rip out the pain and throw it away.

Gabe had a flashback of the first time he'd seen her in the throes of such pain and remembered the prescription medicine that had given her ease.

"Your pills! Annie! Where did you pack your pills?"

She didn't answer. Couldn't answer. Instead, she groaned and went limp against him as he slid his arms around her shoulders and tangled his hands in her hair, massaging the taut, corded muscles at the back of her neck in a helpless effort to ease her pain.

"Annie...where did you put your pills?" he repeated.

"Kitchen...kitchen...kitchen," she moaned, saying the word over and over like a litany. "Oh God, oh God, make it stop."

Her fingers dug into her hair and pulled as Gabe lifted her from her feet and quickly carried her back to her room. Tears streamed down her cheeks as he bolted from the room, leaving her alone in the dark with the pain.

Gabe hit the light switch in the kitchen with the flat of his hand as he ran past. Seconds later he had every cabinet door swinging open as he searched the dusty shelves for the brown prescription bottle he'd seen before. And when he saw it, his sigh of relief coincided with her shriek of pain.

"My God," he muttered, realizing that in his entire life he'd never been this afraid before. Not even when he was about to be hanged.

He grabbed a glass and filled it with water, unmindful of the puddle he left on the floor by the sink as he bolted back down the hall, the pills in his hand.

By the time he got back, Annie had rolled in upon herself. She was curled into a ball so tight that he had to fight her to get her upright enough to swallow.

"Open your mouth, damn it," he yelled when she fought him for making her move, because movement only increased the pain.

And somehow she heard...and obeyed. Gabe slid the pills between her teeth and chased them by pouring water down her throat, unmindful of the liquid that once again spilled, this time going down her neck and onto her gown.

Then he crawled in beside her, rolled her up into his arms and held her until the tremors subsided, her breathing slowed and the pulse he felt beneath his fingertips was no longer racing toward cataclysm. And when she finally slept, he could only hold her, staring up at the ceiling, wide-eyed and shocked, until daybreak came calling.

# Chapter 6

Annie brushed the toast crumbs from the table into her hand and then tossed them into the sink. Breakfast had come and gone with little conversation. Gabe kept looking at her as if he expected her to self-destruct at any moment, and Annie kept looking away, afraid that he would learn more about her than she was willing to reveal.

"Do you want more coffee?" she asked as she topped off her own cup and then turned to Gabe with the pot in her hand.

He shook his head.

"Did you get enough to eat?" she asked as she began dumping grounds and rinsing out the inner components of the old percolator she'd unearthed from her mother's cupboard.

He nodded.

She twisted the tie onto the bread wrapper and shoved the loaf into the wooden bread box beneath the cabinet. Without looking around to see if he was watching, she took a dishcloth from a drawer, doused it into some sudsy water and began scrubbing needlessly at the countertops.

"Annie..."

She grimaced. It was the tone of his voice that warned her. That and the look he'd been wearing that she'd tried all morning to ignore. Last night had been unexpected...and it had been hell. He was bound to wonder. There was only one way to stop the interrogation before it started, and that was to take the offensive.

"Migraines are hell," she said.

*Migraines? Was that what those were?*

Gabe frowned. He'd heard of their ferocity. After the second episode that he'd witnessed, he could vouch for the truth of that statement—in spades.

"Are you sure that's all they—"

"Would you add dish soap to the grocery list, please? I need some. I just used up what was left."

She rinsed the dishcloth before going on to the next set of cabinets.

Gabe frowned and did as she'd asked.

"You *need* a car," he muttered, and added it to the top of the list just for spite, as if she could just walk into a supermarket and pick one off the shelves.

The thought of Annie alone up in these woods with who knew what for neighbors made him nervous. Thinking of Annie alone, period, made him angry with himself. Thinking of himself without her made him sick.

Annie shrugged. "I'll see to it in good time," she said. "There's no hurry."

He gawked at her. Her answer made no sense at all. Of course there was a hurry. "How will you get food?" he asked. "How will you get to town? How will—"

A car horn honked, interrupting Gabe's questions. Annie dropped the dishcloth into the sink and parted the curtains over the window to peer outside.

A new model electric-blue pickup truck with silver running boards had just pulled up and parked beneath the big oak at the edge of the yard. Annie watched as a hulking figure of a man squeezed himself out from behind the steering wheel and stood, looking anxiously toward the house and the big Harley parked in front.

"Davie! It's Davie Henry!" she said, and headed for the door.

*So who the hell is Davie Henry?* Gabe shoved himself out of the chair, abandoning the list he'd been helping her make, and followed.

The screen door banged against the wall as Annie raced outside. In three steps she was off the porch and headed toward the big man who stood waiting beside the truck with a huge grin on his face.

"Annie...Annie, it *is* you!" Davie said, and caught her on the fly, swinging her up into his arms and then turning her around and around beneath the shade tree.

Gabe sauntered out, leaned against the porch post and tried not to glare. It was obvious they were friends. From the way the man was holding her, damned good ones, at that.

A slow rage filled his belly, building layer by layer at the injustice of it all, and just when it might have erupted and ruined whatever existed between himself and Annie, she was released and set back on her feet.

At that moment Gabe felt hatred. He hated Annie for laughing with that man in a way she'd never laughed with him. And he hated the man for being able to make her do it.

"Gabe!" Annie motioned for him to come closer. "There's someone I want you to meet."

"I can't wait," he muttered, and took his time about complying.

Davie Henry's shock was evident as he looked past Annie to the man on the porch. The smile on his face disappeared as he watched the big biker come toward him. He looked from Annie to the man and back again, unable to believe that these two were actually traveling companions.

The man she called Gabe didn't look like anyone he'd ever seen her with before. The expression on his face could only be called menacing. And even though he was wearing blue jeans and a near-white shirt that might pass for Western-style, those high-top leather boots and leather vest of shiny obsidian that matched the too-long shock of unruly hair framing his face, made Davie nervous—along with the silver spurs on his boots that jingled when he walked. Davie thought he'd never seen a more likely outlaw. He frowned and watched. The man reminded him of a big black panther stalking his prey.

Oddly enough, if Annie saw the animosity between the two men, she chose to ignore it.

"Gabe, this is Davie Henry. One of my oldest friends." She punched him playfully on the shoulder and looked up into his face. "Would you believe I used to baby-sit this big lug?"

Gabe stared. *Baby-sit? Then that meant . . .*

"Only until I was eleven," Davie added, and ruffled Annie's hair as if she were a puppy at his feet. "That was the year I outgrew you by six inches."

Annie rolled her eyes and slapped his hand away. "It's true," she said, turning to fix Gabe with a smile that dropped his heart to his feet. "My parents made me baby-sit a moose."

Davie laughed so openly at the joke on himself that Gabe had to grin. The man *was* big. And Annie wasn't all that tall. He looked back at her, trying to imagine her as a young child and then a teenager, and suddenly he realized how little he really knew of this woman who'd stolen his heart.

The time was nearing when he would have to leave her. But it was suddenly a little bit easier, knowing that Annie would be among friends when he did. He held out his hand.

"Gabe Donner," he said, introducing himself. "Annie and I don't go quite that far back. But it's nice to know that she's got friends nearby."

Davie nodded and shook Gabe's hand. "Our place is just a hoot and a holler from here as the crow flies. By car, about a mile and a half."

Gabe grinned. He couldn't remember the last time he'd heard anyone talk like that. It reminded him of his life before.

"Someone's been taking care of the place," Annie said, and looked at Davie.

The blush that ran up his neck toward his ears was answer enough for her, although she verified it with a grin.

"It wasn't much," he said. "Just cut a little grass and made sure the roof didn't leak."

Annie thanked him with a hug.

"You here for a visit?" Davie asked. "I haven't seen you since your daddy's funeral."

She shook her head. "No visit, Davie. I'm moving home."

He grinned. "It'll be just like old times."

A strange shadow passed over Annie's face. Davie was too busy rejoicing in the news to see, but Gabe saw it. With Annie, he missed nothing. He saw regret and something else . . . something that looked suspiciously like . . .

Fear!

Annie was afraid. Of that he was certain. Gabe didn't know how he knew, but he did. And for the life of him, he couldn't understand why she should be afraid. What did she have to fear? Damon Tuttle was out of the picture permanently. Here in Missouri, she had a chance at a fresh start, which was more than he would ever have. So why in hell was she afraid? Everything around her was familiar. She should be waltzing on air. But she wasn't. Annie O'Brien was afraid.

"I have a girlfriend," Davie said, and then ducked his head, suddenly embarrassed that he'd announced something so personal so abruptly.

Annie hid what she'd been thinking behind a grin. "Who on earth would have you?" she teased, and then watched an odd expression come and go on Davie's face. She'd unintentionally hit a sore spot somewhere.

"You don't know her," Davie said. "Her folks moved into town about six years ago... right after you got that teaching job in Oklahoma City. They own and operate a feed-and-seed store."

"What's her name?" Annie asked, trying to smooth whatever it was that she'd stirred up.

"Charlotte. But I call her Charlie."

Gabe walked away, leaving the pair to hash over old times. The knowledge that he had no place in the conversation and no place in their lives was eating at him like a festering sore.

Minutes later Gabe heard the sounds of an engine starting up, and then Annie's footsteps in the dirt behind him. He squatted down beside his bike, picked up a wrench and a pair of pliers, and began tightening stuff on his Harley that didn't need tightening. But it didn't matter. It would give him something else to do when he had to loosen it up again.

"Seeing Davie was great!" Annie said as she knelt beside Gabe and handed him a screwdriver.

He took it from her and then dropped it onto the ground with a thud.

"I don't need that," he said sharply, and refused to look at the shocked expression he knew she would be wearing.

In all the months they'd known each other, he'd never been rude to her. And yet he'd done it today with a vengeance.

"And I don't need to see you act like a jealous baby," she said, and jerked to her feet.

She would have walked away, but Gabe caught her before she'd taken the second step.

"I'm sorry," he said. "And I wasn't jealous."

She fixed him with a stare he tried to ignore. It was no use.

"Is that your 'teacher' look?" he asked with a grin.

She shrugged.

"Okay...I *was* a little bit jealous. But not enough to count."

Her lips pursed as she continued to stare. This time she crossed her arms across her chest and waited for him to fold. He did. Like a table with three broken legs.

"Look, honey," he said, and swept her into his arms, "I admit it." He kissed the end of her nose. "Now are you happy? I saw red." He grinned against her neck as he felt her arms sliding around his shoulders. "I even saw stars. I also saw myself wiping that grin off his face and replacing it with a big fat lip. Now...does that make you happy? I have confessed my worst thoughts to you regarding Davie Henry, and I expect to be rewarded for telling the truth."

"You can quit worrying about my lack of transportation. Davie is loaning me his father's car. And I think I want you to take me to bed."

Gabe was at a loss for words. He now had to consider the knowledge that Davie Henry was about to step into his shoes by providing for Annie's well-being and welfare.

Okay... he knew the reality of leaving her. Someone had to be there for her when he was gone, and it might as well be Davie. He kicked the dirt with the toe of his boot, and then he thought about the second half of her statement. In spite of his need to stay angry, he caught himself grinning.

"So, pretty Annie, you want me to take you to bed? Once we get there... just exactly what do you expect me to do?"

She leaned forward and whispered in his ear. It was reflex that made Gabe sweep her off her feet and into his arms. But then he stopped, staring down into her face at the moisture glistening on her lower lip and the promise of passion in her eyes.

She waited. Quietly. Impatiently.

Desire for this woman turned him pale as he stumbled toward the door with her in his arms. It was one of the few times in his life that he thought to say a prayer. And his prayer was that he would make it to the bedroom in time to do what she asked before he came unglued at the thought.

"Do you know what you're asking?" he said as he set her gently in the middle of her bed.

*I asked you to make love to me until I begged you to stop. But what I want is never to forget this day... or you.*

"Yes, I think so. I just don't want you to forget me when you're gone," Annie said, and started to pull her T-shirt over her head.

*Oh, my God. When I'm gone.*

"Damn you," Gabe said harshly, and yanked the shirt from her hands. "As if I could, Annie Laurie. As if I could."

In seconds he had her naked. Within the next heartbeat he'd joined her, body to body, heart to heart, upon the bed.

Now all he had to do was exert enough control over his own emotions to make certain that *she* never forgot *him*, either.

In that moment, before they joined, Gabe knew that knowing Annie and the love they'd shared would be the closest thing to heaven he would ever find on earth. And when the time came for him to leave, existing without her was going to be a living hell.

"Gabriel."

His name was a sigh on her lips. A plea to begin and, at the same time, a prayer that, for sanity's sake, it would not end too soon.

"I'm here, Annie. I'm here."

His whisper slid across her face. She closed her eyes and let herself go, giving herself up to the emotions he was so skillfully able to create, and refused to contemplate the fact that she would spend the rest of her life alone.

*The rest of her life!*

She sobbed once, and then reached for him.

His hands moved across her breasts, and his lips followed. She arched beneath his touch as his tongue rasped the end of her nipple. She moaned as sensation upon sensation flooded her limbs, making her weak and achy, but yearning for more.

When she would have wrapped her arms around his neck, he grabbed both her wrists, pinning her arms above her head with one hand, while he raided tender territory with the other.

Gabriel shivered at the satiny feel of her skin beneath his fingertips. He closed his eyes and inhaled the essence of Annie as his mouth closed around her breast. And when the tip of it hardened and throbbed incessantly against his tongue, he felt the wild coursing of her lifeblood and knew with joy that it was because of him.

Every touch, every caress he gave her had a rhythm that matched the one pounding wildly within himself. When he longed to plunge his aching body inside her, he sent a searching finger instead. And when honey flowed and heat increased, and muscles began winding too tight to bear the strain, he stroked her body, up one side and down the other, in long, even motions, gentling it for the release that was to come.

Gabriel was lost to all but the woman moving beneath him. The same woman who was urging him to move inside while she made a place for him in the cradle of herself. But he remembered what she'd asked of him and knew that, even if it killed him, he could give her that. He *would* make love to her until she begged him to stop. He *couldn't* promise her anything else, but he would give her that.

A harsh groan ripped up his throat and tore out of his mouth. As badly as he wanted to sheathe himself inside, in the heat, in sweet Annie's fire, it wasn't time. Before he could change his mind, he turned loose of her arms and slid down the length of her body.

Annie felt weightless. Seconds ago Gabriel had been pressing her deeper and deeper into the mattress as he drove her mad with his touch. Now cool air moved across her breasts, bringing the love-swollen nubs to tight, hard peaks. And just when she would have moved in search of him, his mouth found its target and threw Annie's body into instant spasms of satisfaction she had never expected.

"Oh, Gabriel," she moaned, and reached down.

Her fingers slid through his hair, then curled into fists. All she could do was hold on for dear life as his mouth opened, then closed, centering on the throbbing pinpoint of her arousal and yanking her backward through a tunnel of sensuality. It went on...and on...and on...until it became a pleasure she could no longer bear.

"No more. No more," she moaned, digging tighter and tighter into his hair with her fingers as her head thrashed from side to side on the pillow. But it didn't end, and still the tremors rocketed through her body, leaving her burning alive from the inside out.

"Gabriel!" Her body arched as if from a violent jolt of electricity as she screamed his name.

Perfect pleasure. Pounding pain. Where one started the other ended. Gabe had done what she'd asked. She was begging him to stop. To put out the fire of perpetual pleasure while there was enough left of her to survive it.

Her passion. He felt it. Moving beneath his lips, pounding with the rhythm of his own blood that coursed through his veins to near boiling point. And when he heard her begging him to stop, it was all that kept him from dying on the spot. It was what he'd been waiting for.

With a gasp, he lifted himself from where he'd been. Before Annie could react to the abandonment, he moved up and covered her body. The muscles in his back and arms shook from the violent emotion of his own needs as he braced himself above her. Before the last syllable of his name had died on her lips, he was inside her. Just when Annie thought there was no ability left in her to savor what came next, the feel of him moving in and out in a desperate rocking motion started everything all over again.

She groaned, wrapped her arms around his neck and her legs around his waist, and knew that if this was the moment . . . she would and could die happy.

He climaxed, spilling into her over and over in shuddering thrusts. Bright sunbursts of light went off behind his eyelids as he called her name. And then, like the quiet after a storm, he collapsed on top of her, wrapped her in his arms and rolled until she was the one on top. Only then could he relax. Only then could he close his eyes and let exhaustion and sleep overtake him.

Annie lay with her ear against his heartbeat, her hands splayed across the hard, muscled expanse of his chest, and knew that she would never feel this safe and this loved again.

But it had been worth it, she kept telling herself. *At least when he's gone I'll have the memories.* And then she raised herself up and stared long and hard into the face of the man who had stolen her heart.

"It isn't fair," she whispered. Her mouth trembled as she lay back down and searched again for the place nearest his heart. "It just isn't fair."

It was mid-afternoon, and Annie was almost finished unpacking. The moving van had arrived with what was left of her things, and the next half hour had been devoted to dealing with the meager assortment of boxes that the movers carried into the house. When the men finally pulled away, Annie was left with her clothes, a few personal mementos that Damon Tuttle had missed when he'd trashed her apartment, and a small box labeled Books that she seemed unwilling to put down.

Now Gabe sat on the edge of the bed and watched as she walked from a box of clothes to the closet and back again, methodically slipping each garment on a hanger and hanging it up in the closet before retrieving the next item.

Her shapely legs looked long and lean beneath the short cutoff jeans she was wearing. And her body, the one that he'd loved to distraction such a short time ago, moved without constraints beneath the loose pink T-shirt she'd pulled on in her haste. The bra she'd put on this morning was still on the floor where Gabe had tossed it in their haste to make love. And her bare feet padded against the floorboards with a faint, slap, slap sound as she walked.

His eyes narrowed, darkening with remembered passion as he watched. He knew her body so well, yet he knew next to nothing of what went on inside that pretty head. She shared the physical, but never the personal. And there was one thing about Annie O'Brien that just didn't add up.

No matter how organized and thorough and by the book she was in her professional life, from the moment they'd met, she seemed to have simply thrown caution to the winds and done everything a "good girl" wasn't supposed to do.

Somewhere in Annie O'Brien's background was a secret he hadn't unearthed. But unless the revelation came within the next forty-eight hours or so, he didn't think he was ever going to know the truth. He sighed and pushed himself off the bed as he noticed that the small box of books had yet to be unpacked.

"Where do you want me to put these, honey?" Gabe asked as he parted the flaps and pulled out a handful.

"Give those to me!" Annie said, and all but snatched them out of his hands.

Two of the books fell to the floor between them as Gabe stared at her expression. Panic filled her eyes. Certain that he was mistaken about her emotion, he bent down and picked up the books, casually reading the titles as he handed them back.

"*Neurosurgery in the Nineties* and *Life After Death,* two of my all-time favorites." His sarcasm sliced through the silence of the room as he dropped the books into Annie's outstretched hands. "So... now your secret's out. You like to read weird books. But don't worry, I won't tell," he drawled.

She blanched. *Could he have guessed?*

"I didn't mean to..."

"Save it, lady," he said. "No apologies necessary. Obviously I've somehow overstepped my bounds... again. You don't owe me anything...not even an explanation. I'm leaving. Remember?''

The sweet smile she loved so dearly was back to a bittersweet smirk as he turned and walked out of the room, leaving Annie alone with her guilt...and her fears. After the passion they'd shared earlier in the day, she couldn't bear to see pain on his face and know that she was the cause.

She dropped the books onto the bed and hurried after him. But before she could catch up and apologize, she met him in the hallway. He was coming back to her.

She looked up into eyes blazing with a blue-white heat, saw a muscle jerk at the side of his jaw, and wanted to run her fingers through his unruly hair in the hopes that she could smooth the frown away from his forehead in the process. Instead she did nothing. Only waited.

"You make me so damn mad," he said.

"I know." Annie sighed and shrugged, as if it were inevitable that sparks flew between them.

"I didn't mean to pry. I just wanted to help. Since the day we met, that's all I've been trying to—"

"I know," Annie said. "Please...don't apologize for something that's my fault."

"You let me do what I want with your body...but you keep your heart and soul to yourself...don't you, Annie Laurie?" Gabe's hand hit the wall with a solid slap as he spun away from her in anger, and she jumped as his accusation sliced through what was left of her conscience.

She flushed. It was too close to the truth to comment.

"Why is that, Annie? Why would a lady like you let a man like me into her life...and into her bed?" Before she could make up an excuse, he continued. "And don't give me that crap about trying to find yourself. You're the most together woman I've ever known." He turned back to her, and his anger escaped in a slow sigh as his hand cupped her cheek. "You're also the most beautiful woman I've ever known. You could have any man you wanted. Why don't you?"

"Before I met you, I wasn't looking," she said. "After I met you...you pretty much laid it on the table for me. I had a choice. I could take you as you are...or leave you." She walked into his arms. "I just chose to take what I could get, Gabriel. You can't blame a woman for that."

He groaned. Again it all boiled down to the fact that happy ever after and growing old together had no place in his life. It had never been part of the deal.

"I'm sorry...so sorry," Gabe said, and crushed her to his chest. "I wish I could explain...."

Annie shook her head and buried her nose against his shirtfront, searching for that particular spot she'd come to love. The place where the curve of her cheek fit directly over the beat of his heart.

"I don't need explanations, Gabe. I don't even need promises. I had more with you in the short time we've known each other than in all the years I've lived." Her voice shook as she wrapped her arms around his waist. "For me...it's enough."

*But it's not enough for me,* Gabe thought. *This is the first time since my journey began that I'll leave part of myself behind.*

He dug his fingers into the thick, heavy length of her hair, tilted her face up to meet his descending mouth and captured what tasted suspiciously like a sob.

They stood together in the hallway, absorbing each other's pain, and wondered how the hell they would survive when it was time to say goodbye.

Pain engulfed her as she watched him pack. He'd dragged it out until there were no more excuses left to use. No more reasons to stay. She was safe and snug in a house in the hills, with a borrowed car to drive. Her phone was hooked up. Her house was clean. And Davie Henry had stopped by again to give her his number as well as an assurance that he'd be Johnny-on-the-spot if she needed anything... anything at all.

The only problem was, what Annie needed, Davie Henry couldn't provide. Annie needed a miracle. And she'd long since given up believing in those.

"I still wish you'd let me pay you," Annie muttered, then refused to look away from the fierce glare he gave her.

"Well...I do," she continued. "After all, if it wasn't for me, you never would have stopped in Oklahoma. At least, not to stay," she added, on seeing him clench his teeth and viciously shove a pair of jeans into his duffel bag.

"You'll call Davie if you get frightened, won't you?" Gabe asked, and paused in the act of zipping the bag he'd been packing. He couldn't bear the thought of her alone and afraid.

"I won't be afraid," Annie assured him. "There's nothing on this earth that can frighten me."

Gabe stared long and hard at her, mulling over the odd answer she'd just given him as he watched her expression for a reason to stay. *Nothing on this earth?* It was an odd way of putting things. *As opposed to something not of this earth?* He shrugged. He was reading too much into a few simple words.

"Yeah, right. Tough little teacher, aren't you, Annie?" He tried to grin. It didn't quite make it.

"I'll write," he said.

"Don't make promises you won't keep," Annie said quietly, and bit her lower lip to keep from begging him not to go.

"Ah, God," Gabe said, and swept her into his arms.

Kisses rained upon Annie's face and neck until she thought she might faint from the power and passion with which they were delivered. Frantically they clutched each other, willing something...anything...to happen that would stop this insanity. This parting. It didn't come.

"Don't forget me," Annie said, tears sliding down her face in numb profusion. "I would hate to think I'd come and gone without one single person to regret my passing."

She tried to laugh, but it turned into a choking sob, instead. Gabe shook his head and turned away, dry-eyed and aching inside in a place too deep to heal. He walked outside with his bag slung across his shoulder, then tossed it onto the back of the bike and fastened it down with short, angry motions.

His hands trembled as he yanked his helmet off the handlebars and shoved it over his head. Without a sound, he flipped the smoke-tinted visor over his eyes and snapped the chin strap in place.

Annie watched as he swung a long, leather-clad leg over the bike, started the motor and then stood with the Harley rumbling between his legs and stared at her, imprinting her image into his brain for all time.

He looked just as he had when she'd first met him, back in disguise. The hardcase who rode the highways on a Harley. But she knew better. Beneath that leather was a man, not a monster. A man who deserved more out of life than she had to give. It was because of that knowledge that she didn't cry out when the Harley began to roll. She didn't cry, "Stop!" She didn't cry, "Come back!" She just cried.

And he rode away.

# Chapter 7

Hours passed. Hours in which Annie roamed from room to room, trying to find a focus. Trying to find a reason to do something other than cry. But it didn't come. And the emptiness inside her echoed like the painful quiet of the small frame house. She was so lost in her own misery that she didn't even hear Davie drive up.

"Hey, Annie!"

The familiar voice boomed a greeting through the open screen door. Without waiting for an invitation, Davie Henry walked inside with a petite blonde in tow.

"I thought I'd stop and see if you wanted something from town," Davie said. "Mom gave me a list the length of my arm, so if you need anything, don't hesitate to say so. I'll be in that grocery store for an hour trying to find everything. Besides, I wanted you to meet my Charlie."

He grinned and winked as he looked down at the pretty young woman at his side.

"Charlie...this is Annie O'Brien. Annie...Charlotte Thomas."

Annie smiled at the woman. She reminded her of a pixie. Turned-up nose. Big round eyes. Pouty lips and bashful dimples. Such an odd contrast to Davie's hulking appearance...and yet, somehow, perfect.

"Hi, Charlotte. It's so good to finally meet you. Davie has told me all about you." And then she grinned impishly as she added, "You do know that he's never full?"

The unexpected remark about Davie's constant state of hunger set both women into a fit of the giggles.

Charlotte rolled her eyes and nodded. "Do I ever." And then she added, "Davie's talked about you for years. I'm pleased to finally be able to meet the infamous Annie." And then she turned to Davie with an innocent expression. "Davie...she does *not* have horns and a forked tail. Shame on you!"

Davie turned red. He was dumbfounded by the fact that both women had instantly turned on him. "I never... Well, Annie, I swear it was only a joke. I wouldn't..."

They burst into laughter as Davie breathed a sigh of relief. As long as they weren't mad at him, they could laugh all they liked.

"So, Annie, do you need anything from town, or would you two rather stand here and make fun of me some more?" Davie grumbled.

"The only thing I really need is to have a prescription refilled," she said, thinking about the small number of pain pills that were left in the bottom of that little brown bottle.

"Is Parker's Drug still in business?" Annie asked.

He nodded as she handed him her written prescription.

"Wait while I get you some money."

"Naw...just pay Parker the next time you go into Walnut Shade. He knows you're good for it."

She sighed to herself as she thought, Oh, the luxury of small-town living. It felt good to be home.

"Need anything else?" he asked.

"Thanks, Davie, but I don't think so," she said, and shrugged to make her point. "I bought plenty when Gabe was still here. It'll take me a week to eat it up by myself."

*The biker is gone!* Davie frowned. He'd noticed that the bike wasn't out front. But he hadn't known it was a permanent absence. He'd imagined the man was off on an errand. He stared at her face and nearly missed seeing the emptiness with which she smiled back at him.

*Oh damn! She was in love with the guy,* he thought.

Davie recognized the signs. He should. He felt the same way about Charlotte. He looked at her, and then stared at the floor in front of his boots.

Charlotte realized something was amiss and thought to give the two old friends some privacy.

"I'll wait in the truck," she said. "Annie . . . it was great to be able to meet you. Come see me sometime."

Annie nodded and waved, masking regret as the tiny blonde left. *I would have liked her for a friend.*

Davie kept staring at Annie's sad expression. Something felt wrong, but he couldn't put his finger on what, or figure out a way to offer his help.

"You sure you don't need anything else?" He walked across the room, closing the space between them in three easy steps and wrapped her into a warm, engulfing hug. "You better promise me that if you ever—and I mean *ever*—need anything, you'll let me know."

Annie smiled past her tears. For a single moment she let herself imagine that it was Gabe who was holding her. That it was Gabe who was asking for promises. And then Davie turned her loose and stepped back as a cocky grin slid across his mouth. The feeling disappeared.

"Oh, right! If I ever need baby-sitting, I'll call on you. I wasted half my sunny days keeping you out of mischief. I guess it's only fair that you have to reciprocate."

A frown furrowed his forehead. "I'm not real sure what you just said I should do...." And then he grinned and poked her playfully on the shoulder. "But if it doesn't hurt my manhood—or my feelings—I'll do it."

"'Reciprocate' means pay me back, you goof."

He flushed. "Okay, just don't be using all those big fancy words on me. I never left Walnut Shade, you know."

"But I would have sworn that before she died, Mother wrote and told me about you getting an athletic scholarship to Missouri State."

"Well, I did, but it didn't work out," he muttered, then turned away.

He stuffed his hand in his pocket as he searched for his truck keys, looking more uncomfortable by the minute. Annie couldn't imagine what she'd said that had made him so defensive.

"I better be going," Davie said, yanking out the ring of keys he'd been looking for as he headed toward the door.

A small white piece of folded paper fluttered to the floor behind him as he turned away. Annie bent down and picked it up. Tiny, unintelligible scribblings and a few, minute line drawings were written in neat, perpendicular order in three equally neat rows. She frowned. It looked like childish scribbles. It was probably nothing, but since he'd thought enough of it to keep it, the least she could do was return it.

"Davie...you dropped this," she said, and held out the folded paper.

He turned. "Oh, man, my list," he muttered. "If I'd lost that, Mom would have had a fit. I've got a good memory, but it's not that good." He grinned, took the paper from her

outstretched hand and shoved it back inside the front pocket
of his jeans.

"Thanks, Annie. Be seeing you," he said, and missed the
look of utter shock sweeping across her face.

He climbed into his truck beside Charlotte and drove
away, leaving Annie to stare in muddled confusion at his
brake lights as he slowed to turn the corner.

"List? There wasn't one single, legible word on that paper." But there was no one around to hear her, or argue with
the truth of the statement.

She shrugged and walked back inside, certain that they'd
just misunderstood each other. Davie hadn't looked, he'd
just assumed that it was his list he'd dropped. The real list
was probably safe, tucked away in another pocket. She
smiled to herself, imagining him pulling out that paper and
then trying to find a list of groceries amid that mess of hen
scratching. He was going to be so mad at himself, she
thought.

She walked back toward the kitchen in search of something to still the grumbling reminder in her stomach that she
hadn't eaten all day. Hunger was the least of her problems.
But starving herself and adding another problem to the already insurmountable ones she was facing was out of the
question.

She opened the refrigerator and leaned down, saw a half-
eaten meat loaf wrapped in plastic wrap, and caught her
breath at the pain that knifed through her. It reminded her
of the first meal she'd prepared for Gabriel.

"Damn you, Gabe. Are memories of you going to haunt
me for the rest of my life?"

As soon as she said it, she laughed. But it was a harsh,
bitter laugh. The rest of her life. That was rich.

She slammed the refrigerator door shut, her hunger forgotten in the loneliness that overwhelmed her. With a sigh, she retreated to the living room.

She stood in the doorway, watching...listening. But there were no answers to her problems in there. Her gaze fell on the narrow bookcase, where she'd stacked her books from home. Without conscious thought, she walked over to it and then paused, looking at the second shelf from the top. Her fingers traced the spines, mentally cataloging the titles as she braced herself for what she was about to do. With a forefinger, she hooked the top of the book and pulled it toward her. It slid out of the tightly fitted stack like toast popping out of a toaster.

"Okay," she muttered, as she headed for the sofa with it clutched against her chest. "If there are answers to be found, maybe you have one for me in here."

In seconds she was stretched out on the couch, the book open before her at the place where she'd stopped last.

*Life After Death.* She sighed, ignoring the burning sensation in the back of her throat where unshed tears hung at the ready, and began to read.

Compulsion to understand the words made her grip the edge of the book so tightly that when it came time to turn the page, she couldn't. Her fingers were stuck to the paper.

And as she read, she became lost in the images called up by the words swimming before her. Finally she slept, certain only that at some point and time in their lives, all mankind came to the same, inevitable end.

"Annie! I'm back!"

She woke with a start. The book that she'd been reading slid off her stomach and onto the floor with a thump.

"I'm in here," she called as Davie walked into the room alone.

He walked to the couch and leaned over, dangling her prescription in front of her.

Annie took the bag out of his hands. "Thank you."

She tried unsuccessfully to sit up, and Davie held out a hand, pulling her to her feet in one smooth motion. As he did, his foot kicked the book that had fallen on the floor. He bent down and picked it up.

Annie's stomach jerked, and a guarded expression crossed her face. She wasn't in the mood for explanations...or conversational detours. But she needn't have worried. Davie's actions were stiff and awkward as he slapped the book shut and held it out in front of him.

"It won't bite," Annie muttered, and started toward the kitchen with her medicine. "Would you mind putting that book back on the shelf? Just poke it in anywhere you can find space." She waved her hand in the general direction of the book shelf, and didn't look back to see if he was following orders.

Davie sighed as she walked out of the room, then looked long and hard at the book in his hand before heading toward the bookcase at the other end of the room.

In less than a minute Annie was back. Her bare feet made little noise as she walked, and she entered the living room undetected. She opened her mouth and started to speak, but the words dangled unspoken on the tip of her tongue as she watched Davie's odd behavior.

He was standing by the bookshelf. She couldn't see his face, but she saw what he was doing. And when she did, warning signals went off. She couldn't quite pinpoint the urgency of what she was feeling, but she watched, silently and intently, as Davie moved from book to book.

Reverently he touched each book's spine with his forefinger, tracing the letters in the titles with the tip of his finger as a blind man read braille, as if trying to absorb what he read by touch alone.

Annie shivered. Davie wasn't blind.

She watched him studiously struggle with the shape of each letter, tracing it over and over before going on to the next. It reminded her of something she'd seen before. Something in the classroom. Something one of her brighter students had done during her first year of teaching.

What was it? Annie pondered. *What am I trying to remember?*

And then Davie turned unexpectedly. The guilt... the shock... the overwhelming embarrassment on his face was the last clue to the memory she'd been trying to unearth. It was the same look of panic. The same guilt that her student, Varlie Hudson, had worn when Annie had realized what was wrong.

*Davie can't read!*

The knowledge came swiftly. She didn't even have to ask as she watched Davie turn away in sudden horror and quickly shove the book back on the shelf.

"I'd better be getting home," he said. "Mom's ice cream will be starting to melt."

"Davie..."

Annie started toward him. He began backing to the front door, dodging chairs and grabbing at table lamps to keep them from tumbling to the floor as he tried to escape the certainty on her face.

"You know how Mom is," he continued. "She likes crisp things crisp, and cold things cold. If I dawdle, she'll nag for a week."

"Davie, don't," Annie said, and grabbed him just as he reached the screen door.

He looked away, unable to face the question he knew she was going to ask.

"You know that I'm your friend," she reminded him.

He nodded, still unable to meet the look in her eyes.

"You know that you can trust me."

He sighed. "You don't let go, do you, Annie?"

She didn't answer.

He started to talk. It came out in bits and pieces, but she understood just the same.

"I can remember anything," Davie said.

Annie nodded and slipped her fingers across the massive muscle in his forearm. It jerked uncontrollably beneath her fingertips. She squeezed once for comfort as he continued.

"I don't remember a time when I ever really understood them . . . the words, you know." He looked away in embarrassment as he explained. "And every time I asked a question, or stumbled over the sounds, the kids laughed and the teacher would get frustrated with me. I thought I was just stupid. I think so did my teacher."

"Why did they keep promoting you to the next grade?" Annie asked.

Davie smiled. But it wasn't a happy smile. It was full of pain and regret.

"I don't know," he muttered. "Every year I was the biggest one in my class. It was hard being so damned big. . . and different. I guess they just didn't want to fix someone else's mess and kept moving me up. But I got by."

Tears puddled in Annie's eyes. "Why didn't you tell me? When we were kids together, why didn't you tell me, Davie? I would have helped."

He shrugged. "By then it was too late."

"How on earth have you managed? How did you get a job? How did you get a driver's license? Does anyone else know about . . . ?"

"Whoa," he said, and ran a hand through his curly blond hair in confusion. "First things first, teacher."

Annie waited.

"I can't get the good jobs," Davie admitted. "Luckily there's plenty of heavy-labor, part-time jobs around. Even some farming. You don't have to be able to read to plow or cut wood. And I can write my name real good."

"Oh, Davie, I'm so sorry."

He shrugged. "As for the driver's license…" He grinned, as if it were one of his more innovative stunts. "I walked into the office with a patch on my eye. Told them I'd hurt myself and needed an oral test. That I couldn't come back later because I was leaving town on a job. They read it to me. I only missed one question. After that, driving was easy. I know what the shapes of the traffic signs mean. And I can drive as good as anyone. The rest was easy."

Annie hugged him. Davie Henry had been running on guts for years. And then something occurred to her. Something so overwhelming she knew that the message had come from somewhere other than inside herself.

"Davie … I could teach you to read."

He stepped back, astounded by the thought.

"I could," she persisted. And then she added, before he could object, "No one has to know a thing. We could do it here, in my house. Everyone would think you were just helping out with odd jobs."

He swallowed harshly, his Adam's apple bobbing up and down several times before he got out the words.

"You would do that for me?"

She nodded, her eyes filling with unexpected tears. "But I can't promise anything. All the work will have to come from you."

"I'm a real hard worker," Davie said. "And I'm stubborn as hell."

"I remember," she said.

"I'll do it!" he cried, and hugged her, holding her in a near-frantic grip, as if he couldn't believe his luck or was afraid that she might disappear. "When can we start?"

"Come back tomorrow," she said. "When I have time, I'll pick up some proper books, but for now, we'll start with what I learned on," she said, remembering the stacks of children's books that her mother had saved from her childhood.

"What time?" Davie asked.

"You decide," Annie answered. "I'm here. I'm not going anywhere." *At least . . . I don't think so . . . not yet.*

"See you!" he shouted, and bounded out the door and off of the porch.

Annie smiled and waved, then went back into the house. The weight in her heart was still there. After losing Gabe, that would never change. But a small part of the ache was gone, and she knew it was because now she had a purpose. She had a reason to get up each day. For the first time in longer than she cared to remember, she had a goal. Before it was too late . . . for herself and for Davie . . . she was going to teach him how to read.

She headed toward the kitchen, yanked the half-eaten meat loaf out of the refrigerator and began slicing it to make a sandwich. Now she had a reason to keep up her strength.

The night sounds around her home were becoming familiar. Annie had gone to bed just after sunset, weary beyond words at the emotional upheaval she'd been forced to face today.

Losing Gabe had nearly killed her. Then she thought of Davie and his revelation and knew that it had come at just the right time to save her sanity. All she had to do was focus on Davie's problem, instead of the huge, aching hole Gabe's exodus had caused. Surely she could do that.

But the tension of the day had been too much. Three hours into her sleep, she bolted awake. Heart pounding, sweat seeping from her body, hands shaking with dread at the onslaught of what was coming. And it *was* coming. She'd learned to recognize the signs.

"My pills," she muttered, and stumbled as she rolled out of bed.

The small table lamp clattered to the floor as she reached to turn on the light. A loud thud and then the tinkle of glass were enough to tell her that she would have to navigate the darkened room by instinct until she got to the light switch at the edge of the doorway.

But on the second step, she fell, going down to the floor in unexpected pain as a shard of glass from the broken lamp pierced her foot.

"Oh, no," she muttered, as the throbbing at the back of her head increased to blinding proportions.

Carelessly brushing her hand over the bottom of her foot, she swiped at the area that was causing her pain. And as she did, she broke the glass off in her foot. Ignoring the pain and the trail of blood she was leaving behind her, she staggered toward the kitchen with single-minded intent. She had to get to her pills. She had to stop the pain before it stopped *her*—permanently.

She didn't remember turning on the light in the kitchen, pouring a glass of water or holding the open cabinet door to steady herself before reaching inside to grasp the new bottle of pills that she'd placed there earlier in the day.

The cap wouldn't budge. In that moment she hated the invention of the childproof cap with a vengeance. But she continued to struggle, convinced that unless she got the bottle open, this would be the end of her.

Without warning, the cap came away in her hand, scattering tiny pills all over the countertop and at the floor near her feet. Without looking to see where the others had rolled, she grabbed the nearest pill, stuffing it shakily into her mouth. Excess water cascaded onto the front of her gown as she tilted the glass to wash the pill down.

"Now...now..." she groaned as she clutched her head and staggered, swaying drunkenly as she tried to see through the pain-induced haze. Somewhere in front of her, she knew there was a doorway that would take her back to her bed.

But she'd left it too late to move any farther. She went down in a heap near the table in the center of the room, her resting place the floor on which she'd left an assortment of pain pills, water and blood. For Annie, it was far enough. She rolled into a ball, closed her eyes and waited for the medicine to take effect, longing for the blessed relief she knew would come.

Gabe hurt. He ached from the inside out. Anger at fate and himself kept his foot heavy on the pedal while the Harley ate up the miles, widening the gap between himself and Annie.

The sun beamed down on him in relentless persecution. The blowing dirt and wind stung his bare neck and chest as he rode. Once he thought about stopping and putting on a shirt beneath that black leather vest, and then he instantly nixed the idea. He deserved misery. He'd certainly left plenty behind.

There was a crossroad ahead. He stopped to look both ways and flipped up the visor of his helmet, inhaling the hot, dry wind, relishing it over the stuffy air that he breathed behind the helmet. He frowned as a memory tried to surface. Something about this day was so familiar, and yet he couldn't quite put his finger on it.

And then he grinned wryly to himself. It reminded him a little of that hot, dry day so long ago in the Kansas Territory when this had all begun—or ended, depending on the way one chose to view it.

A girl drove by and waved, her smile and her wink nothing more than a reminder to Gabe of what he'd left behind. With an angry curse, he flipped the visor back down and accelerated across the intersection.

Miles and hours passed. And with them came the growing certainty that leaving Annie had been the wrong thing to do.

He knew the unspoken rules governing his time here on earth. He knew that to undo the wrongs of his past, he had to keep on the move. Personal happiness had to be of lesser importance in his life. Personal involvement had no part in what he had to do. And still his gut instinct told him to turn around.

"But why?"

He pulled off the interstate, hit the kickstand with the toe of his boot, then killed the engine. He hung his helmet on the handlebar and walked a distance away to get his bearings.

Stiff muscles reminded him that it had been months since he'd ridden the bike so continually. He stared blindly off into the small brushy canyon below and tried to bring some order to his jumbled thoughts.

When he'd first met Annie, the reason why he'd stayed was obvious. She'd asked. He could even, he told himself, justify why he'd stayed after Damon Tuttle had gotten himself killed. After all, he could hardly have left her in the lurch after nearly all her belongings had been destroyed. And…she'd asked him to bring her home. He couldn't turn down a personal request from someone in need. He just…couldn't.

"Oh, hell," he muttered, and bent down, grabbing a handful of gravel from the shoulder of the road, then absently tossing the pebbles one by one down the hillside. "Face it, Donner. You lost your focus the first time you kissed her."

The ache in his belly grew as he remembered. That was the day he'd first rescued her. When she'd fainted at the gas station, and he'd held her in his arms while he waited for her to regain consciousness.

He closed his eyes. Even now he could remember the feel of her mouth beneath his and how soft her skin was to the touch. He frowned as that thought brought another, more sinister, memory bobbing to the surface.

*Fainting.*

She did a lot of that.

*Migraines.*

He knew people had them. Hers had even brought on some of the fainting spells he'd witnessed. But he couldn't bear to see someone he cared for so deeply, so deeply in pain. He wondered if she'd ever had these bouts at school. Teaching would have been impossible during one of the episodes.

With the thought of teaching, another sinister memory rose to the surface, sitting alongside the first, like little sores festering in his mind.

*Books.*

She loved books. She shared her love of them, and what was inside, with everyone. So why had she been so defensive about the ones he'd been helping her unpack? They were on such offbeat subjects that he would have expected her to joke about them instead of trying to hide them.

*Neurosurgery... Life After Death.*

He started to laugh. But the sound turned into a harsh, ugly gasp as everything he'd just assembled in his mind stirred itself into a thick, ugly heap and began steaming with possibilities he didn't want to contemplate.

*Fainting . . . migraines . . . pain . . . pain pills. Neurosurgery . . . even dying.*

A flashback of the day they'd attended church together in Oklahoma City set his teeth on edge. He thought of how oddly she'd behaved, and suddenly one fact became irrefutably clear.

*Something's wrong with Annie! Something bad!*

"Why did I decide that?" Gabe muttered, and stuffed his hands into his pockets to keep them from shaking. "What in God's name made me think of that?"

And with the speaking of His name, came the knowledge. He knew Who had made him think of that.

"No," he groaned, and looked up into the nearly cloudless sky, as if trying to see past infinity to One beyond. "Tell me it isn't so."

But no answer came. All he felt was a growing fear and the need to hear Annie deny it to his face.

He ran to the bike, calculating how long it would take him to get back to her. If he had it figured right, he would be there around midnight.

He shoved his helmet on his head, snapping the chin strap as he swung one long leg over the bike. In seconds he was on the move. He raced across the highway, crossing the grassy median and leaving grass flying in the air behind him as the tires hit pavement on the other side.

One way or another, he and Annie weren't through with each other. Not by a long shot.

# Chapter 8

Dawn was a thought on the horizon as Gabe finally wheeled the Harley into Annie's yard. After missing turns and once even taking the wrong highway in the dark, he'd misjudged the time it would take him to get back.

He slipped off his helmet and hung it on the handlebar as the motor coughed and died. After hours and hours with the sound of the wind and the roar of the engine in his ears, the sudden silence seemed like a warning.

In one motion he put the kickstand in place and swung his leg up and over, dismounting from the bike as he'd always dismounted from his horse. The rowels on his spurs jingled once as he took a step away from the bike and stared silently up the path that led to the house.

It looked the same. Nothing seemed ominous...or out of place. But if that was so, then why did he have this overpowering feeling of dread? What made him think he might already be too late?

Gabe glanced down at himself, realizing as he did that he probably looked like hell. A day's worth of black, spiky whiskers and twenty-four hours on the back of a bike would do little toward making him presentable. But a bath and a shave would have to wait until he'd seen her... until she'd laughed in his face at his fears and cursed him for coming back just to say goodbye again.

He walked around the bush at the edge of the yard, heading for the path that led to the front door. His heart skipped a beat as he saw the light on at the back of the house.

"She can't be up already." He glanced down at his watch and squinted as he tried to read the luminous dial. It wasn't quite 5:00 a.m.

But he remembered the pain on her face as he'd ridden away, and the knot in his own gut at saying goodbye, and decided that she, like him, had probably just suffered a sleepless night.

Even though he'd already answered all his own questions, he still felt a need to hurry. Just to make sure that she was all right.

*If she's so all right, then why in hell hasn't she come out to meet me?*

He stopped at the door and knocked. Nearly a minute went by without a response, so he knocked again, and this time he called her name aloud. Twice. Nothing happened. No one came.

"Annie, damn it, where are you?" he muttered. "Okay... maybe you left the light on by mistake."

If she *was* asleep in her bed, checking that theory before barreling into the house seemed the sensible thing to do.

With that thought in mind, he ignored the steps and turned the corner at the side of the house on the run. Destination: kitchen window.

A faint beam of light poured out of the window and into the night, cutting the ground in a butter-colored, geometric pattern.

He leaned forward, bracing himself against the outer wall as he peered through the narrow gap between the curtain panels. From where he was standing, all he could see was her foot . . . and the blood . . . and the fact that she was motionless on the floor.

"No!"

The denial was ripped from his lips as terror spread through his system. This was what he'd been sensing! This was what had sent him riding back through the darkest of nights! She was hurt . . . or worse.

"Annie! Annie!"

She didn't move. She didn't answer.

He banged the flat of his hand on the window in sick frustration, and then ran back to the front door.

The door was locked. He'd expected that.

But just as he started to kick it in, he remembered the old, dusty key that she'd retrieved from above the door frame the day of their arrival. He reached up and ran his fingers along the dry, splintery wood. The key was still there! He was inside in seconds, running to Annie's aid.

As he entered the kitchen, he started to shake. Small patches of blood were spattered everywhere. She was lying halfway beneath the table, her thin, white nightgown twisted around her legs. All he could see was the back of her head and the back of her body. Silent. Unmoving.

Within the space of a second, his heart stopped and then changed rhythm to a frantic, pounding pace that left him gasping for air.

Small yellow pills lay scattered across the counter and the floor, haphazardly interspersed with the drying blood stains to form an odd, garish pattern.

Bile rose and burned the back of his throat. But his legs refused to move. In the countless years that he'd been traveling the earth, he'd witnessed almost everything. Births, accidents, even deaths. But this was something he wasn't ready to face. He didn't want to lose the woman he loved. Not now... not like this.

He'd known for weeks that Annie O'Brien meant more to him than she should. But not until now—not until it might be too late—had he been able to admit, even to himself, the magnitude of his feelings for her. For the first time in his life, he felt love for a woman.

"Annie!"

Her name became a prayer as he knelt at her side. With a sick heart and a frantic touch, his hands swept the sides of her face. And when he touched her shoulder, she rolled limply onto her back. Too quiet, too still. He shook as he searched for signs of life.

The flat of his hand splayed across the center of her chest as he felt for her heartbeat. If it was there, it was so faint that it was undetectable.

"Annie...please, baby, don't do this to me," he begged, but she didn't respond.

He leaned forward, so close that the faint, tiny pores of her skin were visible. He held his breath and listened until he heard the slight but steady sounds of her even breathing. His knees went weak, and his heavy sigh of relief echoed in the utter silence of the kitchen.

"Thank you, God," he murmured. "She's still alive."

The mess she was lying in gave birth to all sorts of implications that Gabe didn't even want to consider. There were pills everywhere. To someone who didn't know her, it might look as if she'd tried to take her life. And yet Gabe knew that the pills did not explain the blood.

"Annie... baby... if only you could talk to me."

She didn't respond, and in panic, he began to check her for further sign of injury. It was then that he noticed the seeping wound on the bottom of her foot.

"Thank God," Gabe whispered. Suddenly the blood made sense. Whatever had happened to her must have been an accident. "I've got to get you to a doctor," he said, and started to pick her up from the floor.

But his intentions were momentarily forgotten as Annie's eyelids fluttered, and with a soft moan, she opened her eyes.

"Gabe?" Her chin quivered, and she blinked over and over, unable to believe what she was seeing. "You're gone . . . not here . . . just a dream. Bad dream."

"Ah, damn." Regret tinged his voice as he lifted her into his arms and pressed hot, thankful kisses across her face and neck, tasting the place where her lifeblood pulsed. "It's not a dream, honey. I'm here. What happened?"

"Head . . . headache."

He cursed beneath his breath. With a frown, he carried her toward the bedroom. This didn't look good. In fact, it was just as he'd feared. The headaches were becoming too frequent, and each time they occurred, the pain seemed to be more intense.

He moved through the house, her head bobbing limply against his arm as he held her carefully within his embrace. But when he walked into her bedroom and saw the lamp shattered on the floor, his reaction was anything but proper.

His curses were few but colorful. And he made no apologies for them. There was nothing else that would describe his emotions so well.

Imagining Annie alone and in pain made him sick to his stomach. He turned on the light, and as he did, she moaned.

"I'm sorry, Annie," he said softly, and quickly laid her on her bed. "Let me get you settled. I want to get a better look at your foot."

Confused by his reappearance, in addition to fighting the aftereffects of the painkillers, Annie struggled against the weight of his hand on her shoulder.

Gabe gently pushed her back into a reclining position while angling her foot for a better look.

"Don't move, baby. Let me look."

She lay back on the bed with a moan and swallowed a mouthful of tears. His gentleness was her undoing.

"Oh, God. Why did you come back? I can't take any more goodbyes."

Gabe's vision blurred. The pain in her voice was an echo of the pain in his chest. But he didn't have time for recriminations, from her or from himself. He was too busy trying to ascertain the extent of her injuries. His fingers shook as he examined her foot for the place where the blood had originated. But there was so much of it that it was difficult to tell.

"How bad did you hurt this time?"

Annie opened her eyes and peered down the length of her body. Her foot was propped on Gabe's lap.

"Hurt what? My foot?"

"No, damn it! Your head. How bad was it? Was it worse than before?"

She didn't answer. With a muttered oath, Gabe got up from the bed.

Annie looked away as he walked into the bathroom. Moments later, the sound of running water told her that he wasn't through with her foot . . . or her. She didn't like this. She didn't like it at all. His questions were too pointed for comfort.

He walked back into the bedroom with a wet washcloth in his hand. From the corner of her eye, Annie saw a look on his face that she didn't want to decipher.

She refused to meet his gaze. Gabe wanted to shake some sense into her.

The mattress gave beneath his weight as he maneuvered her foot back onto his lap and carefully began washing away the blood.

"I said . . . how bad was the headache this time?"

Once again, he waited for an answer that didn't come. And then he let her silence slide as his fingers traced the initial wound and finally found the reason for the continuous blood seepage.

"Annie, there's still glass in your foot. It's got to come out. Do you want me to help you change, or do you want to go to the emergency room dressed like that?"

She sat straight up in bed, shock chasing away the last remnants of the painkiller. Her answer was short and succinct.

"I don't want to go to the hospital," she said.

He frowned. "You don't have a choice, lady. We go like this or you can change. But either way, we go."

A very unladylike curse split the air. Gabe smiled and raised his eyebrows at her opinion of his ultimatum.

"I've heard that one before," he said. "Don't get me started. You'll lose."

She flushed and then waved her hand toward her closet. "If you're so insistent on doing this, at least hand me some clean shorts and a shirt."

Moments later he tossed the garments, as well as fresh underwear, into her lap.

"Want some help?" He started to bend down.

"You can either leave or turn your back."

Hurt beyond words that in less than twenty-four hours she'd completely shut him out, he could only mutter, "I've seen it all before."

"That was then . . . this is now," she said.

He turned his back, closed his eyes and tried to ignore the spreading pain in his gut. Leaving her had obviously been the wrong thing to do. For her to behave like this, whatever trust she'd had in him must be gone.

He seethed in angry frustration. It was back to square one with Annie O'Brien. At the moment, giving her space seemed to be wise.

"I'm going to clean up the kitchen while you finish dressing." He walked out before she could argue.

By the time he'd rebottled the pills and wiped away the blood, the sun was just coming over the horizon. A vivid slash of fiery orange coupled with an undulating swath of hot pink clouds painted a welcome on a new Missouri sky.

Gabe parted the curtains and looked outside, wondering as he did how many more sunrises and sunsets he had left in him, and how difficult they would be to endure without Annie's love.

"I'm ready," she called.

The curtains dropped back in place as he stepped away from the window. He started out of the kitchen, then made a sudden U-turn. Retrieving the brown bottle of pills from the cabinet, he stuffed them in his pocket and went to Annie.

Davie's loaner was an older model car, and for that Gabe was grateful. The back seat was larger and roomier than a newer one would have been. It gave Annie plenty of space to recline, and the pillows Gabe stuffed under her ankle kept her foot elevated. The constantly oozing blood made him nervous. From what Annie had told him, the accident had happened around midnight. The fact that it was still bleeding told him that it was very deep.

"We're here," he announced unnecessarily as he turned the car into the hospital parking lot.

Annie grumbled beneath her breath from the back seat and started to open her own door. Gabe bounded out and caught her in mid-scoot.

"You're not hurting me by acting like this, Annie. You're hurting yourself. Now stop it, damn it, and let me help you."

She flushed. His rebuke was justified. The simple truth was that she wasn't mad at Gabe for coming back. On the contrary. She'd been overjoyed when she'd opened her eyes and realized he was truly there.

It was fear that made her act as she did. Fear that he would find out what she'd been trying to hide, and that pity would replace what they'd shared. No matter how fleeting their relationship had been, Annie treasured it.

"Gabe?"

The sound of her voice was soft, almost nonexistent. He sighed and pressed his chin against the crown of her head as he lifted her into his arms and started carrying her toward the emergency room entrance.

"What?" he asked, and kissed a curl that slipped across his lips, wishing it was Annie's lips he was kissing instead of her hair.

"I'm sorry."

He stopped in mid-step, looked down, then nodded his acceptance of her apology.

Her lower lip trembled, and he sighed and smiled gently as his gaze swept down her face. Her eyes were dark, nearly jade, and her hair seemed to catch fire as the morning sun's rays played hide-and-seek within the tangles of her curls.

She looked vulnerable and miserable and so damned beautiful it made his heart hurt.

"It's okay to be scared, darlin'," he whispered. "I should know. I've been scared so many times in my life I can't even count them, and yet all of them stacked together were nothing to the scare you gave me when I saw you on that kitchen floor."

"I'm sorry for behaving so badly. Really, really sorry."

"Don't apologize to me. Save it for the man who's going to dig that glass out of your foot. If you give him half of what I got this morning, he'll be the one needing an apology."

She groaned and made a face at the thought.

"Let's get this over with," she muttered.

And then, as he started toward the door, she spread her hand across his chest, found the spot where his heart beat loudest and closed her eyes in silent thanksgiving that he was back. For whatever reason . . . and for however long . . . she would take it as the gift that it was and appreciate it.

At the sound of the emergency door opening, a nurse looked up. She raised an eyebrow at the sight of the big, leather-clad biker who'd just entered, carrying a woman whose injury was leaving persistent drops of fresh blood in their wake.

The nurse read the look on his face and made an instant decision. This man was not the kind who would willingly wait to fill out the necessary papers.

"This way," she said, and motioned them into a curtained-off area near the door. "You can put her down here. The doctor will be in shortly. There's a waiting area right down the hall, if you'd care to—"

"No. I'll stay here," Gabe said, and gave the nurse a cool look, daring her to argue.

She didn't. If someone wanted him moved, someone else could move him. She was a nurse, not a policewoman. She took down the patient's name, made note of the time and the type of injury, then left the chart at the foot of the bed.

Minutes later, a doctor arrived.

"What have we here?" he asked, and gave them a confident smile.

"I stepped on some glass," Annie said.

"She passed out," Gabe interrupted.

The doctor looked from the big man to the smaller woman and masked a weary sigh. With one on the defensive and the other ready to argue, this looked like it was going to be a nuisance.

"Let's start over," the doctor said. "I'm Dr. Pope." He picked up the chart that the nurse had started. "And you're Annie O'Brien?"

She nodded. "This is my...um, my friend...Gabe Donner."

Gabe hated it. They didn't even have a way of categorizing their relationship. He wasn't just her friend, damn it. But there was no getting past the fact that although they'd made love with sweet abandon, he'd never given Annie reason to think there was anything emotional in their relationship.

"So, Mr. Donner. You're telling me she passed out," he said, as he bent down and began examining the cut on the bottom of Annie's foot. "How do you know? Did you witness it?"

"No. But I saw her lying unconscious on the floor with blood everywhere and *assumed* she didn't choose that location in which to spend the night."

Dr. Pope's eyebrows drew together at the sarcastic tone of Gabe's voice.

"So you're telling me that you weren't there when this happened."

Gabe swiped an angry hand across his face and cursed beneath his breath.

"No...I wasn't there. I left yesterday morning." Gabe stuffed his hand in his pocket and pulled out the bottle containing Annie's pills. Her harsh gasp as she saw what he'd done told him more than he wanted to know. "She takes these for pain...headache pain. She says she has migraines. I didn't know people could pass out from headaches."

Elevated eyebrows were the only sign of surprise that Dr. Pope allowed himself as he took the bottle from Gabe's hands and read the prescription, as well as the dosage.

Gabe turned and fixed Annie with a hard, pointed stare.

Her eyes were wide, the pupils transfixed. All color had drained from her face as she waited for the doctor's reaction.

Dr. Pope looked up. Annie shook her head once in a negative motion. He assumed she didn't want anything further said about the matter, and because she was his patient, he recognized her right to privacy.

Dr. Pope set the pills down on the table beside her bed and resumed his inspection of her foot.

"Let's get some local anesthetic around this cut and then clean out the glass. I think it'll need a few stitches, too, but I can't be sure until I see how deep the glass is. Wait right here, Miss O'Brien. I'll get the nurse."

Annie rolled her eyes and flopped back onto the bed. *Where on earth would she go—and how?*

She looked up at the ceiling, then over at the door. Everywhere and anywhere except at Gabriel's face.

"You're mad at me, aren't you?" he asked quietly.

"No. Of course not," she said shortly. "Whatever for?"

He almost bought it. Almost...but not quite. Because no matter how sweet her smile or how innocent her look, he still saw a deep and abiding fear in the depths of Annie's eyes. Before he could press her for more of an explanation, the nurse arrived with an ominous-looking tray bearing an assortment of bottles and needles.

"You'll have to wait outside," she announced.

Gabe glared. Annie intervened.

"Please, Gabe," she said. "I'll be fine. You did your job by getting me here. Now let them do theirs."

He nodded—reluctantly. Then, before he changed his mind, he leaned over and kissed her gently on the lips.

It was unexpected, and because of that, Annie reacted before she had time to hide her own feelings.

When their mouths merged, sighs traded places. Gabe reluctantly tore away from the seductive pull of her lips and walked away without looking back.

The nurse raised her eyebrows and winked at Annie. "He's a tough one, isn't he?" she asked, eyeing the stiff, unyielding back of the man in black.

Annie didn't answer at first, and then when she might have, she was too busy trying to get past the sharp little needle jabs around the cut on her foot, as the nurse went about her business of deadening the area for the stitches that were to come.

The waiting room chair was small and uncomfortable as hell. But Gabe was unaware of anything or anyone except the muted sounds of conversation going on between Annie and the doctor. He could hear their voices, but not clearly enough to discern what was being said. It was making him crazy. If he could only get a little bit closer, he knew that he would have the answers to his own questions regarding one Annie O'Brien.

He sighed and shifted restlessly in his seat. It wasn't going to happen. Not here. He'd been relegated to being on the outside looking in, and for now, that was the way it would have to be.

A small, determined smile slid across his mouth. But, he told himself, there was always later, after he got Annie home. After she'd rested. When she wasn't in so much pain. Then she had some explaining to do, and he wasn't going to be happy until she did.

"All done," Dr. Pope said a little while later, coming to stand in front of Gabe.

Gabe stood.

"You can take her home," the doctor continued. "I want to see her again in seven days. Earlier if she has unusual soreness or swelling around the area. I gave her an antibiotic. She should be fine."

"What about the headaches? What about the pills? Is that normal?"

A weary, time-worn expression of sympathy moved across the doctor's face. He could see that the man was sincerely worried. His concern for Annie O'Brien was obvious.

But a long time ago the doctor had taken an oath to be faithful to a patient's right to privacy. And this patient had certainly been adamant about hers. He simply shoved his stethoscope into the pocket of his lab coat and answered Gabe's question without actually revealing any confidential information.

"The pills are Miss O'Brien's regular medication."

He'd told the truth . . . as far as it went. It was up to Miss O'Brien to reveal the rest . . . if she chose.

"Exactly what *is* her condition?" Gabe persisted.

The doctor shrugged. "You should know better than to ask me that. If you want to know more than what I've told you, it will have to come from Miss O'Brien, not me."

He walked away, leaving Gabe to read between the lines of his vague remarks. And what he read there didn't make him feel any better. In fact, it made everything worse. It seemed to confirm his own worst fears.

"Annie . . . are you ready?" he asked as he stepped inside the curtained cubicle.

She nodded.

"I'll get a wheelchair," the nurse said.

"It won't be necessary," Gabe answered, and scooped Annie gently from the bed.

Moments later, they were gone.

He watched her sleep.

With her still groggy from the painkillers and the shock of the accident, it had been all he could do to get her inside and in bed before she succumbed to exhaustion. The moment her head hit the pillow, she rolled over on her side, curling up like a child in prayer, with her hands clasped beneath her chin. She never knew when he left the room.

He hadn't gone far, and he wasn't gone long. As soon as he was satisfied that all was as it should be within Annie's domain, he went back to her room. And there he remained, slumped down in another chair too small for his large frame, staring at each separate feature on her face, trying to understand what made her so special to him.

Dissecting her face with his eyes, feature by feature, was a revealing experience for Gabe. He saw past the externals to the woman beyond, and he finally realized that what he loved most about Annie was what was invisible to the human eye. It was a combination of her spirit and her unswerving trust in the face of what should have been insurmountable odds.

He groaned quietly and buried his face in his hands. She was so loving, and too giving, and he couldn't help but wish their lives had been different. He wanted to stay here forever. To go to sleep each night holding her in his arms and wake up each morning by putting a smile on Annie's face. But it wasn't going to happen, and the sooner he faced it, the better—for himself as well as Annie. Giving her false hope was the cruelest thing he could have done, and despite whatever reasons he'd given himself for coming back, it had already happened.

Without thinking of the consequences, he crawled into the bed beside her, then slid one arm beneath her head and the other around her waist. It didn't take much. Just a scoot and a shift before he had her right where he wanted her. Right where he needed her. He closed his eyes, unaware of the painful smile that cut across his features as she relaxed against him.

*My Annie.*

It was his last conscious thought before weariness claimed him, too, and they slept. But only Annie dreamed.

Fateful dreams and flights of fancy had no place in Gabriel Donner's life. He was here on sufferance only, his days marked by a ticking clock and the number of times that he tried to right a wrong. It was what he did, who he was, but this time it wasn't going to be enough.

# Chapter 9

"Juh... Juh-ack and Juh-aisle..."

"That's a short *I* Davie. Try again."

"Juh-ill..."

"Right! Good job! Now continue."

"Juh-ack and Juh-ill wuh... wuh." Davie grimaced in frustration, as he continued. "...Wuh-int up the huh-ill to... Jack and Jill went up the hill!"

The expression on Davie's face was priceless. The sudden understanding of what he'd been trying to read colored his expression with joy. She smiled. That look was the single reason she'd chosen teaching as a profession.

"Oh God, Annie. I read that whole sentence, didn't I?"

Annie nodded. She patted his arm, then pointed to the next line. "You sure did, Davie. But now's no time to stop. What comes next?"

Eagerly he leaned forward, his forefinger still positioned below the last word he'd read so as not to lose his place, and began sounding out the syllables.

Annie's thoughts wandered as she absently listened. It had been a week since their lessons had begun. And in that week, so much had occurred in her life.

Gabe was back and, except for the time she spent with Davie, never far from her side. The stitches had come out of her foot. And Davie Henry was making progress, actual visible progress in learning to read. She should have been the happiest woman on the face of the earth. But she wasn't. Day by day, she became more anxious, more certain that, for her, time was running out.

Each night she was loved to sleep so deeply and so thoroughly that she often found herself pretending that this way of life was going to go on forever. But when morning came and she had to face herself in the mirror, she couldn't lie...not even to herself. It wasn't forever. And it was all because of the secret she was keeping from Gabe. The secret that was eating her alive.

The ragged grumble of the Harley's engine broke her wayward concentration. Annie blinked, looked at the clock on the wall and then over at Davie, who was quickly closing the book he'd been reading from.

"I'd better be going," he muttered, still embarrassed for anyone other than Annie to know about his problem.

"Take this with you," she said, shoving the book toward him. "Practice reading aloud. Sound out the letters the way I showed you, and we'll do the next page tomorrow."

Davie nodded, glancing nervously toward the back door as Gabe's footsteps sounded on the porch.

"He won't interfere," Annie said, and she squeezed Davie's arm reassuringly, remembering the understanding with which Gabe had received the news of Davie's handicap. "So what," he'd remarked. "I was older than him before I learned. It's the learning that counts...not when it happens."

Annie sighed, wishing she could share that bit of Gabe's conversation with Davie. She suspected it would go a long way toward making him feel better about himself.

The two men passed each other with nods and furtive smiles. Gabe imagined Davie didn't approve of him and his relationship with Annie, and Davie imagined that Gabe could see into his soul and read his shortcomings in a single glance.

Gabe stopped just inside the doorway, his gaze sweeping across Annie's face as the screen door banged behind Davie Henry's exit.

Her familiar smile was in place. Everything about her seemed so open and aboveboard. But instinct told him that she was hiding something. Something she was afraid to tell him about.

"I'll be right back," Annie said, and gently touched Gabe's shoulder before following Davie to his truck.

Just as she left the kitchen, the phone rang in the front part of the house. She paused in the doorway, indecision catching her in mid-stride.

"I'll get it," Gabe offered. "Go tell Davie whatever it is he needs to know."

She nodded, waved her thanks and hurried out the door, anxious to give Davie some more last-minute instructions regarding his lessons.

Gabe picked up the receiver on the third ring.

"Hello...O'Brien residence." Then he frowned. The man's voice on the other end was unfamiliar, the tone of his question far too serious for Gabe's peace of mind as he answered, "Yes, she's here, but she's outside. Could she call you right back?"

A slow sigh slid through the line and into his ear. For some unknown reason Gabe shivered. And then the man spoke again.

"So...she's actually there...as, in residence?"

Gabe frowned. "Yes, of course," he answered. "If you'll wait—"

"I can't right now," the man answered. "I'm due in surgery." And then, as if he felt compelled to continue, he said, "My name is Dr. Peter Barnes. Miss O'Brien is...was...my patient. She's missed her last two scheduled appointments, and I was extremely concerned about her welfare. In fact, I was actually relieved to know that she missed them because she moved, not because...well..."

Gabe inhaled slowly. His belly muscles clenched as he closed his eyes and said a small, silent prayer. Something told him that if he handled this right, he would get the answers he'd been wanting, and no one would be the wiser.

"That's too bad," Gabe said. "I wish I'd known about her appointments. I would have made sure she'd called and let you know about the move. We made it together, in fact." He let the doctor digest the information he'd planted before he continued. "So...how did you find out where she was?"

He thought he could hear Dr. Barnes shuffling papers. "I had a request for the transfer of her medical records come across my desk today. I took a chance and called Walnut Shade for a number. After I realized that a doctor there...a Dr. Pope...had already treated her, it only made sense that she had to live nearby."

"Right, that was late last week," Gabe said. "When she had one of her fainting spells and cut her foot. I took her to the emergency room myself."

Gabe imagined that he could actually hear Dr. Barnes absorbing this news. "So...you know something of her condition, then?" he asked.

Gabe bit his lip. What he was about to say wasn't a lie. He did know something. He just didn't know why or how it mattered.

"Yes, I do," Gabe said. "And it's a constant worry to me. I care very deeply for Annie. I could be wrong . . . but it seems to me that her episodes are more frequent and more intense than when we first met."

Dr. Barnes sighed heavily into the phone. And as he did, Gabe absorbed the sound with a sick shudder.

"That's to be expected. Does she still have plenty of medication?" Dr. Barnes asked.

*My God . . . to be expected? What the hell did the man mean?*

"Yes," Gabe assured him. "We make sure she's never out of those. I don't think she could survive without them."

"Unfortunately, as you know, the time will come when that point is moot. I'm really sorry about that. I liked Miss O'Brien immensely."

*Liked? Why the hell did he say it in the past tense?*

Gabe blinked in shock and turned his attention back to the doctor's comments as soon as he realized that the other man was still talking.

"It's a damned shame that something like this had to happen to someone like her . . . someone in the prime of her life, with so much to offer," Dr. Barnes continued.

Gabe grunted. But it wasn't in agreement, it was from pain. Had Dr. Barnes been able to see the look on Gabe's face, he would have realized that what he'd unwittingly revealed had provided the worst kind of shock.

"Please tell her that I wish her well, and if she has any questions regarding her condition, she should feel free to call me and talk anytime. Even though she's asked for Dr. Pope to be her doctor of record in the last phases of her illness, I can't help wishing she hadn't moved. There's going to come a time when even the strongest medications won't help. After that, as I'm sure you know . . . it's only a matter of time.''

Gabe went weak. *Last phases of her illness*. He felt himself sliding down the wall with the receiver still held against his ear. *Only a matter a time*.

He knew he must have been saying all the right things, because he vaguely remembered hearing Dr. Barnes telling him to call if he needed advice, then hanging up. But the memory of what he'd said was gone. All he could hear was the echo of Dr. Barnes's statement. . . . *"It's only a matter of time . . . only a matter of time."*

"Oh, damn . . . oh, Annie. Not *my* Annie."

But there was no one around to refute the horror of what he'd learned. Only an overwhelming sickness that kept threatening to engulf him.

The edge of the chair rubbed the back of his legs, just at the bend of his knees. Luckily for Gabe, it stopped his fall. He found himself sitting in it rather than sliding all the way to the floor, and was oddly thankful for its unexpected presence. It was a less-compromising position in which to be as Annie walked back into the house, calling his name.

"Gabe, where did you . . . ?"

Whatever she'd been about to ask was lost as she walked into the room and saw him sitting in the chair with the telephone receiver lying on his lap.

His long, jeans-clad legs were stretched out in front of him, as if bracing him against sliding out of the chair. As usual, he'd rolled up the sleeves of his long-sleeved gray shirt and had only buttoned it halfway, revealing more of the taut muscles across his chest and belly than would have been considered polite out in public.

Annie smiled. She knew Gabe. It was obvious to anyone who cared to look that Gabriel Donner cared little for so-

ciety's demands. And because she knew him so well, she saw
past the obvious to the shock on his face and felt an un-
named fear.

"What is it? Is something wrong?"

Gabe couldn't answer. All he could do was look at her
and remember the doctor's words. *It's only a matter of time.
It's only a matter of . . .*

He loved that dress she was wearing. The skirt was softly
flared and moved with her body as she walked. The sleeve-
less bodice showed off her narrow waist and slender, tanned
arms to perfection. The narrow red-and-white stripes that
ran throughout the fabric reminded him of peppermint
sticks, one of the few Christmas presents that he'd ever received as a child back in the Territory. Her hair was loose
and full around her face, and bounced when she walked like
the coils of a spring. Her eyes were sparkling with joy, full
of . . . *life?*

"When the hell were you going to tell me?"

The question was harsh, the words guttural, torn from
deep inside in short, jerky clumps.

Annie took a step backward in defense against the unexpected anger of his attack.

"What are you talking about?" she asked. "I already told
you why Davie comes to the house . . . and why you have to
leave. I thought you understood."

Gabe tried to smile. But the smile was lost as he was
forced to grit his teeth to keep from shouting at her. Rage
and an ungovernable sense of injustice swept over him.

He picked up the phone and held it out to her in a taunt-
ing gesture. "You missed your call," he said harshly.

Annie felt sick. She didn't know what had happened, but
whatever it was, she knew it had made Gabriel as angry as
she'd ever seen a man.

"Did they leave a number?" she asked.

Gabe laughed harshly, but the joke was on himself.

"No. You already have the number." He stood up jerkily. "In fact, you have everybody's number, as well as all the answers...don't you? The only problem is, you just weren't of a mind to share."

She was afraid. What terrible thing had happened that had changed Gabe from the tender lover of last night to the cold, angry man standing before her now?

"What are you talking about?" Annie asked. "And stop shouting at me, damn it! You're scaring me."

Her chin trembled, but she held her ground. And as her words hit home, she watched Gabe's defenses crumble.

"Well, excuse the hell out of me, darlin'," he whispered sarcastically, and wiped a shaky hand across his eyes, as if trying to remove the traces of what he'd learned from his mind. It was no use. He knew that the horror of the last few minutes would stay with him forever.

"Who called?" Annie asked.

His hands trembled, and he shook his head, as if in denial of her question. His arms dropped limply to his sides as he stared at her.

Annie watched his eyes turn cold, boring into her until she couldn't look away. Finally he answered.

"It was your doctor."

She turned pale. "Dr. Pope?"

"No, Annie. Dr. Barnes. Dr. Peter Barnes from Oklahoma City. You missed your last two appointments."

Her lips moved, but no sound came out. Understanding began to invade her mind. In sudden terror she started to shake.

"When were you going to tell him that you'd moved, Annie? Or were you planning to give him a dose of the same medicine you've been giving me and just wait? Were you going to let us find out the hard way? Were you going to wait until you died in my arms and he read it in a paper somewhere?''

"Oh ... my ... God."

Her worst fears had been realized. He knew! The room began to spin around her.

Gabe grabbed her by the shoulders, pulling her toward him, pressing her intimately against him in fierce denial of what he'd learned.

"Annie." Her name was torn from his lips. "Please! Tell me it isn't so!"

Gabe winced as she buried her face in her hands. He knew then that every harsh word, every cruel accusation he'd uttered, was true. He heard her struggling to breathe past the overwhelming shock and realized that he'd gone too far.

"Dear God, sweetheart, I'm sorry. I didn't mean to say it...not like this. But have mercy, Annie...." His lips moved across her cheeks as he shoved her hands away from her face and made her look at him. "Were you ever going to tell me?"

"No."

He groaned. The pain of her admission nearly doubled him over.

"Why?" he begged as his thumbs traced the tracks of her tears.

Her voice shook as her hands wrapped around the edges of his vest, holding on to the only stable thing in her world. Holding on to Gabe.

"I only wanted your love, Gabriel. Not your pity. If I'd told you...I couldn't have had the one without the other. It was my choice to make. I made it. You don't have to approve...but you have to understand." And then her voice broke as she clutched at him. "Tell me you understand."

Blind to everything but the pain in her voice and the touch of her hands, Gabe wrapped his arms around her shoulders and held her.

"I can't believe Dr. Barnes told you," Annie whispered, as Gabe's hands stroked across the width of her back in a gentling motion. "He shouldn't have. He wasn't supposed to tell."

He drew back. The guilt on his face was impossible to miss.

"He didn't actually come right out and say it. Mostly I tricked him into believing I already knew what was wrong. What he said was too simple to miss. What he didn't say was impossible to ignore."

"Damn you," she said, and struggled to pull away from his touch. "I needed to do this by myself."

Gabe shook. "Why, Annie? Why cheat the people who care for you most?"

She shrugged and looked away.

"Because...ultimately, Gabe, no one can help me do this. It's a trip I'll have to make alone."

His eyes closed in sudden shame. The truth of her statement was too close for comfort. And then the need to know more—to know everything about this woman—drove him on.

"Exactly what is wrong with you?" Gabe asked.

"What did the doctor say?" she countered.

"That it was only a matter of time."

The words hung heavily between them. Annie struggled through the anger and injustice of the moment to find the right way to say what was in her heart. Finally she decided there was no easy way to say what had to be said and just started talking.

"There is something growing inside my head that doesn't belong there. A tumor. Ultimately, it will kill me."

Gabe groaned softly and threaded his hands through the thick tangles of her hair, feeling the silky strands bounce against his fingers and wondering, as he did, how something this beautiful could hide something so unwanted and ugly.

Annie closed her eyes, relishing the touch of Gabe's hands as she continued, letting everything spill out in a rush before she lost her nerve.

"It will only get worse, and, in time, one of the episodes will be my last."

At the moment the words were uttered, Gabe saw her wilt. It was then that he knew what strength of character, what strength of will, it had taken her to hide the fears she'd been living with.

He had a sudden flashback to the Sunday morning weeks ago when they'd gone to church. He remembered how quiet and uptight she'd been on the way. And then how she'd focused on the pastor's every word, and the intense way she'd had of listening to every nuance of his voice. He remembered the books that he'd seen and the way she'd reacted to his discovery of them. The way she hid her pain and denied the reasons for its existence. Suddenly it all became clear.

Annie was afraid to die! He knew it as surely as he knew his own name. And in that moment, he also knew why God had sent him back to her. If there was anyone on earth who could show Annie O'Brien how to die, it would be him. After all, he'd been where no living man had gone before and returned to tell the tale. He alone knew the beauty and the peace of what awaited Annie.

He slid his arms around her waist and held her close as she tried to regain her composure.

"It'll be all right, darlin'," he whispered. "I promise. It'll be all right."

"I didn't want to tell you, because I didn't want you to feel sorry for me. If you couldn't stay with me when I was well, then you shouldn't stay with me just because I am...just because I will..."

"I came back, didn't I?"

She grew quiet, then finally nodded.

"I came back before I knew the truth, too, didn't I, lady?"

She nodded again.

"Then you can't tell me...you can't accuse me...of staying out of pity. I came back because I had to, Annie. I came back because leaving you behind became impossible to bear."

Annie began to sob.

"Life isn't fair," she said, and felt his arms as they enfolded her.

Gabe closed his eyes and buried his lips in the crown of her hair. Together they stood, rocking back and forth within each other's embrace, and knew the full measure of truth in Annie's words.

Life was anything but fair. But it *was* for the living. And if it was the last thing he did, he would make damn sure that Annie O'Brien's last days on earth were full and perfect.

"Gabe, this is crazy."

Annie's hissed complaint was coupled with a soft giggle as she bumped into his backside when he stopped unexpectedly on the path in front of her.

"Slow down, woman," he teased, and then peered carefully through the inky darkness of the trees before them, searching for the path that had been highlighted only moments earlier by moonlight. "That damn cloud came out of nowhere," he muttered, wishing again that he'd thought to bring a flashlight.

But when they'd left the security of Annie's house for their nighttime excursion to the hilltop behind her home, there hadn't been a cloud in the sky. Only the bright, beaming face of a three-quarter moon shining down to light the way.

Annie smiled to herself and hooked her fingers over the waistband of his jeans. "Whither thou goest and all that stuff," she said.

At that moment the cloud slid away, and the moonlight illuminated Annie's face. She seemed rejuvenated by the short respite.

"Finally," Gabe muttered, and started back up the path through the trees, hurrying now that the light had returned, anxious to get where they were going before it disappeared altogether.

The safe thing to do would have been to return to the house, retrieve the flashlight he'd left behind and venture back through the trees with light in hand. But safe wasn't necessarily the wisest move. Not anymore. A man—or a woman, as the case might be—could waste precious hours practicing safety. When there were no hours left to waste, safety could go begging.

Annie's pulse quickened with excitement as well as apprehension. She could see only as far as Gabriel's ramrodstraight back. She had to squint to see the slim, muscled curve of his buttocks, as well as the long, lean legs she knew were there. He was too big, and it was too dark to see more. But it was her opinion that there were a lot of worse things than having to look at his backside.

She hooked her fingers a little tighter in the belt loop on the back of his jeans and let him lead her up the slow, sloping Missouri hillside toward the bald knob, framed by a ring of trees that shone silver in the moonlight.

"We're here."

This time, when he stopped, she was ready. She unhooked her fingers and then turned, looking for the first time down the hillside toward the shallow valley where night shadows hid everything but the highest treetops from view.

She turned in place until she'd made a complete three-hundred-and-sixty-degree turn. And when she had, she found herself looking up into his face. From the shadowed expression he was wearing, Annie realized that he was anxiously awaiting her verdict. It wasn't long in coming.

"Oh! Oh, Gabe! It's so beautiful!"

His smile was a slice of silver in the moonlight as he grinned at her delight.

"Then it was worth the climb?"

She threw her arms around his neck. "It was worth everything," she said. "I've lived here all my life, and I never—absolutely never—knew that this place was so beautiful in the dark."

Gabe slid his arms around her shoulders and pulled her close to him, letting himself revel in the way she melted against him with no reservations.

"I just wanted you to know you don't have to be afraid, Annie. The dark isn't something to fear. It's just another way of looking at the world in which we live."

She sighed and smiled through her tears, unwilling for him to know how moved she was by his constant need to lessen her fears of her final destination.

"You don't fool me," she said as she watched him move away from her and begin spreading a quilt that he'd brought with them on the ground. "You just can't wait to get me naked."

Surprise came swiftly, followed by a desire so fierce that he nearly choked on the sound of his own laughter. He took a deep breath and hoped that she hadn't noticed. If he hadn't known himself better, he might have thought it sounded like a sob.

But Gabe didn't cry. He hadn't cried in so long that he'd completely forgotten what it even felt like. He vaguely remembered that, as a child, he'd cried once for a beating he hadn't deserved. But that was long ago in the Kansas Territory. Long before he'd taken that wrong road and gotten himself into the mess that had started this whole cycle of regret. Long, long ago, before Annie.

The quilt was a pattern of smoky shadows—pale, fuzzy blues, foggy whites and misty yellows—densely bordered with darker shadows of reds and browns that looked black in the moonlight. It made a perfect bed upon which to lie.

Annie stepped out of her slippers and then walked into the center of the patchwork pattern, doing a quick little two-step of delight from the joy of it all. She turned and clapped her hands, smiling and laughing at Gabe as she did, and caught a look of regret and sadness on his face before he had time to hide it.

"Don't," she begged, and held out her hand. "Not tonight. You've shown me something so special...so very, very wonderful. Don't let things get in the way."

He grinned, ignoring the blinding pain in his chest as she smiled up at him, and pulled off his boots, joining her on the quilt before he had time to think.

Her nightgown was soft and sheer, and the fabric felt slick against his fingers as he pulled it up and then over her head. She lifted her arms to help him. At the moment the gown fell away, it left her arms upraised toward the beckoning moon in a gesture of supplication.

Gabe caught his breath and stared down at her slender beauty. She sighed and dropped to her knees. Seconds later Gabe shed what was left of his clothes and went to meet her.

"Annie, I..."

Her fingertips moved across his face and caught the words before he'd finished.

"No vows or promises. Just love me."

Gabe groaned as he moved across her body, pinning her to the quilt with gentle finesse.

*Love her?*

That was the easy part.

*Telling her that he loved her?*

Knowing what he did about his own fate . . . that was improbable.

*Letting go when it was time?*

Impossible to face.

A swift and sudden wind gusted across the hillside, fanning the edges of the quilt and Annie's hair. It tugged haphazardly at the curls around her face, blowing them gently across Gabe's lips and hands, flirting like a wayward lover as it made impossible tangles in the silky length of them.

Gabe buried his face in their heavy depths, savoring the lingering aroma of lilac-scented shampoo, and knew that for the rest of his life, no matter how far he rode, whenever he saw lilacs he would remember Annie . . . and the hillside . . . and their love.

Annie laughed aloud into the night from the simple joy of being one with this man. Of knowing that with nothing more than a nudge from her body or the touch of her hands, he would come undone. That she could bring him to an aching hardness with only a look, or make him lose complete control with nothing more than a whispered word.

She arched her body up to meet the forceful demand of his mouth, clasping his head against her breast as she stared up and over his shoulder to the inky depths of the starlit sky above them.

Gabe had given her something truly wonderful by showing her this night. It was up to her to give something special
back.

She was fire and rain, sweeping across his senses in a
maelstrom of emotions too fierce to contain. Consuming
him by degrees, she burned for him far into the night. Then,
raining kisses upon his weary body, she washed away the
might-have-beens that hovered in the nighttime, beyond the
quilted square upon which they lay.

Sometime during the early morning hours, when the dew
was gathering on the grass and soaking persistently into the
patchwork of their quilted dreams, they gathered themselves and their belongings, and made their way along the
path that led down the hillside.

And when they quietly entered the small frame house that
had patiently waited for the lovers' return, they knew that
the night had been magic. It had been with them like a
friend, filling their memories with only the best of what had
been, sifting out the fear of what was to come.

# Chapter 10

"Gabriel, come look."

Poised in the act of tightening a nut on the bike, Gabe wiped a bead of sweat from his forehead and turned to see what Annie was up to now. The last time he'd noticed, she'd been cleaning fallen leaves from the chrysanthemum bed that lined the front porch. Now she was nowhere to be seen.

"Annie? Where are you?" He dropped the crescent wrench he'd been using and straightened up to look around.

"Up here. In the tree."

Gabe walked to the porch, then tilted his head back until he was staring up into the wide, overhanging branches of the old oak that shaded the front of the house, peering intently through the thick growth in search of Annie.

She was perched about halfway up the tree, sitting in the fork of a branch while her feet dangled downward in thin air. All he could see was a bright splash of yellow that he knew to be her shirt and shorts, and an expanse of bare arms and legs.

"You'll fall," he said, and instinctively reached up as if to catch her.

"No, I won't." Laughter was rich in her voice. "As a child, I used to spend hours upon hours up here. I never once fell."

"That was then, this is now," Gabe reminded her. "Come down . . . please?"

She smiled. Bracing her arms against the limb that was her seat, she leaned down and blew him a kiss.

His heartbeat jerked, a painful reminder that the world was never going to be the same without Annie's smiles, and that he was never going to be the same without her kisses.

"Okay, I'm willing to concede you're part monkey." He shrugged and put his hands on his hips in pretend defiance. "If you didn't intend to mind me, lady, then what the hell did you want?"

Annie grinned. His anger was all bluff. And he knew that she knew it.

"I hadn't realized until I got up here that the leaves are turning. I wanted you to see."

Annie reached out and picked a leaf from just over her head, then let it drop slowly downward, drifting through the gaps in the limbs until it came to rest at Gabe's feet.

He bent down and picked it up. It was still soft and supple to the touch, but she was right. The colors were changing. A faint hint of wine red and burnt orange highlighted the places between the leaf's fragile veins.

Gabe's anger came unexpectedly. Time was running out. The season was changing and taking Annie with it. He looked away, suddenly in need of something else on which to focus, and tried to ignore the fact that he was looking at the world through a blur of tears.

"Fall is great . . . but winter is my favorite time of year," Annie said, and then leaned back and stared up through the branches to the bits and pieces of clear blue sky overhead. "I like the snow . . . and I love Christmas."

Gabe stared down at the leaf in his hand and then slowly crushed it in his fist.

A low string of curses filtered up through the branches, to the spot where Annie was sitting. Shocked by his unexpected reaction, it took several moments for understanding to come. And when it did, she, too, felt an overwhelming sadness.

Unwittingly she'd just reminded them both that these were the last leaves of fall she would see. That she might never see this year's first snow or enjoy another Christmas.

"Gabe!"

It was no use. He was already gone. She looked down through the branches in time to see him walking away toward the creek below the house.

Annie leaned back and looked up, taking a last look around at the world from above, and then scrambled down through the branches. The lowest limb was her last firm handhold. To get down from there, she had to let herself dangle, then drop to the ground, trusting that it wasn't too far.

The bark of the branch was rough against her palms as she scissored her legs to find the perfect landing. From where she was hanging she was enveloped by leaves, a thick umbrella above her, another multicolored barrier between her and the ground below. Yet Annie knew firm ground awaited. All she had to do was trust her judgment and then turn loose. She held her breath, closed her eyes and let go of the limb.

Small clumps of leaves brushed against her underarms and the sides of her face as she slipped through the opening and dropped to the ground, landing safely upright just as she'd known she would.

Dusting her hands on the seat of her shorts, she started to run after Gabe when something stopped her. She turned in mid-stride and stared back at the heavily laden branches of the old oak tree that she'd just vacated.

"Oh!" Her gasp was soft as understanding came quickly.

She'd known before she climbed the tree that there was a way down. And when it had come time to vacate her perch, she'd known that all she had to do was trust in the obvious.

"All I had to do was believe that the ground was there," Annie whispered.

Her eyes grew round and her mouth went slack with surprise as she stared intently at the tree. There was nothing else to consider, because she had just been given the answer to something she'd been trying to come to terms with for months.

She'd faced everything about her illness except how she would behave when it ended. All along she had been—and still was—dealing with the pain. Another bridge that she'd already crossed was the knowledge that she would be leaving things and people behind that she'd come to love.

But the one thing—the single most important thing—that she hadn't understood was what she had to do. What was her part in leaving going to be?

She'd made herself sick worrying about the way it would happen. Where would she be? Would it hurt? Would she even know it was coming? The unknowns had been driving her mad.

"That's it!" Annie said as a slow sigh of relief flooded her system. "I don't have to know when or where. All I have to do is trust. A firm foundation has already been laid. All I have to do is let go, just like I did when I climbed out of the tree. I won't fall. Someone will be there to catch me."

And with that thought came the knowledge that it wouldn't be Gabe. He was part of what had to be left behind.

Tears shifted across her vision, but she blinked them back with rough determination. She had no time for tears. There was too much left to do to waste time crying over things that couldn't be changed. She remembered where she'd been going, turned toward the creek and began to run. He needed to know that she was going to be all right.

Somewhere between the tree and the creek, Gabe had started undressing. A grease rag lay on the ground where he'd dropped it. His vest was hanging from a low branch, dangling from the armhole where he'd looped it. She saw his shirt hanging across a bush in a haphazard fashion where he'd obviously tossed it.

And then she saw him, bare to the waist, with water droplets running from his seal-black hair down the middle of his back and onto his jeans. His head was thrown back in a gesture of defiance, his legs braced for an invisible blow only he saw coming. He stood without moving, staring blindly down into the gentle flow of water while the world went on without him.

Annie felt his pain as if it were her own. The love she held for him went deep and was without reservation. Everything about him was at once familiar to her and, at the same time, unique, right down to the stillness that was so much a part of him. The strength of his body, as well as his character, that she'd come to rely on more each day. She knew him so well . . . and yet he was very much a stranger.

She accepted the secrets that were a part of him, because she understood his need. The unabashed way in which they made love was what kept her going from day to day. For Annie there was nothing else left in this world that mattered to her except this man.

And yet, in spite of his constant denials, she knew that staying with her was killing him. She saw his pain. She felt his regrets. She, after all, was the one doing all the taking. She took what he offered, knowing that she had nothing left to give back. And he never complained.

Unobserved, she continued to watch, but when he drew back his arm, she saw for the first time the thick, clublike stick he held in his hand. Uncertain what to expect, she was not prepared for the rage that exploded within him.

Anger came up and out of him in a roar, a painful denial of Annie's fate that went out with the stick he threw into the air. It crossed the creek with deathlike force and exploded against the side of a tree trunk. Helpless to deal with his fury, he let it tear through him. With the release of his rage came an ebbing of adrenaline that sent him to his knees.

"Gabe . . . don't!"

In seconds Annie was at his side, wrapping her arms around his neck, absorbing the shudders that ripped through him while he held her in desperation.

"I don't know how to let you go."

His heartbroken words wounded her and, at the same time, consoled her. At that moment, the depth of his love for her was unmistakable.

"You don't have to, Gabe. I finally understand what you've been trying to show me. I know that I don't have to worry about anything. When it happens, I'll know what to do."

"No, no," he begged, and pulled her roughly across his lap. "Surely there's another way. Another doctor. Someone else with a . . ."

Annie closed her eyes against the pain of his words, realizing, as she did, that she was also closing herself off from everything that could have been. It didn't bear thinking about. The decision had already been made.

"Stop it, Gabe. Please don't make this any harder than it already is."

Her quiet plea was all he needed to get his maverick emotions in check. And the only way he knew to change the subject was to pick another one she couldn't ignore. It was all he could do to laugh through the pain, but for Annie's sake he made the effort.

He jiggled her lightly on his lap and nuzzled her neck. "So... you don't want this any harder?" he asked.

Annie flushed, knowing full well what he was referring to.

"What I *want*, at this minute, is beside the point." She gave him her best teacher look for good measure.

A wry smile changed the expression on his face from one of despair to one of beauty.

Annie caught her breath, and then, before she thought, she clasped his face in her hands. "You are so beautiful," she whispered as their lips met, then danced back and forth in little nips and tastes, savoring each other as passion built.

Gabe nearly blushed. "Oh, hell, Annie, men aren't beautiful."

"Tell that to your mother, then," Annie said, and sighed with regret as the smile slid off his face. "What? What did I say?"

He looked away in shame, remembering his life before. Old fears and bad memories came calling. And then he thought of Annie and knew that whatever she saw in him, she saw through the eyes of love.

"I never knew my mother," Gabe said. "Or my father... or any single person who I might be related to."

Shocked by the unexpected revelation, all she could ask was, "Who raised you?"

Gabe shrugged. "Mostly I raised myself. There was an old trapper... and a few others. It was a long time ago... lifetimes ago, darlin'. You wouldn't understand."

Annie leaned forward and pressed her mouth against the faint pucker of scar tissue ringing his neck. She felt his shock beneath her lips. Blood raced and muscles jerked as his throat worked and he tried to speak past the surge of emotion her touch had aroused.

"I would understand anything about you, Gabriel. Even how you came by this." Her fingers traced the edge of the scar. "When you love someone, anything is possible."

Everything faded except the sound of Annie's voice and the wide, green stare of her eyes. He was stunned by her admission.

She watched anxiously for his reaction. It was the first time that either had said aloud the thing that was in their hearts. Emotion filled him.

"So... you think you love me?"

Shyness accompanied the joy in his voice as he looked into Annie's face.

She laughed softly. "I don't think. I know. And why shouldn't I?"

He took her fingers and laid them against the scar at his throat. "Because you just shouldn't. Because I don't deserve it," he said quietly.

Annie shook her head in denial. "What you were doesn't count, Gabe. You could have been an outlaw for all I care. What matters is that right now... for as long as it takes... you're my outlaw."

He laughed wryly and rolled her beneath him before she had time to think.

*Outlaw. Oh, Annie, if you only knew.*

"I'm going to make love to you, Annie Laurie."

She looked up, startled by his announcement.

"Right here? In broad daylight?"

He grinned. "Sure, lady. That's what outlaws do."

* * *

Nearly a week had passed since the incident at the creek. And in that time Gabe had almost been able to convince himself that Annie was getting better. It had been weeks since she'd had any pain. Her days were spent in doing whatever she wanted. All she had to do was think it and he would put the thought in motion.

He went to bed each night with her in his arms, and then lay awake watching her sleep, trying not to think of a world without her in it. Everything revolved around Annie's wants and wishes. Everything else had been put on hold. To him, she was all that mattered.

Her days were full of immediate plans. And each day a certain portion was set aside for Davie and his lessons. Watching his progress and knowing that she was partly responsible was a large part of what kept her going. Because of Davie's need, she had something to look forward to . . . a purpose in life. It seemed as if, while Davie still needed her, Annie refused to give up and give in to the thing growing inside her head.

"Gabe! You're still here!"

Annie's shock was evident as she stared at the part he'd removed from the Harley and the oil dripping from his fingers. A nervous glance toward the clock on the wall told her that Davie would arrive almost any minute for his reading lesson.

He waved the length of tubing as he walked past her toward the kitchen sink. "Fuel line's clogged. I'm not going anywhere today."

"But . . . Davie will be here any minute. What's he going to think when . . . ?"

"I think Davie's a big boy," Gabe said shortly. "He'll survive."

Annie resisted the urge to stomp her foot. It wouldn't do any good, and she knew it. When Gabe got that look on his face, there was no changing him. Obviously the fact that his bike was on the fritz had put him in a disgruntled mood.

"Oh, Lord," Annie muttered, as Davie pulled up and parked beneath her climbing tree.

She peeked out the window. Even from here she could see the frown on his face as he neared the front door clutching his small stack of books. There was only one thing to do, and that was to pretend nothing was different.

"Hi!" she said as she went to meet him. "Come in. I'm on my way to the kitchen. I was just taking brownies out of the oven."

"Why is he still here?" Davie muttered, glaring over his shoulder at the black Harley still parked at the edge of the yard.

"He's working on his bike," Annie said. "He won't bother us."

Davie stopped short and stood in the doorway. "Maybe I should come back tomorrow," he said, and started to make a U-turn.

"Hey, Davie, how's things?"

Gabe's simple question stopped him from leaving and left the trio standing at the door, staring mutely at one another while Gabe waited for his answer.

Davie shrugged and tried to grin. "'Bout the same, I guess," he said. "Can't complain."

"Well, I sure can," Gabe said, holding up the piece of tubing. "I thought this thing was clogged. Now I find it's got a pinhole in it somewhere. The darned bike sucks air instead of fuel."

Davie frowned. "You know...I just might have something in the toolbox behind the cab. Come on outside and we'll look. Might save you a trip into Walnut Shade."

Gabe nodded and walked past Annie, giving her a slow wink that Davie missed.

Annie watched them go through the doorway, their heads together like two little boys with one frog, and smiled to herself at the mental image.

One was blond, broad and brawny, the other tall, dark and deceptively deadly. And yet, somehow, she knew that in another time, another place, they could have been friends.

"Sorry," Gabe said as he watched Davie digging through the odd assortment of bits and pieces in his toolbox.

"What for?" Davie mumbled as he shoved a greasy glove and a half-used box of shotgun shells aside. "I know I've got some tubing somewhere. I'm just not sure if it's the right size."

"I'm sorry you're going to miss your lesson because of me."

Davie grew still. A deep red flush stained his face and neck as he backed away from the toolbox. "Damn it, she promised," he said, glaring at the ground as shame overwhelmed him.

"She didn't actually tell me anything," Gabe said. "I just recognized the signs. I've been there myself."

Davie looked up. Shock spread across his face as his gaze swept up and then down the big biker.

"You? You didn't know how to...I mean you couldn't...?"

"Oh, hell. Come out and say it. I couldn't read. I never even went to school until I was full-grown. You're not so damned special after all, are you?" Gabe grinned wryly to lessen the sting of his words.

Davie sighed. "Thanks to Annie, I'm getting real good at it," he offered.

Gabe clapped his hand roughly on Davie's shoulder and grinned. "I know. Congratulations."

Davie grinned back. "When I can read the want ads in a newspaper, I'm going to ask my girlfriend to marry me."

The smile died on Gabe's face. A sudden and intense surge of jealousy filled him as he considered the simplicity of Davie Henry's life.

Davie had a problem. His problem was that he couldn't read. All he had to do was learn how and his problem was over.

Annie had a problem, too. And it wasn't going to be cured by learning anything. In fact, the more they learned, the worse her situation became.

Gabe cursed softly and spun away, unwilling for Davie to see his pain and anger.

"That's good. Really good. I'm happy for you. A man needs to have a place to call home and a woman to come home to," Gabe said quietly.

"So, what's between you and Annie, then?" Davie asked, then resisted the urge to take a quick step backward. The look Gabe gave him as he turned was anything but friendly. "And I'm not going to apologize for asking," Davie said. Instinctively he curled his fingers into fists and waited for the blow that never came.

Gabe's anger dissipated when he saw how fiercely Davie would have defended Annie. And he knew Davie's reasons for asking were fair ones. After all, he'd known Annie all her life.

"There's a lot between Annie and me," Gabe said. "But that's where it's going to stay...between us." He fixed Davie with a cool blue stare. "I can't help it if you don't like that answer, but it's the only one I've got to give."

Davie shrugged. "None of my business, really," he said. "If Annie's happy, I'm happy."

"That just about sums it up for me, too," Gabe said. "Now... about that tubing."

Minutes later Davie dashed back inside the house, using the scent of brownies to lead him to Annie.

"Where's Gabe?" She looked past Davie toward the open doorway.

"I loaned him my truck to go to town. The tubing I had didn't fit."

"Oh."

Davie grinned and pointed toward the brownies cooling on a rack. "Do I get any of those?" he asked.

"What happened between you two?" Annie asked, ignoring his question in favor of another.

"Not much," Davie said, and helped himself to two brownies without waiting for her approval. "When you get to know him, I guess he's a pretty decent guy. Right?"

Annie nodded and sat in the nearest chair with a plop, unable to mask her surprise. Would wonders never cease?

Thunder rippled through the hills and down the valleys, running with the storm front that was moving across the state. Lightning cracked as it tore across the skies, rocking the lamp on the bedside table and rattling the glass in the windowpanes.

Gabe rolled over and, at the same time, reached out for Annie. The flat of his hand slid across her pillow and then down the length of the bed.

Seconds later he was crawling out of bed in panic. She was gone! He stepped into his jeans as he walked out of the bedroom, calling Annie's name.

The wind whipped her nightgown, molding it to her slenderness like a second skin. Annie tilted her face, catching the first raindrops as they began to fall upon the thirsty earth. She closed her eyes and inhaled slowly, letting her skin savor the moisture in separate, single increments. It was as if every cell in her body had come alive, dancing with the same electrical force as the lightning that threaded the skies.

The thunder, an angry grumble of nature, rumbled overhead. Annie's toes curled against the rough-hewn boards of the porch as she felt the house quaking from its power.

Like a daring child, she stood at the edge, just beyond the safety of the rooftop, and let the storm have its way with her. In those few moments, before the full onslaught of the rain, she felt joyously alive . . . and knew no fear.

And then she heard his voice and turned toward the sound, waiting on the edge of the steps for him to come to her. To become part of the immensity of what she was experiencing.

"Annie! Annie! Answer me, damn it! Where are you?"

"I'm here," she said softly, knowing that he would hear her voice and follow it with unerring instinct.

He walked outside, intent on nothing more than rescue, when a bolt of lightning slashed through the darkness just beyond the trees and momentarily illuminated her in a glow of eerie light.

It was then that he saw her face and knew that she was locked under the spell of the elements in which she stood.

"What the hell are you doing to yourself?" Gabe growled as he grabbed her by the forearms and hauled her back beneath the safety of the porch.

His hands ran rapidly up and down her body, touching, testing, to assure himself that she was still in one, albeit fragile, piece. That she was not as storm-tossed as she looked.

"Feeling the storm," she whispered. "Oh, Gabriel . . . come feel the storm with me!"

He couldn't tell her no.

She took him by the hand and led him to the edge of the porch, where the wind whipped wildly beneath the over-hang, digging through the thick, damp tangles of her hair. She turned to him, needing to know that he understood. That he felt what she was experiencing in the same special way. The look on his face made her knees go weak.

The wind caught and lifted the dark, heavy length of his hair, whipping it back and forth across his face and into his eyes in stinging fury, and yet he stood unmoving, watching Annie's joy. Rain began to come down in earnest, pelting against the broad, muscled strength of his chest and belly, only to slide downward in rivulets toward the spiral of hair that began just below his navel, visible in the V of his un-zipped jeans.

Annie's eyes narrowed, and she took a step forward, fas-cinated by the path of the rain and its destination. She splayed her hand across his chest and watched, eyes wid-ening with desire, as the wind-driven water hammered against her own skin, too. She closed her eyes and breathed deeply, imagining that she was melting into him, becoming part of him, always with him.

"Annie."

Her name was a prayer as she came to him, unto him. And when her rain-slicked body moved against him, he knew he was lost.

"Come inside," he urged, and started to move her to-ward the doorway.

"No," she whispered, and pressed her mouth against the curve of his lips, letting him feel, as well as hear, her words. "You come inside. Inside me."

Denial was impossible.

With little loss of motion, he let the wind tear away what was left of her gown as he pulled it up above her waist. Shaky with desire, he groaned as she laughed aloud, lost in the driving need and the rain pelting down upon them. And when she wrapped her arms around his neck and her legs around his waist, the pleasure and the passion nearly sent him to his knees.

Staggering backward in desperation, now buried so deeply inside the woman in his arms that he feared he might lose the way back, he felt the porch post behind him and knew a moment of thanksgiving that they wouldn't fall.

With legs braced, he centered her once again on the hard, jutting thrust of his body, and relished the cry of delight that flew out of her mouth and into the night. With a shaky groan he took them both over the edge and into the storm, and never knew which ended first, the rain or their pleasure.

All he remembered was struggling for breath and feeling a cool wind drying the last raindrops from his bare back. The rest was a blur. Just a collage of lightning, power, the touch of Annie's hands, her laughter and the rain upon her face. It was only later that he thought to wonder if it had been tears, and not the rain, that he'd seen running down her cheeks.

But it didn't matter, and it wouldn't have changed a thing. Sometime during the night, he'd taken Annie on a ride to heaven and back. Much later, as he set her in bed, he watched her curl up in weary satisfaction against his passion-spent body. Annie seemed to be at peace with herself and the world. It was Gabe who now struggled to find the sense in it all.

Annie's life mattered so much to so many, and yet it was about to end. His had been of no consequence in the beginning, and now, no matter how long he rode and how hard he tried, he feared he would never know the peace of heart that Annie possessed.

# Chapter 11

"Annie! Annie! You'll never guess."

Annie looked up from the book she'd been reading and smiled at the man who burst through the front door.

"Don't you ever knock?" she asked, and grinned at the shock that came and went on Davie's face as Gabe's arm slid off her shoulder and back into his own lap.

"Oh...yeah...right," Davie mumbled, suddenly embarrassed by his behavior. "How ya doin', Gabe?" It was such an obvious afterthought that Gabe laughed, catching Davie off guard.

It was the sight of those black boots propped up on the coffee table alongside Annie's sock-covered feet that told him he might have walked in on a serious hugging-and-kissing session.

"Am I interrupting anything?" he asked, knowing full well he probably was.

Gabe stood up and stretched. "Just the possibility of a nap. It's too cold outside for anything else."

Davie nodded, and then remembered why he'd come.

"Annie! I've got great news!"

"You won the lottery."

"Nope!" Davie grinned and shoved his hand through his hair, ruffling the thick wheat-colored curls even more than they already were. "Guess again."

"You're getting married."

Davie blushed as Gabe laughed softly from across the room.

"Well, yeah, actually I am, but that's not it, either," he said.

"Okay, I give up," Annie said, and spread her hands in defeat. "What's the big secret?"

"The head of the history department at Walnut Shade High School just quit. There's going to be an opening next semester. What do you think about that?"

The smile froze on her face.

Gabe's stomach turned as he looked at Annie.

Twice she started to speak, and both times the words wouldn't come.

"Son of a bitch," Gabe said succinctly, and walked out of the room, unable to watch Annie's pain.

Davie was in shock. "What? What did I say?" he asked, and touched her anxiously on the shoulder.

Annie shrugged and tried to smile, blinking over and over in rapid succession to clear her vision of a sudden spurt of tears. "Nothing," she said, and hugged him to prove her point. "Absolutely nothing at all."

"Then why's everyone so uptight?" he persisted. "Something made Gabe madder than hell, and I'm the only new face in the room."

"It's complicated," she said. "But it's nothing you did, I promise."

Davie shoved his hands in his pockets and shrugged. "Okay, okay. I get the message. I'll drop whatever it was I said... if I can figure out what it is I'm supposed to drop."

A small niggle of pain dug into the muscles at the back of Annie's neck. She rolled her head and winced, trying to loosen the tension before it became full-blown.

"Davie... about the job." Annie struggled to find the right words. "Thanks, but I don't think I'd be interested." The smile on her face broke. Unable to contain her misery, she turned and walked out of the room.

"Well, I'll be damned," Davie said.

But there was no one around to hear him, and rather than risk another outburst, he left the same way he'd come in. Unannounced.

He was halfway up the path when he saw Gabe walking toward the creek behind the house. In seconds he'd made the decision to follow him and find out what was going on. He would get answers out of that damned biker or know the reason why.

Gabe hurt from the inside out. Every step he took was a step away from Annie's pain, but it didn't lessen the impact of what he'd seen in her eyes. He would have bet his life—if he'd had one left to bet—that she wanted that job, and badly.

He knew how important teaching was to her. He'd witnessed her determination in the classroom back in Oklahoma. He'd seen her willingness to risk personal safety just to fulfill a contract, as well as her duty to the students. He'd also seen the life go out of her when they'd had to leave Oklahoma City. At the time, he hadn't understood.

The real inner joy, the thing that kept Annie motivated, had returned only after she'd discovered Davie's handicap. It was after that that she seemed to have taken a new lease on life. Looking back, the reasons for it were so simple, so obvious. Annie was at heart a teacher. She needed to be needed.

Even with the knowledge that Davie would be her last student, she'd still dealt with the disappointment of giving up a much-loved career. Day by day, she'd struggled with the fact that she had to let go, a little bit at a time. And she'd done it.

But that was before Davie Henry had come barreling through the door offering something she desperately wanted, something she couldn't have. A future.

Heavy footsteps pounded the trail behind Gabe. He turned, his fists doubling instinctively, then relaxed almost as quickly.

It was only Davie. But when he saw the concern on the big man's face, he cursed softly to himself, sickened by the entire mess. He should have known Davie would want answers. In his place, he would have done the same.

"Donner! I want to talk to you!" Davie shouted.

Gabe waited for him to catch up.

"What's the damned deal with Annie? She hardly ever leaves the house, and when she does, you're always with her. You have no job, and she expects me to understand, without any explanation, that she isn't interested in teaching. *Why?*"

"What did she tell you?" Gabe asked, ignoring all of Davie's accusations except those concerning Annie.

Davie spat angrily, then ground the moisture into the dirt with the toe of his work boot.

"She didn't tell me a thing. She just started crying."

"Damn. I was afraid of that." Gabe looked away, unwilling for Davie to see his pain.

Davie grabbed him by the arm and spun him around. A long, slow minute passed while the men took each other's measure.

Finally it was Davie who made the first move by loosening his hold on Gabe's arm. "All I want to know is, what the hell's going on," he muttered.

"I can't tell you more than Annie wants people to know," Gabe said. "And that's all I'll tell you. If you find out more, it'll have to come from her."

"What are you saying? What's the big secret?" Davie shouted.

"It's not my secret to tell," Gabe said softly. "You above all others should understand that. After all, you asked Annie to keep your secret, and she did. Why do you expect me to do less for her?"

But Davie still persisted. "What could be so bad that she doesn't want it told?" he asked.

Gabe didn't answer. He couldn't. All he could do was turn away and try to focus on something—anything—besides the pain eating away inside him.

"Okay," Davie said shortly. "But if I find out later that you've had anything to do with Annie's problems... anything at all... I swear I'll fight you to hell and back."

Gabe turned. All sound unexpectedly ceased. The mockingbird that had been scolding from a tree limb took sudden flight. The squirrels that had been playing above the creek bank, jumping from limb to limb like furry acrobats, disappeared from sight.

Sunlight haloed behind Gabe, making his shadow larger than life. Davie shuddered. He had a moment's impression that Gabe was not of this world, and then he scoffed at his own flight of fancy as Gabe's deep voice echoed within the silence on the creek bank.

"There's no coming back from hell. Pick another location."

Davie's eyebrows arched, and then he laughed abruptly. His anger was gone as quickly as it had come.

"Damn, but you're a cool one," he said.

Gabe shrugged. "I am what I am. Just know this. What I do, I do for Annie's best interests... always." He took a step forward until he was nearly toe-to-toe with Davie. "For as long as I'm with her, she's safe. I'll kill the next man who harms her. Know *that* for a fact."

*Thou Shalt Not Kill!*

The celestial warning sifted through his mind, but Gabriel shrugged it off as he continued to stare long and hard into Davie Henry's eyes.

"The next? What happened to the first?" Shock splintered the concern on Davie's face.

"The cops got him," Gabe said shortly, aware that what he'd revealed was something about her life in Oklahoma City that Annie had obviously kept to herself.

"Cops?"

"Just remember what I said," Gabe warned, ignoring Davie's wild-eyed, slack-jawed expression. "No one messes with Annie. She's been hurt more than any woman should have to endure. If you want to know anything more about her business, you'll have to ask her yourself."

Gabe turned and walked away, disappearing into the thicket of trees above the small spring-fed creek, leaving Davie Henry alone with the warning still echoing in his ears.

For two days Annie moped around the house, no longer able to find joy in the little things as she previously had. All she could think about was Davie's news and the fact that she couldn't even consider the job. Anger and self-pity for what fate had dealt her crept back into her daily routine and held on with insidious persistence.

Gabe found himself being rebuffed for even offering to do the smallest things for her, and he was at a loss as to how to fix what ailed Annie. But then an advertisement in a local paper gave him an idea. He began to set his plan in motion, remembering that spontaneity had worked before. Why not now?

When she was busy at other tasks, he began packing a bag for what would amount to an overnight stay. Little by little, he secreted her belongings, along with his own, in the duffel bag.

Just after dark, while she was taking a bath, he buckled it onto the back of the bike and then hurried inside. He yanked off his boots and jeans and crawled quickly into bed, excited about the prospect of what he planned. He took slow, deep breaths to calm his racing pulse, anxious that when Annie came back, she would not suspect he'd ever been gone.

A few minutes later she came out of the bathroom, her nightgown billowing around her legs as she walked. With only a dim light in the hallway to serve as illumination, she sat down on the edge of the bed to brush her hair.

At first glance she looked unbearably young and innocent, all white lace and long, rambunctious curls. And then she turned slightly as she struggled with the length of her hair, trying unsuccessfully to brush out the knots. The incoming light silhouetted her sensuous shape against the sheer fabric of her gown and left Gabe in no doubt as to how much of a woman Annie really was. It made him want. It made him hard.

She lifted the hairbrush again and began to brush another swath through her hair when she came to a tangle and winced. The motion of her arms unintentionally pushed her breasts tightly against the thin, cotton fabric. Gabe's swiftly indrawn breath was the only clue to his instant desire.

Unashamed of his nudity or the obvious ache in his manhood, he rolled over onto his knees and took the brush from her hands, scooting her gently until she was braced against his body.

Annie sighed and let her head loll back against his bare chest with relief. Everything she did nowadays seemed to take too much effort to bother.

"Let me," he begged, and began to pull the brush through her tangles in slow, firm strokes.

"Be my guest," she said shortly, and then blinked quickly to stifle the film of moisture that distorted her vision.

She was being rude and she knew it, but it was beyond her to accept his gentleness without bursting into weak tears. She hated herself for feeling it, let alone thinking it. She didn't want to be weak.

*Damn it! I want to be well!*

"Your hair is so beautiful," Gabe whispered softly, feathering kisses along the curve of her ear as he pulled the brush through her hair, letting it rake lightly against her scalp in a sensuous motion. "It's one of the first things I noticed about you."

Annie shivered. She remembered the first thing she'd noticed about him. His size...and his mouth. How a smile had changed his appearance from menacing to marvelous simply by turning it up at the corners.

"There's something I want to tell you," Gabe said.

He dropped the brush onto the table and slid his hands around her shoulders toward the front, cupping his palms to fit the thrust of her breasts beneath the gown.

For days he'd been living with the knowledge that, for whatever it was worth, he was in love with Annie O'Brien. And yet telling her without making her think it was said out of pity was impossible. He'd struggled with the how of it for so long that he ached.

"Don't talk to me, touch me," she begged and leaned a little farther back, allowing him easier access. Within an instant of his touch, she became lost in the sensuality of Gabriel's hands.

Gabe shuddered as his body answered the call by thrusting uncontrollably against the softness of her backside. He closed his eyes and swallowed harshly, imagining her cupped tightly behind him on the back of his Harley without this ache being eased. It was impossible. He had to make love to Annie before they rode or he would land them both in a ditch.

They would ride. Of that he was certain. But that would be later. After he'd healed both their respective aches and pains.

And then he forgot what he'd wanted to say. He forgot about everything except his need to lay claim. Gently his hands feathered across her body in seeking strokes, in much the same way as he'd brushed her hair only moments before.

"Annie, Annie...so much woman..."

"...And so little time."

He paused in mid-stroke, stunned by the finality of how she'd ended his sentence for him.

"Damn you," he groaned, and rolled her beneath him. "Damn you for making us both remember."

A sheen of tears puddled across her eyes. Even in the faint half light, he saw her lips trembling around a smile.

"Then make me forget," she whispered, and slid her arms around his neck.

"I don't want to forget," he said harshly, as he yanked her gown up and off her body. "I don't want to forget a thing about you...ever."

Annie's sob was lost as he lowered his lips to hers. Tears blended with passion as he swept across her body, moving like a marauder through the night, taking what he needed from her to survive, leaving behind a trail of pleasure for which Annie burned.

She took what he gave and tried not to wish for more. And while she could hide it from Gabe, she could not hide it from herself. Just once... even if he didn't actually mean it...she would have given a precious minute of what was left of her life just to hear him say he loved her.

Gabe left his trail across her body. A path of mind-drugging kisses that left her shaking and breathless and yearning for more. His hands coaxed and caressed her to the point of explosion and then gentled her back into a waiting game.

And as he rebuilt the fire within Annie, his own body ached, pulsating to the point of explosion as her tiny cries of pleasure echoed in his ears. When it was nearly too late to make the move, he lifted himself up and then thrust. Falling too deep to pull back, he came apart in her arms.

Ripple after ripple of pleasure exploded within him. Gabe shook from the exertion of his release. Unaware of Annie's arms around his neck, unaware of her legs around his waist, he buried his face against the curve of her neck and knew that the tears upon his cheeks were not his own.

"You're mine...mine. You're my love," he muttered over and over as shudders racked his body, forgetting, in his weakened state, that he'd meant to keep that secret to himself.

Her heart stopped as his soft, urgent whisper nearly missed its target.

*Oh, Gabriel,* Annie thought, as she clutched him to her in desperation. *If only you meant it. If only I'd met you sooner... before it was too late. I might have had the nerve to take the chance.*

But Gabe was unaware of her thoughts. He was too lost in the feeling of having died and been reborn in Annie's arms.

They slept. An hour before dawn, Gabe woke with a start, knowing that it was now time to implement his plan. He rolled out of bed and quietly began to dress. Soon he was ready.

A small, indistinct sound filtered through Annie's mind. Sleepily, she rolled over and then sat upright, staring directly at the shadow of the man who was standing in the doorway across the room.

Just when she thought about screaming, she realized that it was Gabe. And as she did, she knew that the sound that had awakened her was the slight jingle his spurs made when he walked.

*Spurs!* That meant he was dressed!

"Gabe? What on earth are you doing?"

"Kidnapping the school marm."

She imagined she saw his smile, although it was really too dark for her to have done so. But it was there in the sound of his voice just the same, and it reassured her as nothing else could have done.

"It's still dark outside," she said, and then began backing up against the headboard of the bed as she saw him coming toward her.

"The better to steal you away, teacher dear."

This time she was certain he was smiling. She heard a distinct chuckle as her back connected with the headboard.

"Nowhere left to run, girl. You're mine. All mine."

With a practiced growl, he swooped, lifting her from the bed in a tangle of bed sheets and laughter.

She struggled weakly, laughing too hard to put up much of a fight. But truth be known, she was too intrigued by what was happening to argue.

"Go do your thing, woman," he grumbled in a gentle but teasing voice. "You've only got minutes to spare before I come in after you."

Annie headed toward the bathroom to "do her thing," as he'd suggested. She had a sudden suspicion that it would be hours before he let her off that darned black Harley.

She stared at herself in the mirror over the sink, realizing as she did that the woman who looked back was laughing and full of anxious anticipation. Her eyes sparkled; her hair was a wild, sleep-tossed tangle. Her lips were still slightly swollen from last night's passion. She should have looked like hell. But Annie knew she'd never looked better.

"You've got two minutes, and then I'm coming in after you," he warned.

Annie squealed in mock fright and began running water and yanking on clothes with wild abandon.

On the other side of the door Gabe grinned sadly to himself. God willing, this trip would be perfect. It had to be. It might very well be their last. At the thought, he went to double-check, just to make certain that he'd packed that damned brown bottle of pills.

It was a heady thing to ride in the dark, with the throttle on the Harley wide open and the sound of the engine roaring in your ears. Annie imagined that it was like flying blind, trusting that instinct would keep you on the right path and luck would get you to your destination.

She inhaled deeply, reveling in the freedom of the moment and pretending that if they went fast enough, she could outrun the inevitable. For Annie, sitting behind Gabe on the back of the Harley was her past, present and future. Wherever he went, she was ready for the experience.

Sunrise was waiting for an audience. Through his mirrored sunglasses, he saw the faint rosy hue and the change in the texture of the air just above the horizon. Without announcing the fact, he wheeled off the highway onto a small lookout point above the autumn hues undulating throughout the thickly wooded valley below. He nudged Annie with his shoulder to get her attention.

Thankful for the opportunity to divest herself of the ungainly helmet, she pulled it up and off, unaware of what she was about to witness. At Gabe's insistence, she turned in the direction he was pointing and stared.

It came over the treetops in a burst of color, moving up and out in a spasm of rebirth. A soft, pure white and thick, creamy gold, with a faint crimson lining to remind the onlooker that pain as well as joy came with new life. The day had begun.

"Oh!"

Her gasp of delight was all he needed to hear.

"So beautiful," Annie sighed, and rested her forehead against the bulge of muscle on Gabe's arm, unaware of the tension beneath her cheek or the tight grip he still had on the bike.

*Just like you, my love,* Gabe thought.

She smiled up at him, then saw that he was still wearing the glasses, still hiding his feelings behind those mirrored walls.

*Oh, Gabe. You never let me in.* And then her thoughts became lost as she watched his face.

His lips tilted into a gentle smile. Something told her that he was feeling more than he was saying. It had to do with the muscle jerking along the cut of his jaw and the way the skin seemed to tighten across his cheekbones.

*But you care. You can't make me believe you don't care,*
Annie thought.

"Seen enough?" Gabe asked roughly.

It was for damn sure he had. Feeling Annie's soft body
pressed firmly against the back of his for mile after mile had
done nothing to ease his aching libido. Seeing the beauty
that sunrise had put on her face made everything
worse... and at the same time made everything better. This
trip was meant to take her out of herself and her worries.
From the way she was smiling, he'd done it in spades.

"The prelude was spectacular. What's next?" she asked,
still willing to play along with the game.

"Breakfast in Branson," he said, and handed her the
helmet.

"Branson? I haven't been to Branson in years. Especially not since it's become the 'New Nashville.'"

Nearly every country and western singer of any merit,
plus half the entertainers who had once played solely in Las
Vegas, played Branson, Missouri, now.

Elaborate music halls had sprouted up nearly overnight
and dotted the small, cramped hillsides surrounding the tiny
town to the point that tourists drove bumper to bumper on
a quest to see their favorite stars.

"Me either," Gabe said. "Besides breakfast, there's
something I want you to see."

"What?" she asked, her stomach suddenly growling at
the mention of food.

Gabe grinned. "Food first. Surprises later. Now, quit
asking so many questions. You're supposed to be my pris-
oner, remember?"

She smiled beneath the smoke-tinted visor of the helmet
and wrapped her arms around his waist as the Harley's
powerful engine made the bike leap forward beneath them.

# Chapter 12

Gabe sat in the small café with his back to the wall, nursing a cup of coffee. He watched with satisfaction as Annie cleaned the last of her biscuits and gravy from the plate and then looked around the table to see if there was anything left that she might want to eat.

It was the most food he'd seen her eat in a week. Their outing had put color in her cheeks and a growl in her belly, but there was no way he could stop the destruction that was happening inside her head.

She looked up from her plate with a smile on her face. But it was impossible to look at her and not see the shadows beneath her eyes or the deepening hollows in her cheeks. Annie's health was failing, and there wasn't a damn thing he could do to stop it.

"You're frowning at me," Annie accused, and nodded when the waitress sailed by with a fresh pot of coffee and stopped to top off her cup.

"No, baby, only at how much you ate," Gabe teased. "You ate the last biscuit."

She laughed. "Some kidnapper," she chided. "You let me have it."

He leaned close until his lips were only a whisper away from her face before he answered. "I'll let you have it all right, darlin', but not now...and not here."

A woman in the next booth choked on her food. At the same time, Gabe and Annie turned to look. They saw the guilty expression on her face and knew that she'd been eavesdropping. Gabe's sexy innuendo had left her gasping for air.

Annie leaned over and whispered conspiratorially to the curious woman, "He's real good at it, too."

Gabe grinned as he hauled Annie out of the chair. "That does it. You're coming with me, lady. Remember...you're my hostage for a day. Now let's go before you get me into something I can't fight my way out of."

Annie's eyes sparkled. Gabe was a wonderful kidnapper.

"I can hardly wait until later," she whispered as he dug in his pocket to pay for their meal.

His eyes widened and a grin slid across his face. He could tell by the look in her eyes that she wasn't through playing with him.

"What happens later?" he asked, and knew the moment he'd asked that he'd fallen right into her trap.

"That's when I pay my ransom. What did you have in mind? A little bondage, or just some—"

Her feet barely touched the floor as Gabe yanked her out the door.

"Lord, lady. You're gonna get me arrested yet," Gabe swore, then looked around nervously to see who else might be listening to their byplay.

Annie shrugged. "Can't help it. That's what usually happens to the bad guys."

A strange expression crossed Gabe's face. "Not always. Sometimes they just string 'em up and ask questions later. Here, put this on," he ordered, and stuffed the helmet in her hands without waiting for her to respond.

Annie tucked in the strands of her hair and did as she was told. But she couldn't help wondering what she'd said that had put that guarded look on Gabe's face.

"Gabe . . . ?"

"What?"

"If my teasing embarrassed you, I'm sorry. I was just..."

He lifted the visor of her helmet and leaned inside.

Lips met. His hard and demanding. Hers soft and ready to please.

Gabe groaned as he reluctantly released her from the kiss.

"Gee, Miss Annie, for a schoolmarm, you're a real good kisser."

She blushed.

Gabe laughed and then added, "And you ought to know that you can't embarrass an outlaw, darlin'. Now mount up. We're ready to ride."

The grin was back on his face. She sighed with relief. Whatever she'd unwittingly said had been forgiven.

As he guided the Harley out into traffic, Annie slid her arms around his waist, searching until she found her familiar handhold. Locking her thumbs into the two front belt loops of Gabe's jeans, she leaned forward, bracing herself against his back, ready for whatever was to come.

An hour or so later she heard him gearing down and looked around in surprise. As they pulled off the highway and into a huge parking lot, she craned her neck, trying to see where they were going. All she could see was row after row of cars.

"What on earth?" And then she saw the sign up ahead and started to smile. "Oh, Gabe!" She squeezed him in delight. "It's Silver Dollar City."

Gabe heard the excitement in her voice and knew he'd chosen wisely. But Annie would be surprised to know the real reason he'd chosen to visit the old-time, frontier-style theme park.

Annie waited impatiently while he buckled down and locked up everything they weren't taking inside.

"I haven't been here in years," she said.

He stuffed his sunglasses in his front pocket, then used his fingers for a comb, roughly shoving the black, shaggy length of his hair away from his face in haphazard fashion.

"Me either. I came once, a long time ago, when it first opened. It made me homesick," Gabe said quietly.

And then he slid his hand along her neck, tugging gently at the silky thicket of hair hanging down her back. "It's only fair that a man show all he can about his past to the woman he loves."

Annie's eyes grew round. Her lips parted, but no words would come. Her heart pounded, and she clasped her hands together to keep from throwing herself into his arms.

"Don't look at me like that," Gabe growled, and pulled her into his arms, anyway, ignoring the constant influx of tourists pulling into the theme park.

"Oh, Gabe," she whispered, moved beyond belief that he'd admitted his feelings to her.

"I know, darlin'," he said softly, and bent down. "It takes my breath away, too."

When their lips met, she was smiling. When he came up for air, Gabe was smiling back.

"Don't get me wrong," Annie said, as they walked toward the entrance gate. "I love being here. But how can bringing me to Silver Dollar City have anything to do with your childhood? This kind of life-style disappeared over a hundred years ago."

"By all rights, I should have, too." He gave her an odd sort of grin, one that held more regret than humor. "Don't ask me to explain, honey. Just know that I'm more comfortable with the way of life in there than what's out here."

Annie nodded, accepting him on his word alone, as she'd done since the moment they'd met. It was a fact that, by all rights, their meeting each other, much less becoming lovers, should never have happened.

She sighed and leaned her head against his shoulder as they walked through the entrance gates to the theme park nestled deep in the verdant hills of southern Missouri. She didn't care that they came from two different worlds. She didn't even care that he was an enigma she couldn't explain. Gabriel Donner loved her. It was all that mattered.

And so they walked the narrow streets of the town, marveling at the reclamation and resurrection of an older and slower way of life, and pretended, as did everyone else who ventured inside, that they were in another world.

Their footsteps echoed on the wooden sidewalks as they crunched candy apples and savored the hand-pulled saltwater taffy only hours old. And all through the day, as Annie saw the old mountain town through Gabe's eyes, she realized that she was also seeing another man emerge.

Gone was the cynical tough who'd climbed off a Harley and into the middle of a gang of hoodlums without giving it a second thought. Gone, also, was the daredevil who'd run into a burning building and rescued a child without thought for his own life. She tried to picture this Gabe walking into the middle of a robbery with fists doubled and couldn't quite make it fit. The Gabe who dared life to take him down seemed to have disappeared. In his place was this young-hearted, easy-spoken man from another era.

More than once, Annie found herself turning around to tell him something, only to realize he was no longer walking beside her. And when she checked to see where he had gone, invariably she would find him standing somewhere behind her, lost in thought as he stared wistfully at the old-time displays in the store windows, not even aware that Annie had gone on without him.

The wood-carver's shop fascinated him. Deep in a discussion with a clerk over the price of a figurine, Annie heard laughter and turned to see Gabe kneeling on the floor in the wood curls and sawdust. With two small towheaded boys for an audience, he was showing them how a hand-carved wooden man could dance on the flat of his hand. Annie grinned in delight. At that moment it was difficult to tell the adult from the children.

Soon afterward, as they walked outside in the cool autumn air, she saw Gabe stop and listen. An eager, almost boyish expression crossed his face, and before she knew it, he was dragging her down the street, through the crowds, all the while coming nearer and nearer to the sound that had caught his attention.

It was the village blacksmith, bare to the waist, covered with an old-fashioned leather apron, hammering a piece of iron he held fast upon an anvil.

"Would you look at that forge!" Gabe said, and whistled softly through his teeth.

Before she knew it, Gabe had ducked under the roped-off area, taking the blacksmith by surprise as he was about to demonstrate an old-style method of foundry work, pouring hot pig iron into a mold that had been buried in the earth.

Within minutes Gabe had talked the blacksmith into letting him try his hand. A crowd gathered, and they, along with Annie, watched in fascination as Gabe shed his shirt, donned the leather apron to protect him, and picked up a hammer and tongs. The onlookers watched as Gabe eagerly pulled a piece of hot iron from the fire.

Annie held her breath, unable to believe what she was seeing. Gabe hammered with skill, placing firm, steady blows on the iron, constantly bending and shaping, reheating and then hammering some more. He never seemed to tire or lose his concentration. And before her eyes, a perfect horseshoe began to take shape.

Heat from the fire seared the tan of Gabe's skin, and sweat began to run across his forehead and down onto his belly as the blacksmith obligingly pumped the bellows to keep the fire in the forge at optimum heat. But Gabe was oblivious to everything but his task.

The blacksmith's bushy beard parted in a pleased smile of surprise as he watched Gabe work. "That's quite a feat," the man told Annie. "It took me years to learn to do that. What's he do for a living, anyway? And don't tell me he's a stockbroker or it'll break my heart."

Annie laughed at the blacksmith's joke and made light of the fact that, when Gabe wasn't rescuing people, she didn't know what he did with his life. Along with the onlookers, she was stunned by Gabe's obvious and unexpected abilities.

What *does* Gabe do for a living? she wondered.

To Annie, he was something between the love of her life and a guardian angel. He often seemed to be a man with a past he kept trying to outrun. She frowned as she watched him finishing his work. What she knew about Gabriel Donner could have been written on one page with space left over.

Suddenly Gabe plunged the horseshoe into a bucket of water. The hot iron hissed as it was engulfed, sending a small cloud of steam into the air. Then he yanked the shoe out and held it up for approval while the water dripped from the tongs and ran down his elbow.

"Good job!" the blacksmith cheered. "Mister, if you ever want to change occupations, just let me know. You could work here any day. That's the best piece of iron work I've seen in a month of Sundays."

Gabe grinned as he relinquished the hammer and apron the blacksmith had loaned him. "It's been a while." And then he laughed aloud. "Ah, hell, who am I kidding? It was a whole other lifetime. But it was fun."

Suddenly he remembered Annie, and a spurt of guilt surfaced. "Sorry, honey. I sort of got carried away. What do you want to do next?" he asked as he dried himself off and then dressed.

For a moment Annie didn't answer. She was too busy fixing his expression firmly in her memory. She didn't ever want to forget how he'd looked filled with excitement and laughter.

"I want to have our picture taken," she said, remembering a studio they'd passed earlier that had period costumes for the customers to wear while being photographed. "I want to remember this day for always."

He grinned and hoped that his smile was steady. Because when she'd said "for always," he'd had a sudden urge to grab her and run and never stop. Maybe if they ran far enough and fast enough, they could outrun Annie's fate.

"Okay," he said, and let her lead him back the way they'd come. "But I get to pick what you wear. I distinctly remember seeing a red satin dress in the window. The one with black feathers around the neck and hem. I think I once knew a Sue from Santa Fe who had a dress just like it."

"Oh, you," Annie said, and punched him lightly on the arm, unaware that, for once, Gabe was telling her the truth, the whole truth and nothing but the truth.

* * *

Annie pulled at the neckline, trying to tug it up to a more respectable position. It wasn't going to happen. She blew at the feathers tickling her neck and chin, and rolled her eyes. Gabe hadn't been kidding about picking out her dress. It *was* red satin and as flagrantly gaudy as it could possibly have been.

She made a face at herself in the full-length mirror and then grinned, imagining what her old principal back home would have said upon seeing her dressed like this. Schoolteacher material she was not. If she knew Gabe, he was probably going to love it.

"I'm ready," she called.

"So am I, little lady," Gabe said quietly as he walked up behind her.

Annie looked up. The smile on her face froze in place.

"Oh, my."

It was all she could manage to say. The outfit she'd picked for him to wear had been chosen in jest. She'd had no idea that he would come out of the dressing room looking as if he'd walked out of one of the daguerreotypes hanging on the studio walls.

Devils danced in his eyes, making them seem brighter and bluer than before. Suddenly his much-needed haircut was no longer an issue. The slightly longer style now fit him to perfection.

His black frock coat bounced against the backs of his thighs, and his matching black pants made his legs seem even longer as he pranced around the studio, testing his appearance in first one mirror and then the next. The white ruffled shirt was a crisp and vivid contrast to the all-black suit, and the red string tie beneath his chin was just right for the riverboat gambler that he'd become.

Annie's eyes widened, and her lips parted on a slow sigh as she watched him jam a black flat-brimmed hat on his head and then buckle on a double holster. She grinned at her sudden urge to fan herself before she went into a fit of the vapors.

"Here you go," the photographer said as he led Gabe toward an array of fake firepower. "Pick your weapon. How about these fancy pearl-handled revolvers? Everyone seems to favor those."

Gabe shook his head and reached for two plain, long-barreled pistols instead. The only thing remarkable about their appearance was the shiny, blue-black sheen to the metal.

"I'll take these," Gabe said, flipping back his coat-tails and sliding the guns into place with little wasted motion.

Annie shuddered as she watched him handling the pistols. They fit too easily in his hands and slid too slickly from the holsters as he fanned them in and out to test his draw. Somewhere between the dressing room and now, she'd lost the Gabe she knew.

She glanced back at herself in the mirror, trying to get in the mood of the moment as deeply as Gabe had done. But it was no use. She was out of place in this silver dollar town, while Gabe looked as if he'd been born here.

"Now...about the pose," the photographer muttered to himself as he began moving Gabe and Annie around like mannequins. "Sir, how about you sitting down in this wingback chair pretending to hold the cards you've been dealt, with the little lady leaning over your shoulder, as if she's peeking at your hand?"

Annie looked at Gabe and shrugged, suddenly out of her element. A few minutes ago it had seemed like so much fun. Now she felt a certain uneasiness.

Gabe sensed Annie's dilemma and thought he knew the reason why. He was too at home in this place. Instead of playing the curious and interested tourist, he'd become a part of the place. The last thing he'd meant to do was make her afraid.

He turned to Annie and held out his hand. She came to him without a word.

"Just take the picture. We'll do the rest," Gabe said.

The photographer shrugged. It was all the same money to him. He fiddled with his cameras and lighting, but finally he was set.

"Are you ready?" he finally asked.

"Do it," Gabe said.

Annie held her breath as his arm slid around her shoulder, then squeezed her gently. Without thinking, she looked up and found herself reading his lips.

"I love you, lady," he whispered.

Lights flashed. The moment was caught forever on film. It seemed as if a dark, devil-may-care rake was about to kiss the woman he loved. Only by tilting the photo a certain way could you see the tears that had been running down her face.

Annie sat in the middle of the motel bed, looking over the array of mementos from their outing. Unable to resist it, she'd bought the small wooden dancing man from the wood-carver's shop. She fiddled with its floppy, jointed legs, trying to make it dance as Gabe had done, and then let it fall onto the bed with a plop. It obviously took a skill she was lacking.

Next to it was the rag doll that Gabe had insisted they buy. She'd resisted playfully until he'd pointed out that the doll had green eyes just like hers. The doll had gone into the bag with the little wooden man.

But it was the picture of them together in costume that she kept coming back to time and again. She picked it up and stared long and hard, unaware, as she looked, of the despair etched upon her face.

Gabe came out of the bathroom, still slightly damp from his shower, to find her sitting among the day's treasures. She should have been tired and happy, but all he could see was defeat.

"Annie, are you all right?"

Gabe's deep voice was husky, suddenly anxious that today had been more than she should have endured.

She looked up, unaware that she was smiling through tears. "Better than all right. Today was perfect, absolutely perfect."

Gabe sighed with relief and made a place for himself on the bed beside her, moving their prizes to a safer place on the bedside table.

"You're probably exhausted," he said, eyeing the clock on the table. It was nearly midnight. "Did you really have a good time today?"

She nodded. "It was practically perfect."

He grinned. "Only practically?"

"Well—" the drawl in her voice should have alerted him "—for a kidnapper, you sure lose sight of what you're doing."

His eyebrows arched, and a sexy grin slid across his lips. "Just what am I doing wrong, teacher?"

"Forgetting to demand a ransom, that's what."

"Oh, no, lady, I haven't forgotten a thing. I'm just still trying to decide what it'll take to get me to let you go."

"Oh, Gabe," Annie whispered, and threw her arms around his neck. "Don't do it! Don't ever let me go."

His hands cupped Annie's shoulders as he held her tight within his grasp. "I won't ever leave you, Annie," he whispered as he pulled her into his arms. "Wherever you go, I'm right behind you. Don't you ever forget it. Not for a moment."

The picture slid onto the floor as Gabe pinned her beneath him on the bed. Then there was nothing between them but the truth as Gabe stripped them of their clothes and made slow, perfect love to her until the sun came up.

And when morning came, they packed their bags in silence, climbed back on the Harley and headed back to reality. For a short while Gabe had done the impossible. He'd stopped time and given Annie one perfect day to remember.

Annie dug through the package that had arrived by post only minutes ago. Inside were the special books that she'd ordered to supplement Davie's reading material. She sorted them by subject matter, leaving the ones she knew he would view as work, putting the ones that she knew he would enjoy on top.

A nagging pressure at the base of her skull kept reminding her that time waited for no man... or woman.

*If only Davie continues with his studies after I'm gone.*

She slammed the stack of books on the table and then winced at the noise. Day by day, the knowledge that she was growing weaker was impossible to ignore. Each morning it seemed to Annie that it took more effort to get up than it had the day before. Often she caught Gabe watching her, as if he were gauging her strength and measuring her weakness, and, in a strange way, she hated him for doing it. She lacked even the privacy to die in peace.

A book slid out of her fingers and onto the floor. With a muttered oath, she bent over to pick it up, and as she did, she felt the room spin beneath her feet.

"No," she muttered, and grabbed hold of her knees until the spinning stopped. "No, damn it, no! I'm not ready for this to happen."

The sound of a truck pulling into the yard warned her that Davie had arrived for his lesson. It was the first time since they'd begun that Annie dreaded his appearance.

"Hey, Annie," he yelled as he burst into the house in his usual fashion. "Ready or not, here I come."

Annie straightened and pasted a smile on her face, determined not to let her weakness show.

"Look what came," she said as Davie began digging through the books. "They'll help you immensely in your studies. Promise me you're going to use them."

Davie grinned and shrugged. "Sure I will, teach," he teased. "And if I don't, you can always give me a failing grade."

Annie frowned. "I won't always be around to give you a kick in the pants, Davie. You'll have to push yourself to gain the skills you're going to need."

His smile died on his face. "Where are you going?" he asked. "Somewhere with Gabe?"

A sharp pain twisted inside her chest. *If only I could run away with Gabe.*

"I'm not going anywhere. I just want you to realize that I'm no longer your baby-sitter...and I won't be your teacher forever. Soon you'll be at the point where all you'll need to do is just practice. You won't need me for that."

"Whatever," Davie said agreeably. "Let's get busy. I've got a hot date with Charlie as soon as we're through."

Annie grinned at his enthusiasm.

"Where's Gabe?" Davie asked as he sat down at the kitchen table and opened his book to the spot where they'd stopped yesterday.

"He's outside somewhere," Annie said. "He won't bother us, remember?"

Davie nodded and began to read. His brow furrowed in concentration as he read the sentences aloud. Soon he was lost in the story, unaware that Annie was less than focused on what they were doing.

*Oh God,* Annie thought. *Not now. Not in front of Davie.*

But the dull ache ignored her warning and spread across the back of her head, pushing persistently behind her eyeballs. She closed her eyes and took a long, deep breath, hoping that she was wrong about the impending attack.

Motioning for him to continue, she pushed back her chair and started toward the cabinet. By the time she touched the countertop, it was all she could do to reach up and open the door. Her fingers curled around the bottle of pills at the same time that the pain burst behind her eyes. The last thing she remembered hearing was the sound of breaking glass and Davie's shout of alarm as she fell to the floor.

Annie curled into herself, digging her fingernails into her scalp as she mindlessly tried to tear out the pain that was killing her by degrees.

She needed her pills. The blessed pills. The reliever and the seducer . . . the thing that took away what she treasured most, her ability to function.

Davie dropped to his knees in a panic. Unsuccessfully, he tried to pick Annie up. He couldn't believe her strength as she fought his touch. Twice he almost had her in his arms, and both times she arched her back and screamed, in so much pain that he was forced to lay her back on the floor.

Finally, Davie thought of Gabe. "Don't move, Annie. I'll get Gabe."

But she didn't hear. And she wouldn't have reacted if she had. She was too lost in the pain that was ripping her apart.

*    *    *

Gabe grunted as he tightened the last bolt on the new carburetor he'd just put in Annie's car. With the weather turning cooler by the day, riding on the back of his bike was becoming less and less of a pleasure.

He'd heard Davie arrive, and imagined that he and Annie were now deeply engrossed in sorting through the new books that she'd ordered.

It was a day like all others until he heard Annie's scream. He was on his feet and running toward the house when he saw Davie bolt onto the porch, his face a dull, pasty white.

Gabe pushed past him and in seconds was on the floor at Annie's side.

"I don't know what happened," Davie kept saying over and over as Gabe knelt beside her. "One minute she was fine, the next thing I know, things are falling on the floor, dishes are breaking . . ."

"Her pills. Where the hell are her pills?" Gabe muttered, as he tried to sort through the broken crockery on the floor and keep Annie from hurting herself in the progress.

"Pills? I didn't see any . . ."

As he spoke, he accidentally kicked an unbroken and overturned plate. Beneath it lay a small brown prescription bottle that rattled as it rolled toward the cabinet.

Gabe grabbed it with a thankful oath and seconds later was trying unsuccessfully to push one of the small tablets between Annie's tightly clenched teeth, unaware that Davie was calling for an ambulance.

"Oh, damn," he muttered when he realized that her pain was so great that her muscles had gone into spasm. "Annie . . . baby, please! Open your mouth!"

Sweat beaded Gabe's forehead as panic began to set in. This was by far the worst episode that he'd witnessed. He couldn't even face the implications of that knowledge.

Harsh, aching gasps of air tore through her windpipe and down into her lungs as she tried to remember to breathe. It would be so easy to just stop. It would be so much simpler to just give up now. *No,* she thought, and opened her mouth wide enough to pull in the next breath.

"Thank God," Gabe whispered, and dropped the tiny pill deep into her mouth, knowing that when she next swallowed, it would go down where it belonged.

And then he braced himself against the cabinets, with his back to the doors and his boots digging deeply into the floor, and held her with a grip that death couldn't have loosened while he waited for the pill to take effect.

Davie sank to his knees on the other side of the room and stared blankly at the mess in front of him, trying to assimilate what he had witnessed. "What's wrong? What in hell's wrong with Annie?"

Gabe shuddered and began to rock her gently, back and forth in a slow, gentle motion. He breathed a sigh of relief as he felt her body beginning to relax. Twice he looked up at the shock on Davie's face and knew that the man deserved an answer. But each time that he tried to speak, nothing came out. It was impossible to say aloud what he knew was happening.

"I called the doctor," Davie finally said. "The ambulance should be here any minute."

"It won't help," Gabe said. He buried his face in her shoulder. "Nothing will help."

Annie moaned and rolled limply against him as the painkillers began to kick in.

"What the hell do you mean, 'It won't help'? Have you lost your mind? She needs attention. She needs it now."

Gabe maneuvered himself to his feet and then shifted Annie's limp body carefully as the distant sounds of a siren became obvious. He glared at the younger man, directing his anger at Davie to keep from crying aloud in despair.

"No doctor can fix what's wrong with Annie," he said harshly, unaware of the sheen of tears in his eyes. "Damn it, Davie, she's dying." His voice broke. "She's dying, and I can't stop it. No one can."

With that, he walked outside to the ambulance that had just pulled up in front of the house. Moments later, the ambulance pulled away, with Gabe on his Harley, only seconds behind.

# Chapter 13

The waiting room was too warm. Gabe sat in a hard-backed chair against the wall and watched the sweat beading across Davie Henry's forehead. He knew that the small blond woman who sat beside him was Charlotte. He'd been introduced. That was as far as the relationship had progressed.

He watched them whispering to each other, trying to get past the bitterness of knowing they had each other and the rest of their lives, when he and Annie had nothing.

Charlotte clutched Davie's hands in her own, touching the worry lines on his face, patting his knee when he fidgeted restlessly in the chair, and every now and then leaned over and murmured in his ear.

Gabe wished to hell that they were somewhere else. He didn't want to see them. Not here. Not now. And yet he knew that Davie cared deeply for Annie, that begrudging him the right to be here was petty. But he couldn't help what he was feeling.

*Oh, Annie...they don't love you like I do,* Gabe thought, and buried his face in his hands.

In doing so, he missed seeing Dr. Pope enter the waiting room. He jerked in surprise when the doctor touched him on the arm.

"How is she?" Gabe asked. "When can I take her home?"

"She's stable. But her condition has progressed a little faster than we'd expected. I'm not sure home is the best place for her at this time," Dr. Pope said.

"Exactly what does that mean?" Davie asked.

"It means that for her to be able to go home and... function normally...she's going to have to be on a stronger medication. That in turn means that she'll sleep for longer periods of time, which in turn means that she's close to needing round-the-clock care."

"Son of a bitch."

Gabe's curse startled them all, and left them staring in shock as he bolted from the chair and stalked out into the hall.

The quick tears that shot to his eyes shamed Gabe. He didn't cry. He never cried. He couldn't let go of his emotions, not even for Annie. If he did, he would never be able to stop.

Dr. Pope followed him into the hall.

"I'm sorry, Mr. Donner. I wish I had better news to give you."

"Hell, Doc, so do I," Gabe said shortly, then shoved his hands in his pockets, and started toward Annie's room. Suddenly he stopped and turned.

A tiny jingle from the rowels on his spurs was the only sound that warned Dr. Pope he was coming back.

"Doc..."

"What is it?" Dr. Pope asked.

"How long?"

"It's hard to say... maybe a month, maybe three."

*A month? A mere thirty days?*

The doctor's prediction was a death knell that knocked the wind from Gabe's lungs. He knew that he staggered, because he remembered seeing the floor tilt. But he never saw the doctor reach out and steady him. All he felt was the firm, reassuring grip, and then the world coming back into focus.

"If you were planning a big Christmas, I'd advise an early celebration," the doctor said, and patted Gabe roughly on the shoulder.

Shock bled the color from Gabe's face. "Christmas," he repeated blankly, as if unable to contemplate a celebration of any kind. His life was never going to be the same. Not without Annie.

Davie and Charlotte came out of the waiting room hand in hand. Gabe saw the way their heads nearly touched as they leaned together, sharing whispered words of comfort as they drew near. In that moment he hated them for having the rest of their lives together.

"It doesn't make sense," Gabe muttered. Annie's life should still be beginning, and instead it was coming to an end.

Doctor Pope overheard Gabe's remark and misunderstood the reason for the comment. And in doing so, he inadvertently revealed the last of Annie's secret. The part she'd never meant to share.

"I agree," Dr. Pope said. "It doesn't make sense. And I told Miss O'Brien so, the first time I examined her. You remember... the day she cut her foot and you brought her in to see me."

Gabe nodded absently and stared at a small water spot on the ceiling, trying to focus on anything but the news at hand.

"There *is* a risk involved. Actually, a big risk. But to blindly turn it down without giving herself a chance..." Dr. Pope shook his head. "I don't know her very well, but it surprised me. I imagined her to be more of a fighter."

Gabe's attention slowly refocused. He turned and stared, suddenly very attentive to the rest of Dr. Pope's opinion.

"Annie *is* a fighter," Gabe argued. "I've never known anyone quite like her."

Dr. Pope shrugged. "That may be. But I was still surprised when she refused to consider the possibilities of surgery."

Gabe's belly turned. What he was hearing didn't bear contemplation.

"Are you trying to tell me that Annie had a choice? That she didn't have to die?" Gabe asked.

Dr. Pope looked startled as he realized that he'd revealed confidential information.

"I thought you knew," the doctor muttered. "This wasn't my news to tell."

Gabe grabbed the doctor by the shoulders. Without thinking, he shoved him against the wall. "I want the truth," he whispered. "I'm sick and tired of hearing everything in bits and pieces. Talk to me...now!"

Davie saw the commotion and ran toward them without waiting to see what would happen next. From the expression on Gabe's face, it could have been almost anything.

"What the hell do you think you're doing?" Davie said, and started prying the doctor from Gabe's grasp.

"Answer me," Gabe said softly, refusing to let go of the man until his question had been answered. "Are you telling me that Annie could have been cured?"

Davie froze. He, too, stood silently, awaiting the doctor's diagnosis.

Dr. Pope shrugged. "There was a chance. It was a slim one, but it was better than no chance at all."

"And she refused to consider it?" Shock was thick in Gabe's voice.

The doctor nodded. "So it would seem," he said.

"Why? Why would she choose to die?" Gabe asked.

"She said the risk was too great. She didn't want to be just alive. If she couldn't be active, she didn't want to live."

"She chose death? She could have changed her own fate, and she chose death?"

Gabe couldn't believe his ears. He'd heard the doctor saying it, but he wasn't processing it as thoroughly as he should. All he could see was Annie, withering away before his eyes, and it had been by choice.

"I don't believe it," he said, and turned away.

"Is it too late now?" Davie asked.

Gabe listened intently for the answer, although he couldn't look at the doctor's face when it came.

Dr. Pope shook his head sadly. "I would guess that the chances now are reduced by more than half. It's hard to tell whether she would even survive the surgery, let alone in what condition."

"Oh, damn," Gabe groaned, and felt his legs go weak. He hadn't been this scared in his whole life. Not even the day he'd been hanged.

"At their best, what were her chances of coming out alive and well?" Davie asked.

"There was about a twenty percent chance of a total cure, maybe less," the doctor said.

"Then that means that Annie now has less than a ten percent chance of living through the surgery," Davie repeated.

"And that doesn't take into consideration what shape she'd be in if she did," the doctor reminded them.

"So what?" Gabe shouted. "Without it, her chances of living are zero."

He slammed his hand against the wall, ignoring the fact that it echoed down the hall and brought several nurses scrambling to see what was happening.

"Damn her! She cheated." Gabe's voice went from angry to empty in one breath. "She lied to me. But what was worse, she lied to herself."

He walked away, leaving Davie and Charlotte to console each other as best they could. For Gabe, there was no consolation, only the overwhelming fact that Annie had given up on life without a fight.

The walls of her room were yellow. A pale, placid color that reminded her of a plate of butter that had sat out too long and lost its shape and consistency. The view wasn't the most appealing she could have had, either. It made her lonesome for her little frame house and the thick ring of trees surrounding it, for the clear running water in the creek and the big moss-covered rock below the spring.

And she missed Gabe. She vaguely remembered hearing his voice when she'd been brought in, but she couldn't remember if he'd visited since.

She shrugged. It was to be expected. She'd lost most of the last twenty-four hours to pills and shots. But no more. Annie wasn't ready to sleep what was left of her life away.

She threw back the sheets and swung her legs out from under them, letting them dangle for a minute off the edge of the bed, just to make sure that the vertigo she'd experienced earlier was gone.

Nothing happened. The room didn't spin. Her head didn't feel as if it was about to explode. *Okay . . . now I'm going to get dressed.*

And then the door swung open and Gabe filled the doorway with his presence.

"Gabe! I'm glad you're here," Annie said, her attention entirely focused on the fact that her means of escape had arrived. She didn't notice his expression. If she had, she might have been ready for what ensued.

"Hand me my clothes, will you? They're in the closet."

He didn't move. He didn't speak.

"I can't wait to get home," she said, unaware of his lack of cooperation. "I'm going to soak in a tub for—"

"I didn't take you for a coward."

Shock spilled across her thoughts like beads of water dancing on a hot griddle. She slid back into bed and pulled the sheets up beneath her chin. It was an unconscious and useless gesture. She had no way of hiding from Gabe or the truth. And from the look on his face, the truth had finally come out.

"I don't know what you're talking ab—"

"Bull."

"You don't understand."

Gabe came toward her, the rowels on his spurs jingling with each long, slow step he took. And when he got to the edge of the bed, he placed an arm on either side of her body and leaned forward until Annie saw her own reflection in the cold blue glare in his eyes.

"Make me understand," Gabe whispered. The bed shook gently from the movement of his body as he slid onto the edge beside her. "Damn you, lady. Make me understand."

Her chin quivered, but it was the only sign she gave of how deeply his behavior moved her.

"I've been alone for seven years," she said.

"And I've been alone for more than two lifetimes," he countered, uncaring of how odd his rebuttal might seem.

Annie tried to glare. It shouldn't have been necessary to defend her decisions about her life to anyone.

"When I first got the news, I was devastated," Annie said. And then her chin tilted in a defiant gesture, as if daring him to begrudge her her fear. "Actually, I was scared out of my wits."

Gabe heard the tremble in her voice, but he gave her no evidence that he cared. He couldn't. He needed her to see her life from another perspective.

"And . . . ?" he said.

"They gave me my options, such as they were. Actually, it was pretty cut and dried." Annie's eyes teared up as she remembered sitting in the doctor's office while her world came shattering down around her. "I could have an operation. But there was a less-than-twenty-percent chance that I'd survive, and even less than that, that I would survive intact. *If* I survived, I might be blind, immobile, unable to speak, unable to think, or—" bitterness colored her last remark "—a combination of the above."

Gabe looked away. He didn't want her to see the sympathy he was feeling.

"So . . . I chose to go out the way I came in. All in one piece."

The bravado in her voice made him furious. He turned and glared. "It all sounds so damn easy. Is that the way you've gone through life? Taking no chances, always choosing the easy way out?"

Annie leaned toward him, her voice shaking with fury. "No! Once in my life I took a hell of a chance, Gabe Donner. I took you home, and I fell in love."

He flushed, unwilling to admit that she'd scored.

"That wasn't much of a chance, lady," he whispered. "You had nothing to lose when we met. How can you look on our relationship as any kind of a risk? You'd already signed your own damned death warrant. There wasn't anything I could do to you that you hadn't already done to yourself."

Annie gasped. Cruelty from Gabe was something new. Something she didn't know how to fight. It made her angry. In fact, it made her fighting mad.

She kicked out and actually pushed Gabe from her bed with her feet. "Get out!" she said, swinging her legs over and then off the bed. "I don't need your help. I'll get myself dressed."

"So it's like that, is it, teacher? Do as I say, not as I do?"

"What do you mean?" she asked.

"Everyone needs help at one time or another in their life, Annie. I can vouch for that. I've had more help than you'd ever believe. But not you! Oh, no! You're willing to help everyone else, but you won't help yourself."

Annie stomped to the closet and started grabbing her clothes from the hangers in fits and jerks.

"All the years that you taught, you made such a difference in your students' lives," Gabe said. "Look at the ones you left behind in Oklahoma City who'd looked forward to having you for a teacher next year. You walked off and left them without a single thought. And why? Because you were too busy feeling sorry for yourself to fight."

Annie threw a shoe at him and screamed in frustration when it missed.

"Look at Davie. He'd still be hiding behind a wall of ignorance, afraid to tell the woman he loved that he wanted to marry her. And why? Because he couldn't read. You changed all that for Davie, but you aren't willing to change anything for yourself."

Annie pushed her feet angrily through the legs of her jeans, wishing she had enough hands to dress herself and still cover her ears. She didn't want to hear this. She didn't want to face the truth of what Gabe was telling her.

"You have so much to offer, Annie," Gabe said softly as all the anger and fight suddenly went out of him. "Life has so much to offer *you*. How can you give up without a fight?"

Annie slumped forward and buried her face in her hands. But no tears would come. There was no way of hiding from the truth of what he'd said.

"Oh, Gabe," she whispered. "I wish I'd met you sooner. Before all this happened. If I'd had you to come home to, I might have been strong enough to give myself a chance."

"No! No, you don't," he said, his voice harsh and unforgiving. "You don't use me for your scapegoat. You don't choose to live for me, Annie. You either choose life for yourself or not at all."

Annie stared, dry-eyed and sick at heart, as Gabe turned and walked out the door. Long, silent seconds slid by as the echo of his accusations rang in her ears.

Annie shuddered, then stared slowly around the room, as if coming out of a trance. She moved toward the bed, walking as if every muscle in her body ached, and when her knees hit the mattress, she collapsed. Crawling beneath the covers like a recalcitrant child, she turned over on her stomach and buried her face in the pillow, unable to look at the truth of what she'd done.

Gabe sat on the bank of the creek below Annie's house and stared off into the trees beyond. The ground on which he sat was cold, and the seat of his jeans felt damp, but he didn't care. Moving took too much effort. He was weary clear down to his soul and heartsick beyond belief.

"I've been here too long," Gabe muttered, and buried his face in his hands.

"Does that mean you're leaving me?" Annie asked, and then clasped her hands in front of her like a child waiting to be chastised. What she'd overheard had made her panic. She couldn't lose Gabe. Not now, when so much depended on his strength.

Gabe bolted to his feet, then grabbed her by the arms, raking his gaze across her face and then down her body to assure himself that she was really there.

"I didn't mean I'd been too long with you, Annie. That's not what I meant." He stopped there, unable to explain any further. And then he realized she'd come home from the hospital . . . without his aid.

"How did you get home? Why didn't you call? I would have come for you."

Annie sighed and spread her hands in defeat. "I wasn't sure if you would even talk to me, Gabe, never mind play chauffeur. I called Davie. He and Charlotte brought me home."

He took her in his arms. Unable to hide his pain when she relaxed against him, he groaned softly and pressed a kiss against a curl that strayed across his lips.

"I'm sorry. I'm so, so sorry," he said. "I had no right to say the things I said to you. Please . . . just chalk it up to shock and an inability to mind my own business."

"No," Annie said and pushed him away. "You had every right. And you were right to say what you did."

Gabe closed his eyes against the truth of her words. Being right didn't make what would happen later any easier to bear.

"Come to the house," Annie said. "I have something to show you."

She held out her hand, and Gabe took it. Together they walked back through the trees, then up the path that led to Annie's house.

He shivered slightly as they walked inside. It was the first time they'd been here together since he'd found her on the floor at Davie's feet.

And then he forgot everything he'd been thinking at the shock of what he saw in the middle of the living room floor. There were boxes everywhere.

"What's all this?" he asked, and watched as Annie began opening and sorting boxes with calm deliberation.

"Mother's Christmas decorations. I had Davie get them out of the attic before he left. I want to put up a tree."

"A tree?"

"A Christmas tree," she said, then continued to sort through tissue and tape.

"Davie's father has lots of cedar growing on their place. He's bringing one over this evening after he gets off work. He and Charlotte are going to help us decorate. It'll be fun."

"A real Christmas tree?"

Annie paused in the act of unwinding an old string of lights and stared at Gabe. "I know it's early," she said. "But I thought it would be obvious to you why I'm doing this." She handed him the string of lights. "Here, see if you can get these untangled. I want to test them before we put them on the tree."

Gabe sank into a chair as Annie dropped the string of lights in his lap. He stared down at them, then up at her, as a slow smile spread across his face.

Even though she'd seen it plenty of times, Annie still caught her breath at the amazing beauty of his smile. It made him seem almost angelic. She laughed to herself at the thought and turned back to her task.

"I've never had a Christmas tree."

Annie almost didn't hear him. She stopped what she was doing and turned. Gabe was holding the lights and staring at them as if they'd suddenly turned to gold.

"What do you mean, you've never had a Christmas tree? Surely you've had a—"

"No. Never. It just didn't seem like a thing to do alone."

Annie stopped what she was doing and dropped to her knees beside Gabe's chair. "Gabriel Donner . . . I love you. Very, very much. And for the rest of our days, whatever we do won't be done alone. Somehow it only seems fitting that we share your first Christmas together."

The words were never spoken, but they both heard them just the same.

Gabe pulled Annie into his lap, settling her amid the tangle of wire and bulbs, and then held her face between his hands.

"I don't deserve you, lady," he whispered, then feathered a kiss across her lips.

"I know," Annie said with a sigh, and leaned against him, nuzzling her cheek over his chest until she came to the place where his heart beat loudest.

He chuckled, and Annie heard its origin from deep down inside his chest and smiled.

"We'll put up the tree tonight and open presents tomorrow. And then whatever comes after that, comes. At least we'll have celebrated together. Deal?"

The anxious look on her face made him angry. He'd put it there, and for that he would never forgive himself. Gabe hugged her lightly, willing the swelling pain in his chest to hell, where it belonged.

"Deal, darlin'," he whispered. "Whatever comes."

Annie smiled. With Gabe at her side, she *could* handle whatever came.


"Open mine first!"

"Okay, okay," Annie said. "Hand it to me."

Davie was like a puppy with a new bone. He'd gotten into the excitement of the early celebration as if he'd thought of it himself. His request was duly noted as Annie picked up the small flat box and shook it for effect.

Gabe watched the two old friends and tried to smile, hoping that no one noticed he wasn't nearly as excited about this event as he should have been.

It was impossible not to notice Annie's drawn expression or the dark hollows in her cheeks. When she thought no one was looking her eyelids drooped; she was constantly sleepy from the heavier doses of painkillers she was now forced to take.

Gabe stared at the scene unfolding before him and tried not to let his feelings show.

"Look, Gabe. It's a picture frame. I'm going to put our picture from Silver Dollar City inside. It'll be perfect."

"Now mine," Annie said, handing Davie a wrapped box.

He tore into it with enthusiasm, and his face lit up as he pulled out an old nursery rhyme book.

"It's one of my favorite books," Annie said. "And it's the first one you learned to read. I thought you should have it so that you can read to your own children some day."

"Man..." he whispered, suddenly choking on emotion as he gently turned the pages of his gift. "You've changed my life, Annie. Because of you, I'll never be ashamed again."

"Here," Gabe said, offering Davie some punch. "Annie spent all afternoon mixing this stuff. You'd better check to see if she's spiked it."

Annie smiled as her heart swelled with pride. Gabe was trying so hard... and all for her.

"Okay, you next," Gabe said, and handed Annie a small oblong box. There weren't many gift choices in Walnut

Shade, but when he'd seen this, he had instantly thought of her.

For a moment Annie just held the box, letting the love with which it had been given seep into her soul. She needed all the strength she could get to finish this day. And then the rest of her life was going to be in someone else's hands.

She lifted the lid and pushed back the tissue. When she saw the tiny apple-shaped charm and the long gold chain, she began to smile.

Gabe lifted it from the box and then draped it around her neck while he fastened the intricate clasp.

"An apple a day keeps the doctor away?" Annie asked, and caught the small, golden charm as it dangled in the valley between her breasts.

"No, honey. It's an apple . . . for my favorite teacher."

Gabe leaned over and kissed her lightly on the lips before turning to pour himself some of that punch. Suddenly he, too, was suffering from a lack of words and too much emotion.

"Oh, hell," Davie said, and took another big gulp of punch.

Annie laughed. "You're both pathetic," she said. "I'm not done for yet."

Gabe grinned past the knot in his throat. Damned if this woman wasn't something. She was thumbing her nose at them and at her fate. He couldn't let her down. Not when she was trying so hard.

"Where's mine?" Gabe asked, and began poking playfully beneath the branches of the tree.

Annie clasped her hands together in her lap and took several slow, calming breaths before she began. It was, after all, why she'd planned this elaborate get-together.

"It's here," she said, and slipped an envelope from behind her back. "I was hiding it. I knew you'd peek."

Gabe grinned and took the long white envelope as she handed it over, wondering as he did about the near-panic he thought he saw on her face.

He made a big issue of turning it over and over several times before slipping his finger beneath the flap and pulling it up. And then, just to prolong the issue, he peered inside twice before pulling out the contents.

Davie muttered softly in disgust, and Annie laughed aloud.

Gabe grinned. He'd done his bit toward putting a smile back on her face. It was time to end the ordeal. With an elaborate flourish, he pulled the piece of paper from inside the envelope and began unfolding it with relish.

"Probably a letter from the IRS," he teased as he unfolded the first flap.

"Naw...it's from one of those sweepstakes places," Davie offered, slapping his leg in jest. "You just won the jackpot."

The smile on Gabe's face stopped in mid-formation. Quickly he scanned the printed page, and Annie held her breath, waiting for his reaction. She didn't have long to wait. The paper shook in his hands as the blood drained from his face.

"Why? Why now?" Gabe asked.

Annie shrugged. "Why not?" she retorted. "After all, what you said was the truth."

"What is it?" Davie asked.

"It's a copy of my preadmission form," Annie said, her voice a little too bright and a little too light to fool anyone. "I'm admitting myself tomorrow. Surgery the day after that."

"But I thought..."

"Shut up, Davie. Just shut up." Gabe's voice shook as he leaned over and picked Annie up in his arms.

She slid her arms around his neck and rested her head against the curve of his cheek as he shifted her to a safer place within his embrace.

"Davie..." Gabe stared at the sheen of tears in Annie's eyes.

"What?" Davie asked.

"Let yourself out," he said, and walked out of the room with Annie in his arms.

"So, do you like your gift?" Annie asked a few minutes later as Gabe laid her down upon her bed.

He shuddered as he crawled in beside her and then wrapped her so tightly within his arms that it was hard to draw a breath.

Long minutes passed, and Annie thought he was never going to speak. Where once he'd been the one who gave comfort, now it was her turn to do the same.

Gabe shook. Great, shivering contractions that jerked his muscles and rattled his teeth. The tighter he held her, the colder he felt. He didn't think he would ever be warm again. And in the moment that he thought it, he knew why he'd reacted as he had.

If Annie died, all the light and warmth would go out of his world. That piece of paper was simply a reminder of the awful fact.

"It's not my present to keep," Gabe finally whispered, and buried his face in the warm, thick tangles of her hair. "No one's life can belong to another. The only thing you can give away is love, Annie. Only love."

"Then it's yours," she said lightly. "Now, remind me of what I've got to live for, Gabriel. Make love to me now, while there's still time."

"My God, Annie. I don't know if I can. I've never made love with a broken heart."

He choked on his words and felt her tremble as he wrapped her in his arms.

"Then try. That's all anyone can do—just try," she whispered.

So he did.

# Chapter 14

The house was cold and quiet. Inside, it looked and felt a little bit like it had the day that they'd arrived: drab and lonely. And now it sat empty, just waiting for someone to come back and add the spark to it that made a house a home.

Gabe walked from room to room, making certain that everything was turned off and unplugged.

All morning Annie had gone through the rooms, folding up linens and making up beds, anything she could think to do that would postpone her trip to Walnut Shade. She'd fussed with the little things until she'd made herself sick and ended up leaving Davie with a list of instructions he faithfully promised to complete.

But now she was gone.

Gabe inhaled deeply as he walked into her bedroom. The scent of her bath powder still lingered, as well as a few small, unnecessary items that she'd left behind when she'd packed her bag.

He leaned against the door frame and closed his eyes, recalling his last image of Annie and how small she'd looked as they'd strapped her down in the gurney and lifted her into the helicopter.

MediFlight was airlifting her back to Oklahoma City, to the specialist who'd first begun her treatment. Walnut Shade and the good doctors there simply didn't have the specialists and facilities available for the delicate neurosurgery she needed.

Gabe pushed himself away from the door and cursed softly, trying to forget how pale she'd looked and how frightened she'd seemed when the helicopter lifted off.

He'd watched until it was nothing more than a tiny black speck in the sky. And then a sudden sense of urgency had sent him driving back to the house in a cloud of dust. He couldn't shake an overwhelming urge to race the helicopter to Oklahoma City. Annie might need him.

Because he owned little and traveled light, Gabe had nothing much to pack. What he'd left until last, he now stuffed haphazardly into his bag, anxious to get back on the road.

He started out of the room, then stopped and turned, taking one last look around at the place where he and Annie had loved.

The old stuffed teddy bear, her first and her favorite, was propped against the pillow shams on her bed. Their picture, the one they'd had taken at Silver Dollar City, was safely mounted in the frame Davie had given her as a gift and now sat in a place of prominence in the center of her dresser.

Gabe looked at it from across the room and felt a sense of timelessness, as if all things come full circle. It was as if someday another couple might come upon the picture and know that once upon a time, in another life, a man and a woman had loved as they did now.

"God willing, my Annie, you will be back."

He walked away, his bag over his shoulder, and missed seeing that she'd hung the long gold chain with the little apple charm over the corner of the frame. If he had, he would have known then that Annie had already made peace with herself and her fate. The necklace hadn't been off her neck for a moment since he'd put it on. And yet it was the first thing she'd left behind.

The front door slammed behind him as he walked out on the porch. Gabe dropped his bag and reached up over the door, letting his fingers trace the dusty path until he came to the old, rusty key.

He poked it into the lock and then turned it. The tumblers clicked into place. Carelessly Gabe put the key back onto the narrow ledge, paying little attention to its location, and picked up his bag. With Annie gone, there was nothing here that needed to be kept safe.

In two steps he was off the porch and running toward his bike. He tossed his bag onto the back, strapped it in place and jammed the helmet on his head. Seconds later the engine fired, and the big, black Harley roared out of the quiet little yard, leaving dust and dry leaves flying in its wake.

Hours later Gabe crossed the state line and absently read the sign at the side of the road. Welcome To Oklahoma. He didn't feel welcome. He didn't feel anything at all.

Sometime later he crossed another, smaller state highway to get to the southbound on-ramp leading to Interstate 40. The wind beneath the helmet roared in his ears as he focused on the next leg of his journey. Destination: Oklahoma City—and Annie.

It was nearly midnight when Gabe got off the elevator. A night nurse doing rounds looked askance at his shaggy black hair, dusty boots and faded jeans, then shrugged and entered the next room on her list. In her job, she saw all kinds.

Gabe's spurs made tiny jingling sounds as his long legs quickly covered the distance to the nurses' station.

"Annie O'Brien's room," he said as he stopped in front of the desk and waited for further directions.

"I'm sorry, sir," a nurse said. "But visiting hours were over long ago."

"She's expecting me," Gabe persisted. "I've been on the road since early this morning. I don't think she'll rest until she knows I'm here."

The nurse frowned. She'd already familiarized herself with the case history and couldn't quite fit this big biker with the young school teacher who'd been brought in by helicopter earlier in the day.

Gabe saw her frown and knew it for what it was, disapproval of his appearance, rather than anything that he'd done.

"Please," he insisted. "My name is Gabe Donner. I have to see Annie. I'm all the family she has."

"You're *that* Gabriel? Miss O'Brien's angel of mercy?" She grinned. "Sorry. You just didn't quite fit the image I had in mind." And then, to soften the rudeness of her remark, she added, "I was expecting maybe...wings?"

Gabe grinned wearily. "That's one I haven't heard before." And then the smile disappeared and the shadows came back into his eyes. "Please...I need to see Annie."

"Room 353, down the hall and to the right."

Gabe disappeared so quickly that the nurse was left wondering if she'd imagined him. And then she heard the faint but distinct jingle of spurs and knew that he'd been real. She resumed her work and hoped that Gabriel Donner could withstand some shocks. Miss O'Brien's appearance had undergone a drastic transformation.

Nervous anticipation made him shake as he pushed open the door to the private room, then walked inside. Thick, dark shadows surrounded the bed, making everything, including Annie, seem small by comparison.

A mere lump beneath the covers, she slept in her old familiar position, with her knees drawn up and her hands beneath her chin in a gesture of prayer. Gabe caught his breath and swallowed his shock.

He leaned over and kissed her cheek, trying not to look at the small white cap she wore over her head, trying not to notice that she looked more like a newborn baby than the woman he'd made love to with total abandon only a day ago.

Annie stirred, as if sensing Gabe's presence. She reached out into the darkness and found him reaching back.

"They cut off my hair," she whispered, unaware of a small tear that trickled down her nose.

Gabe hurt from the inside out. "It will grow back," he whispered, and kissed the tips of her fingers before covering her hand with his own.

She sighed and seemed to settle. Gabe sat on the edge of the chair and held Annie's hand in the safety of his own. When he could no longer look at the damage that had been done to her in his absence, he leaned forward, resting his head against the edge of her bed, and closed his eyes.

Twice he swallowed, trying to get past the pain before he was able to talk. "Sleep, Annie. Rest while you can. I'll do the worrying for both of us now."

She seemed to smile and then sighed.

The sigh sounded too deep, too final, and Gabe found himself holding his breath in fear, unable to rest again until he'd heard her inhale. And when she did, he went weak with relief. It was the assurance he needed that she was still breathing.

Guilt overwhelmed him. If he'd minded his own business and accepted Annie's decision about her life, she would be back in Missouri in her own house, in her own bed, waiting for fate to catch up with her. Not here, shorn of her pride, poked and prodded and hooked up to too many machines with too many beeping lights and multicolored wires.

"Annie...Annie." His heartbroken plea slipped into the silence of the room. "What have I done to you?"

But she didn't answer. And the night passed away.

They came with morning, unannounced...unexpected. Bolting in through the doors of her room like the sun springing up from below the horizon. Wearing surgical greens, laughing and talking about the movie they'd seen last night and the pizza they'd had. Making light of the fact that someone had gone off a diet while another had gone off the wagon.

Gabe wanted to shout. He wanted to cry. He wanted to lash out at their lack of compassion for the pain that he was in. He wanted to rail at them...to ask them why it mattered that someone had gained a pound or drank too much, when Annie's desperation should have been foremost in their thoughts.

Were they blind to the way she clung to him as they moved around the room? And when they lifted her with little finesse from her bed to the gurney, Gabe felt empty...without purpose, knowing she would soon be gone.

He didn't know that they suffered with him, that they truly sympathized with Annie's pain. He didn't know that their loud, raucous jokes were the only way they could deal with daily doses of lives gone wrong. He didn't know, and at that moment he wouldn't have cared. The only thing in his world was Annie, and they were taking her away.

"Gabe!"

She called out in panic, reaching for a last touch of his hand as they wheeled her from the room.

His fingers curled around her wrist and then instantly loosened as he felt her fragility.

"I love you, sweetheart," he said huskily.

"Will you wait?" Annie asked.

Gabe shuddered. She hadn't asked him if he'd wait *for her*. She'd only asked him if he would *wait*. Wait until the verdict was in, whatever it might be.

"Sure I will, honey," he said, forcing himself to smile when all he wanted to do was crawl into a hole and pull it in after him. "Forever, if that's what it takes. But you already knew that, didn't you? Outlaws don't run from love, just the law."

"Remember," Annie whispered as they wheeled her from the room. "Remember me."

Gabe had stared at her face until they'd taken her away, too lost in the depths of those unblinking green eyes to tell her that her last request had been unnecessary. Remember Annie? How could he ever forget?

A nurse came in and started to strip the bed. Gabe turned and stared, unable to make even the simplest of remarks.

"I'm just going to make up her bed," she said gently. "There's a waiting room across the hall, and a cafeteria on the basement level. Why don't you go get yourself some breakfast... at least some coffee? Her surgery will take hours, and they haven't even started."

Gabe wiped a shaky hand across his face. The thought of food made his stomach roil.

"I might get some coffee," he said. "But I'll be just across the hall. When you have news, you'll come and get me... won't you? I won't be far."

She smiled sympathetically. "I promise," she said. "Someone will find you. Until then, you need to take care of yourself... for her."

*For her.*

He looked up to see Davie and Charlotte almost running down the hall.

"You just missed her," Gabe said, and pointed toward the end of the hallway.

"No, we didn't. We saw her just as they were putting her on the elevator. We got to say goodbye."

Anger overwhelmed him at Davie's careless words. He shook as fury enveloped him, and then he cursed helplessly, knowing that he was searching for an excuse to take his fear and anger out on someone else. He shook his head and shrugged, telling himself that what had been said, had been said without malice.

Davie flushed. "I'm sorry," he muttered. "I didn't really mean ... goodbye as in forever. I just meant ..."

"Save it," Gabe said. "I knew what you meant. It's hard to find the right thing to say."

"Come on," Davie said. "Charlie and I brought you some coffee and doughnuts. We can eat in the waiting room."

Gabe followed them. It was the simplest thing to do. Having to explain why he would rather be alone would have been impossible ... and selfish.

The waiting room quickly became a prison. The longer he sat, the sicker he got. Imagination was making him crazy. Any minute Gabe expected to look up, see that damned doctor wearing pity and mouthing excuses, and know that it had all been for nothing.

Davie and Charlotte were at it again. Heads together, touching, whispering, even now and then having the unmitigated gall to laugh quietly about things, when he was bleeding to death from uncertainty.

"I'm going to get some coffee. I'll be right back," Gabe said shortly, then jumped to his feet and stomped out of the waiting room before anyone could offer to go with him.

Within seconds he'd made it to the elevator without losing his mind. He pushed the button, then leaned against the wall, taking slow, deep breaths while he waited.

The car came quickly, and when he got on, he was thankful he was alone. Conversation was the last thing he could face. The doors closed behind him as he reached out to punch the button for the ground floor.

His finger never touched the panel. Instead, all around him, the air inside the car felt strangely charged and too rich to breathe. Gabe staggered then fell against the back wall as the pressure inside the car changed from heavy to light.

Suddenly he found himself being drawn upward, quickly now that motion had started, faster and faster toward a bright white light.

Gabe's thoughts spun outward, flinging themselves into the atmosphere until there was nothing left inside him but one single, desperate cry.

"No-o-o!"

But it was too late, and he'd gone too far to be heard. Gabriel Donner was gone.

The Voice came through the air, and when he dropped into the light, he knew who was waiting for him to appear.

"Gabriel."

*Oh, God. Why now?*

"Because it is time. Welcome, my son," God said. "I've been waiting for this day."

Gabriel felt weightless and knew that somewhere along the way he'd left his earthly body behind. And with that thought came the knowledge that he'd also left something else . . . something infinitely more important. Annie!

*I wasn't ready.*

"Oh, but you are," God said, and joy filled the air around them as his laughter echoed within the clouds. "You've done all that I asked and more during your time on earth. You've earned your rest, Gabriel, my son. Come . . . follow me . . . and the sound of my voice."

*Wait!*

God gasped, and the air was suddenly filled with the sound of his displeasure, rumbling across the skies like so much thunder.

"Gabriel! What manner of foolishness is this? You don't *wait* to get into the Kingdom of Heaven. You come when you are called."

*Annie! What about my Annie?*

God's sigh blew the thunder from the heavens, clearing the skies and the air with a single breath.

"She's no longer *your* Annie, Gabriel."

*No-o-o! I have to know. I can't leave without being sure. Will Annie live? Please . . . will she live?*

God's answer was kind, his voice benevolent, and yet Gabriel heard the certainty with which he spoke.

"Her fate is no longer your concern."

An overwhelming pain sent Gabriel to his knees. There at the Gates of Heaven, he felt the first onslaught of tears as they began running down his face.

He never cried. Not even on earth when it had mattered, and here he was, crying at the feet of God.

*Please. Don't let her die!*

God hissed, and the heavens stirred, as with a tumult of thousands upon thousands of angels' wings moving in constant motion, fluttering in unison. And with the wind came a sound, a wailing unlike anything Gabriel had ever heard.

"Now see what you've done," God said.

The accusation in his voice became a violent reverberation of judgment that made Gabriel unable to look up.

"You've made my angels cry. For shame!" He cried as the air was rent with sound. "For shame! There can be no tears in Heaven."

*But she has no one. No one but me, and now I'm gone. I have to know . . . will she live?*

"I tell you now! Come forward into the light."

The voice was once again a command and a demand, yet solace to Gabe's aching soul, peace where none had been. But taking that first step away from Annie was still impossible for him to do.

He lay at the feet of God. Prostrate with grief. Unable to do what his Master had commanded.

*Send me to hell. Cast me from heaven forever…leave me in Limbo, lost between Heaven and Hell for all eternity…just let Annie live.*

The cry came from Gabe's heart.

God heard and at once understood that the man He'd sent back to earth to right all his wrongs had indeed grown in stature and grace. He'd done more than penance, he'd learned the meaning of true sacrifice.

God's manner changed. His voice became the sound of purity overflowing with patience, and yet it held a warning Gabriel could not miss.

"You would willingly exist alone—for all eternity and more, without the sight or sound of another living soul—just to know this woman's fate?"

*Yes…oh, yes.*

"You would never know the meaning of rest, never feel an inner peace, never—"

*Yes! Yes! Yes! I would go now. I would go willingly. If you will only let Annie live.*

"Without you?"

*Without me.*

God smiled. And in that moment Gabriel felt the tears drying upon his face. Felt the wind around him moving, turning, faster and faster, a whirlwind of motion that pulled him up and then flung him out.

Gabe forgot to be afraid. He forgot to say that last goodbye to Annie in his heart. Everything exploded within him, and he felt, rather than saw, a blackness enveloping him.

*So, this is now my existence. . . . This is my Limbo.*

"No, my son! This is life!"

The elevator came to an abrupt stop that sent Gabe to his knees. He reached out as he fell, expecting to touch the empty space of Limbo and instead felt the floor of the elevator coming up to meet his face.

"Where am I?" he muttered as he rolled over and then pulled himself to his feet, thinking that Limbo couldn't be an empty elevator car on its way to nowhere.

And then he heard the squeak of the elevator cables and heard a receptionist's voice coming over the hospital intercom and into the car, patiently paging a doctor by name.

He reached up, felt the tears on his face and knew in that moment that everything he'd imagined had been true. He *had* stood at the feet of God. He *had* been called Home. Then *why* was he back? Why was he *here*?

*Because you cared.*

Gabe started to shake. He knew as well as he knew his own name that God had just spoken to him.

"So . . . how long do I have this time?" Gabriel whispered, almost afraid to ask.

*You are now as other men, my son. Live your life. Love your love. When it's time . . . you will come to me. I will never again come for you.*

The elevator door opened. Davie all but jerked him out of the car and began running with him back toward the waiting room.

"Where the hell have you been?" Davie muttered as he turned a corner with Gabe in tow.

"Talking to God . . . I think," Gabe said.

"Oh! Right. I didn't think to look in the chapel," Davie said. "Sorry." And then they entered the waiting room, where a weary young doctor, still wearing his surgical greens, stood up at their arrival.

"I found him!" Davie shouted, almost shoving Gabe toward the man. "Now...tell him what you just told us." Davie was almost dancing with relief as he pulled Charlotte into his arms.

The doctor smiled and motioned for Gabe to sit.

"I'll stand, if you don't mind," Gabe said softly. "I'm still trying to get my land legs back."

They all smiled at his joke. They had no idea how close to the truth it was.

"It's like this," the doctor said. "We had all the tests results. MRIs, CAT scans, EEGs, every test known to man. We had every reason to believe that the mass inside Miss O'Brien's head was becoming aggressively invasive."

Gabe ignored his own advice and sank into a chair. What were they all smiling about? This sounded like hell.

"But..." the doctor continued. "When we got inside—" his face lit up, and he began gesturing with his hands to describe what had happened "—the damned thing was just...just sitting there. It all but fell out in our hands, so to speak. I don't know what it was we saw on the X rays—shadows...bad films...I can't explain it. All I can say is, in surgery today...I saw a miracle. I can't explain how or why, but Miss O'Brien should recover with few, if any, lingering effects."

Gabe buried his face in his hands. He could have explained it.

*A miracle. Divine intervention. Or just a plain, old-fashioned gift from God.*

He didn't care what they called it. Annie had been given back to him. And in a way none of them could ever have known, he'd been given back to Annie.

"Thank God," Gabe whispered, and reached up to shake the doctor's hand.

*You're welcome.*

Gabe smiled. The Big Man always had the last word.

# *Epilogue*

Sunlight was warm on Gabe's face as he carried the last of the groceries into the house. He passed through the hall on the way to the kitchen and caught a glimpse of himself in the hall mirror. He almost laughed. The outlaw he'd been was nowhere in sight.

His leather and his spurs had been packed away, his haircut was almost ordinary, and he was going to be late for work if he didn't hurry.

Work! It still amazed him that the old skills he'd once thought were useless had been the single most important reason for landing him a job as one of Silver Dollar City's employees.

If old-style, wooden shingles needed to be hacked by hand, he was their man. He also blacksmithed, trading days with another blacksmith who also knew how to make soap, a job Gabe politely refused to do.

Now and then he was even a stand-in for the gunslingers when an exhibition shoot-out was performed. But there was one thing he refused to do. He wouldn't pin on a star to save his life. Being a lawman, even playacting as one, was a little too close to the bone for Gabe.

"Gabe . . . you're going to be late for—"

"I'm never late for the things that count, am I, Annie Laurie?"

He dropped the sacks onto the counter and swung her up into his arms, ruffling her short, thick curls and mussing her makeup just to hear her fuss.

She did. But not because she cared. She did it because he expected her to.

"So your timing is almost perfect," she said, and grinned when his eyebrows shot up into his hairline.

He laughed. The little devil. She wasn't talking about his damned job, and they both knew it.

"What do you mean . . . almost?" he asked. "I give good love. Remember . . . you said so yourself."

Annie blushed, then opened her mouth for the kiss she saw coming.

Gabe sighed and wrapped her in his arms as she snuggled within his embrace. "What?" he asked. "Why, my dear wife, do you always wiggle when I first hold you?"

"I'm just finding my spot," Annie said, surprised that he'd even had to ask.

"What spot?"

Annie smiled and moved the flat of her hand across his chest until she found the spot she'd been searching for.

"This one," she said, and laid her cheek against it. "It's the place where your heartbeat's the loudest. It makes me feel closer to your heart."

"My God," Gabe whispered, and dug his hands deep within the baby curls framing her face. "Closer to my heart? Annie. You couldn't be any closer, darlin'. You *are* my heart. Without you, it isn't capable of beating."

She sighed and relaxed in his arms.

"When I get a little better, I'm going to teach again, you know. Then we won't have all this special time together."

"Then we'd better enjoy it while we can, honey."

Reluctantly he set her aside with a sweet farewell kiss. And when she whispered a naughty promise in his ear as he started to let her go, he laughed uproariously and began swinging her around and around the room like a doll.

It was during their dance that Annie looked up, laughter rich upon her face, and saw them shining in his hair.

"Gabe! Gabe! You have to stop. You won't believe what I just saw."

He stopped and stared, thinking that she'd truly lost her mind.

"What is it now?" he asked. "And don't make up stories. I really can't be late for work. One of the men is out sick."

Annie grabbed him by the hand and dragged him back out into the hall, pushing and shoving until she had him square in front of the oval-shaped mirror.

"Look!"

He bent over and peered carefully. All he could see was the same old face.

"See what?" he asked. "I don't see anything different."

Annie turned his head and then plucked a lock from above each ear and held it out from his head like little horns.

"Look! There! You have gray hair!"

An emotion swept over him that was at once so fierce and so joyful, he didn't know whether to laugh or cry.

"Where? I don't see it!" he said, and tilted his head ever closer to the mirror, desperate to see the proof.

She tilted his head in the other direction and then tugged once again at the thick tufts of hair between her fingers.

"There...just above your ears...on each side. Like little wings. See?" And then she smiled as she had a thought "You know how I always call you my guardian an gel...well...you finally got your wings. I guess this makes it official." She laughed, pleased with the comparison she'd drawn. Gabriel would forever be perfect in her eyes.

"Oh, my God! I see them! They're beautiful," Gabe whispered, and feathered them beneath his fingers, testing the feel against the smoother texture of the rest of his hair. "They're honest to God fantastic!" he shouted.

Annie stared. She'd expected any kind of reaction other than excitement. Some men might have ignored their appearance. Some might have dyed their hair back to a more youthful state. Some might even have panicked and yanked the gray hairs out, unwilling to face the evidence of their mortality. But not Gabriel. She should have known that he would be different.

But Annie would never know exactly what a precious sign this was for Gabriel. It was the final and physical proof that, after more years than he cared to remember, he was at last a man like every other, and he was growing old...along with Annie.

\* \* \* \* \* \*

# COMING NEXT MONTH

### #601 CALLAGHAN'S WAY—Marie Ferrarella

American Hero Kirk Callaghan had returned home in search of peace.
But he soon found himself playing surrogate dad to Rachel Reed's
eight-year-old son—and playing for keeps with Rachel's heart.

### #602 A SOLDIER'S HEART—Kathleen Korbel

Tony Riordan merely wanted to thank the nurse who'd saved his life
so many years ago in a war-torn jungle. But that was before he saw
Claire again—and the unresolved anguish reflected in her eyes. Now his
angel of mercy needed *his* help, and Tony would never refuse her.

### #603 SCARLET WHISPERS—Diana Whitney

His father was no murderer. And Clay Cooper would prove it once and
for all to the closed-minded people of Scarlet, South Carolina. But that
meant convincing Lainey Sheridan, the dead man's daughter. She alone
held the key to the past—and to Clay's heart.

### #604 FUGITIVE FATHER—Carla Cassidy

Sarah Calhoun had successfully kept her secret from the Clay Creek
rumor mill—and Reese Walker—for six years. But once she returned
home, there was no denying who'd fathered her child—and no keeping
Reese from the daughter he'd never known existed.

### #605 ONLY THE LONELY—Pat Warren

Giff Jacobs had one reason for living: retribution. And he would have it
once he gathered the evidence to clear his name. But his agenda radically
changed the moment he encountered Roxie Lowell, the woman who'd
made him trust—and love—again. The woman he'd unwittingly placed
in danger.

### #606 JENNY'S CASTLE—Elizabeth Sinclair

*He'd found her.* Six long years of separation hadn't eased the pain
of Jennifer Tyson's betrayal, but Devin Montgomery would have his
revenge. But Jenny wasn't the ice princess he'd believed her to be.
Instead, she was a victim of the past just like him—and their
five-year-old daughter....

## MILLION DOLLAR SWEEPSTAKES (III)

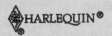 HARLEQUIN®   Silhouette®

## The movie event of the season can be the reading event of the year!

Lights… The lights go on in October when CBS presents Harlequin/Silhouette Sunday Matinee Movies. These four movies are based on bestselling Harlequin and Silhouette novels.

Camera… As the cameras roll, be the first to read the original novels the movies are based on!

Action… Through this offer, you can have these books sent directly to you! Just fill in the order form below and you could be reading the books…before the movie!

| | | | |
|---|---|---|---|
| 48288-4 | Treacherous Beauties by Cheryl Emerson | $3.99 U.S./$4.50 CAN. | ☐ |
| 83305-9 | Fantasy Man by Sharon Green | $3.99 U.S./$4.50 CAN. | ☐ |
| 48289-2 | A Change of Place by Tracy Sinclair | $3.99 U.S./$4.50CAN. | ☐ |
| 83306-7 | Another Woman by Margot Dalton | $3.99 U.S./$4.50 CAN. | ☐ |

**TOTAL AMOUNT** $ _____
**POSTAGE & HANDLING** $ _____
($1.00 for one book, 50¢ for each additional)
**APPLICABLE TAXES\*** $ _____
**TOTAL PAYABLE** $ _____
(check or money order—please do not send cash)

To order, complete this form and send it, along with a check or money order for the total above, payable to Harlequin Books, to: **In the U.S.:** 3010 Walden Avenue, P.O. Box 9047, Buffalo, NY 14269-9047; **In Canada:** P.O. Box 613, Fort Erie, Ontario, L2A 5X3.

Name: _____

Address: _____ City: _____

State/Prov.: _____ Zip/Postal Code: _____

\*New York residents remit applicable sales taxes.
Canadian residents remit applicable GST and provincial taxes.

CBSPR

# "HOORAY FOR HOLLYWOOD" SWEEPSTAKES

## HERE'S HOW THE SWEEPSTAKES WORKS

### OFFICIAL RULES — NO PURCHASE NECESSARY

To enter, complete an Official Entry Form or hand print on a 3" x 5" card the words "HOORAY FOR HOLLYWOOD", your name and address and mail your entry in the pre-addressed envelope (if provided) or to: "Hooray for Hollywood" Sweepstakes, P.O. Box 9076, Buffalo, NY 14269-9076 or "Hooray for Hollywood" Sweepstakes, P.O. Box 637, Fort Erie, Ontario L2A 5X3. Entries must be sent via First Class Mail and be received no later than 12/31/94. No liability is assumed for lost, late or misdirected mail.

Winners will be selected in random drawings to be conducted no later than January 31, 1995 from all eligible entries received.

Grand Prize: A 7-day/6-night trip for 2 to Los Angeles, CA including round trip air transportation from commercial airport nearest winner's residence, accommodations at the Regent Beverly Wilshire Hotel, free rental car, and $1,000 spending money. (Approximate prize value which will vary dependent upon winner's residence: $5,400.00 U.S.); 500 Second Prizes: A pair of "Hollywood Star" sunglasses (prize value: $9.95 U.S. each). Winner selection is under the supervision of D.L. Blair, Inc., an independent judging organization, whose decisions are final. Grand Prize travelers must sign and return a release of liability prior to traveling. Trip must be taken by 2/1/96 and is subject to airline schedules and accommodations availability.

Sweepstakes offer is open to residents of the U.S. (except Puerto Rico) and Canada who are 18 years of age or older, except employees and immediate family members of Harlequin Enterprises, Ltd., its affiliates, subsidiaries, and all agencies, entities or persons connected with the use, marketing or conduct of this sweepstakes. All federal, state, provincial, municipal and local laws apply. Offer void wherever prohibited by law. Taxes and/or duties are the sole responsibility of the winners. Any litigation within the province of Quebec respecting the conduct and awarding of prizes may be submitted to the Regie des loteries et courses du Quebec. All prizes will be awarded; winners will be notified by mail. No substitution of prizes are permitted. Odds of winning are dependent upon the number of eligible entries received.

Potential grand prize winner must sign and return an Affidavit of Eligibility within 30 days of notification. In the event of non-compliance within this time period, prize may be awarded to an alternate winner. Prize notification returned as undeliverable may result in the awarding of prize to an alternate winner. By acceptance of their prize, winners consent to use of their names, photographs, or likenesses for purpose of advertising, trade and promotion on behalf of Harlequin Enterprises, Ltd., without further compensation unless prohibited by law. A Canadian winner must correctly answer an arithmetical skill-testing question in order to be awarded the prize.

For a list of winners (available after 2/28/95), send a separate stamped, self-addressed envelope to: Hooray for Hollywood Sweepstakes 3252 Winners, P.O. Box 4200, Blair, NE 68009.

CBSRLS

## OFFICIAL ENTRY COUPON

# "Hooray for Hollywood"
### SWEEPSTAKES!

Yes, I'd love to win the Grand Prize — a vacation in Hollywood — or one of 500 pairs of "sunglasses of the stars"! Please enter me in the sweepstakes!

This entry must be received by December 31, 1994.
Winners will be notified by January 31, 1995.

Name _____

Address _____ Apt. _____

City _____

State/Prov. _____ Zip/Postal Code _____

Daytime phone number _____
(area code)

Mail all entries to: Hooray for Hollywood Sweepstakes,
P.O. Box 9076, Buffalo, NY 14269-9076.
In Canada, mail to: Hooray for Hollywood Sweepstakes,
P.O. Box 637, Fort Erie, ON L2A 5X3.

KCH